Nora and the Secondhand Bookworm

EMILY JANE BEVANS

First published privately in Great Britain in 2012

Published in paperback and Kindle by Mary's Dowry Productions in 2017

Emily Jane Bevans, publisher

This is a work of fiction. Names, characters, places, organisations and incidents are products of the author's imagination and used fictitiously and are not to be construed as factual.

DEDICATION

This novel is dedicated to Mr. Raymond Dale R.I.P.

NORA AND THE SECONDHAND BOOKWORM

CONTENTS

	Acknowledgments	i
1	POPPY DAY	1
2	MISS READ AND THE ROAD SWEEPER	27
3	THE CHIHUAHUA IN A BIRDCAGE	43
4	IN THE ANTIQUES SHOP	56
5	THE ALMOST-FIGHT AND THE BOOK SIGNER	75
6	Z FOR ZACHARIAH	93
7	HAVE YOU GOT MY KNICKERS?	116
8	THE UNIVERSE OF BOOKS	132
9	MUSHROOM FARMS, CHICKENS AND THE REMAINDER WAREHOUSE	153
10	GEORGINA'S ADMIRER	172
11	THE LADYBIRDS AND THE JET HOSE	188
12	THE WOMAN IN GOLD AND THE MAN IN THE KIOSK	204
13	NORA IN WONDERLAND	221

NORA AND THE SECONDHAND BOOKWORM

ACKNOWLEDGMENTS

I am ever grateful for the ten years I spent working in Kim's secondhand and antiquarian bookshops on the South Coast of England, which afforded me greater experience in the world of selling used books.

Special thanks to Anne Honiball for her patient proof-reading (more to come!)

NORA AND THE SECONDHAND BOOKWORM

1 POPPY DAY

Great gusts of cool November wind sent a big red blind outside an antiquarian and secondhand bookshop flapping wildly. Inside the old Tudor building it rattled against the front wall, causing a young woman to turn around and grimace. Her name was Nora and she was behind an untidy counter, where toppling piles of books stood amidst packaging tape, message pads, a pot of pens, a box full of biscuits baked in the shape of Darth Vader, a cash book, an ancient looking till, a computer monitor and a brand new PDQ machine.

"Splendid." Nora said, looking from the blind to the skies seen through the book-filled window. "Looks like rain."

Two postcard holders stood inside the shop on an area of flagstones before the carpet. Nora had already run up and down the street collecting the pictures of the town, which was situated in the south coast county of Cole, that had taken off like 2D UFOs in a strong gust of wind.

She had dragged the spinners back into the shop and left them inside, deciding that if tourists to the town were out in such weather they would be glad to venture into the warmth of The Secondhand Bookworm to buy postcards.

A man ran past the window chasing a hat that bounced along the pavement in front of him.

Nora pondered him a moment and her lips twitched with sudden amusement. She sighed, picked up an early 'Thomas the Tank Engine' book that Georgina had bought at the weekend while in her Seatown branch and delivered the evening before, and turned to pop it on one of the special shelves behind her.

"There you are James, you lovely red engine." She told the book.

"Are you talking to yourself again?"

Nora clutched her chest and gave a small yelp, dropping into the chair before the computer.

Her colleague Roger stared at her and then smirked.

"Did I make you jump?" He placed a cup of hot steaming tea onto the mouse mat, keeping hold of the other.

"You did actually." Nora admitted.

"That's because I'm so light and nimble on my feet."

"Were you trained by Native Americans?"

"American Indians." Roger corrected.

"Sorry." Nora apologised with a small smile at his being a stickler for political correctness.

The blind outside the shop flapped madly in another blast of wind. Nora and Roger looked at it. According to Roger's weather app, rain was forecast for the week throughout the County of Cole.

"We should reel that in." Nora decided. "In case it takes the whole front of the shop off."

Roger put his mug of tea onto the mouse mat and gloomily pushed his glasses back up the bridge of his nose.

"I'll take care of it," he volunteered and walked around the front of the counter.

Nora watched him stop beneath one of the black beams across the ceiling and unclip a long pole. He then headed out of the shop to hook in the blind and fasten it safely against the wall. When he opened the door he almost fell sideways. The wind was ferocious

The phone rang so Nora grabbed the receiver.

"Good morning, The Secondhand Bookworm." She greeted cheerfully, watching Roger, whose glasses almost blew away while he battled with the blind.

"Hello. Is that The Secondhand Bookworm?!"

"Yes. The Secondhand Bookworm." Nora assured the caller.

"I have some birthday cards for sale, would you be interested in buying them from me?" the woman asked.

"Erm…well this is a bookshop." Nora replied.

"Yes but these are wonderful cards, I assure you."

"We buy and sell books." Nora explained warily

"Oh but these are almost *like* books with the stories that they tell. I have a whole box and they are fifty years old and over! They'd appeal to people who buy cards, especially birthday cards, and special collectors of ephemera. Would you like to make me an offer for them?"

Nora stared blankly at Roger through the window.

"I'm sorry but we only really sell books." She assured her.

"Oh but these are collector's items, they're fifty years old and even older and were all my father's, cards like 'Happy Eighteenth Birthday', 'Happy Twenty-First Birthday', special ones like that, and then ordinary ones like, 'Happy Birthday to a Great Son', 'Happy Birthday

Brother', 'Wishing you a Happy Birthday full of dreams', 'To a Lovely Grandson on his Birthday'...from a variety of cousins, his parents and grandparents."

"I'm quite sure they wouldn't be for us," Nora said, beginning to feel exasperated.

"Well, what would their value be? The ones I have are fifty years old and more."

"Perhaps you would like to phone our other branch and speak to the owner of our shops?" Nora decided.

"Oh, alright. Do you have the number?"

Nora gave it to her, wondering what Georgina's reaction would be.

"I'll phone her now!" The caller decided and hung up.

With a small smirk, Nora replaced the phone, shaking her head.

Roger came back inside the shop, what little hair he had sticking up in several places and his glasses on the end of his nose.

"It is mad out there!" He reached up and replaced the pole. "I feel sorry for the poppy sellers. One lady just chased about twenty across the road."

Nora laughed.

"That was like me earlier with the postcards."

"Must be Monday." Roger said glumly.

"It's been unusually busy again. Busier than is typical for November." Nora pointed out thoughtfully, scanning the cash book where she had written down eight separate sales of books so far and they had only been open for half an hour. Nora had had to stop in the midst of a diatribe about the weekend staff leaving empty pot noodle pots all over the kitchen and pinching her Darth Vader shaped biscuits to serve them all, selling odd titles and volumes such as 'The Correct Way to Brush a Goat', 'Beer-Making for Teetotallers' and 'Knitting Light Houses'.

"That's thanks to the Duke of Cole." Roger said drearily. "Him and his new plans to rebuild that castle of his. So much for our quiet winters."

Nora smiled.

"Yes, it is thanks to him." She agreed, dreamily.

The Duke of Cole was a very good-looking, thirty-something nobleman who spent his time wading lakes, undertaking the grand restoration of old ruins into magnificent properties and giving talks about conservation and rewilding to large stuffy gatherings while running an international architectural business throughout the realm. He had spent most of his life living by himself on the Scottish borders and, despite being an eligible bachelor, was ignored by the national press because the media considered him to be a bit of a bore. He was never seen in social circles, had never caused a scandal and was now turning his attention to the large castle ruins behind the shops as his latest architectural project.

For centuries, tourists had enjoyed clambering over the ancient stones and wandering around the huge hollow rooms that gave Castletown its name. Rumours that the Duke of Cole was planning to rebuild the castle had turned into realities as the Duke's firm had arrived in Castletown at the beginning of October to assess the whole estate, and then building had begun under the supervision of the Duke of Cole himself, who had given several interviews about his rebuilding project including one to Castletown TV.

Nora had watched it on the internet many times, especially fascinated with the Duke's pledge to preserve history and culture and move into his castle even before the entire project was complete. The development had drawn a great deal of interest and a lot more tourists to Castletown. The plan was for tourists to be able to visit the old parts of the castle such as the keep and the gatehouses, the grounds, ancient walls, turrets and dungeons as well as many of the new rooms that the Duke would allow to be opened. Nora expected the Duke would have an unrivalled library and hoped that would be open for viewing too.

Castletown was abuzz with anticipation.

"Can I check my emails?" Roger asked, interrupting Nora's fantasising and nodding at the monitor. "I'm expecting one from my daughter."

"Of course." Nora said and stood up, deciding to tidy the desk.

The bookshop had only been open for an hour and in that time Nora and Roger had taken several piles of books upstairs. They had managed to put some away, left the rest in the appropriate rooms to be put onto the shelves later and decided they needed a cup of tea before tackling the rest.

While Roger checked his emails, Nora set about picking up the tumbling piles of books from the counter and placing them on the floor to arrange in the antiquarian shelves later on. She hummed happily as she did so. Running a secondhand and antiquarian bookshop had been a dream of hers ever since she was a child and five years ago her friend and employer Georgina Pickering, who owned The Secondhand Bookworm, had made that dream come true.

Nora had first made the acquaintance of Georgina Pickering during her long visits to Georgina's first bookshop located in Piertown not far from the village of Little Cove, where Nora was currently staying with her parents while she looked for a new flat, and where she had grown up.

The Secondhand Bookworm in Piertown had been opened by Georgina's mother back in the 1980's. It had commandeered a huge, long antique shop only a stone's throw away from the promenade and the famous pier.

The shop had comprised of an endless corridor lined with bookcases and ten bays full of books branching off the corridor along the whole right side, culminating in a room of sheet music at the very end and an extension filled with three more rooms of books to the left. The counter had been a long desk with a flap in the middle to lift up so as to get behind it, positioned to the right of the front door and located in front of three enormous glass fronted cases that housed all of the rare and antiquarian books.

Georgina's grandpa had lived in the old flats above The Secondhand Bookworm in Piertown, which had been converted into tenant flats linked to the bookshop after he had passed away.

Nora would spend hours every Saturday while she was at school and then at college, rummaging through the bays of books and discussing literature with Georgina until they had started to meet up for coffee in an old Piertown café and then set up their own book club.

When Georgina took over the running of The Secondhand Bookworm in Piertown from her mother she was inspired by a fit of ambition to open two more branches and asked Nora to manage her new bookshop in Castletown.

While taking a walk through nearby Wall Town, Georgina had stumbled upon a little estate agents with The Castletown Bookshop advertised for sale. She had struck up a friendship with Mr and Mrs Lodbrok who had run the Castletown bookshop for several decades and who had specialized in Norse mythology, sagas and poetry and who were looking to retire.

Georgina had purchased the shop and promptly employed Nora as its manager. For five long years Nora had enjoyed the daily ups and downs, chaos and dramas of working in The Secondhand Bookworm, Castletown, with her friend and colleague Cara running The Secondhand Bookworm in Seatown with Georgina. Georgina spent most of her time in the offices upstairs since closing down the Piertown branch several years ago. Cara and Nora were best friends and got on like sisters even though Cara had once thrown a book at Nora's head and another time Nora didn't speak to Cara for one whole week.

It was the perfect set up.

Nora was even sort-of dating Georgina's brother, Humphrey Pickering, who had recently retired from his high-powered company in London and was staying with Georgina until he too sorted out his own place.

Life was perfect.

Her humming turned to singing as she nudged Roger in the small of his back while she attempted to retrieve the polish and duster from under the shelf beneath, accidently pushed the phonebooks onto his lap, dropped a handful of felt-tip pens on his head and spilt some tea on his leg in the process of cleaning the desk until he stood up and volunteered to start putting away the paperbacks in the attic room, finishing his tea with a final loud gulp.

"Take one of the walkie-talkies up." Nora said, picking up one from the stands next to the phone.

The walkie-talkies were a new addition to the shop and saved them bellowing up and down the stairs to each other and scandalising the customers. Also, Nora felt like a cop whenever she used it.

"Okay." Roger nodded dubiously.

He took it and switched it on. Immediately the sound of crackling filled the room.

"Customer at 'Windmill Road'. Over."

"Taxis." Nora glanced out of the window to see if she could spot the local transport car. "Better change the channel."

They upped the channel to number five. Roger clipped his walkie-talkie onto his belt.

"Don't contact me unless absolutely essential." He warned.

"Not even if I get lonely?" Nora teased.

His lips twitched slightly and then he set off.

Nora heard him creaking up the stairs and grabbed the receiver when the phone began to ring again.

"The Secondhand Bookworm." Nora greeted.

"Did you tell that mad woman with the birthday cards to phone me?" Georgina Pickering's voice sounded on the end of the line.

Nora chuckled.

"I didn't think you would believe me if you didn't hear her yourself."

"Well, I wouldn't have." Georgina replied, half amused.

"So, did you buy them?" Nora asked.

"No I did not!"

"I particularly thought the 'Happy Birthday Brother' would have fetched a high price."

Georgina laughed too.

"I wished her luck with them." She said.

"How's it going over there? It's been mad here."

"That'd be because of the Duke of Cole, bringing in all the tourists to Castletown before the season. Have you seen how quickly his castle is being built? He'll be moving in before you know it."

"Yes. It's fantastic."

"It's pretty quiet here." Georgina moaned. "I just bought an enormous amount of books from the back of a man's van. Twelve boxes! I don't know what came over me."

"Twelve?! Was he a travelling library?"

"No, he had cleared out a bibliophile's house at the weekend and remembered seeing my shop here."

"Ooooh, anything nice?"

"A lot of general stock for both shops and some good runs of sets. Also, some yummy Folio Society books including a sparkling run of Andrew Lang fairy tales and some special editions. Very useful and clean. Betty and I are just trying to make some room here for customers."

Betty was the newest member of staff in The Secondhand Bookworm and had been working part-time for Georgina for almost two months. Before that she had often popped in and had sold antiquarian books herself on EBay. She was due to work with Nora on Wednesday.

"So I'll send half of this new stock for you to mark up." Georgina decided.

"Oh okay. I miss the quiet life." Nora teased.

"Silly. It's never been quiet there." Georgina chuckled. "Oh I'd better go. I think there's a customer behind the wall of boxes. Betty, did you trap him?"

Georgina rang off leaving Nora grinning. She replaced the phone and then her smile faded when she noticed a regular customer of The Secondhand Bookworm walking past the front windows, staring in.

"Oh dear." Nora muttered and grabbed the duster, beginning to polish the top of the counter.

The door opened and White-Lightning Joe almost fell into the room. He remained hanging onto the handle and swung with the door until he stepped down with a giggle and a little flourish of his hand.

"He-lo, Nora." He greeted.

"Hello." Nora returned, dusting away some biscuit crumbs.

"Do you have a poppy? Eeeep." He almost tripped where the carpet met the flagstones but straightened up and stood before the counter.

Nora looked at him.

"Hehe. Do you have poppy?" He asked again and the scent of White-Lightning cider wafted over Nora, reminding her as to why they had given him his sobriquet.

White-Lightning Joe was a short, rotund man who had recently been made redundant from his job at the Old Hotel further along the street. He had been a regular of The Secondhand Bookworm when it had been The Castletown Bookshop owned by Mr and Mrs Lodbrok. He collected books and ephemera all about the history of the town because his ancient old mother had once told him he was a direct descendent of the first Duke of Cole's closest servant and dung-gatherer, an occupation that many generations of White-Lightning Joe's ancestors had apparently held with pride until the Sixteenth century when they had gone up in the world and become chimney sweeps.

Ever since Nora had known him, Joe had carried a white plastic bag with a bottle of White-Lightning cider inside and sometimes asked Nora to lend him two quid to buy a bottle. He had strange mannerisms and very little social skills. Nora politely tolerated him and usually felt sorry for him but he was a bit of a menace.

"A poppy?" Nora repeated as he smiled at her stupidly.

"Yes. I left all the ones that I bought at home and I can't be bothered to traipse back there. I've only got five pence and I'm going to the eleven o'clock service in the town square. So have you got one I can wear?"

Nora shook her head.

"No, I don't. Sorry, Joe." She apologised but then remembered that Cara had bought one from a particularly pushy poppy-seller on Friday and it had kept falling off her jumper. "Hang on." She spotted it tacked to the computer monitor. "Here, you can have this one."

"Oh, thanks Nora! Zoinks!" White-Lightning Joe whipped it from her fingers and proceeded to try and zip it up in the front pocket of his jacket.

"I'm afraid I don't have a pin." Nora said.

"It'll stay on like this! Thanks, Nora." He stared at her through his bleary, bloodshot eyes and patted the poppy stuck fast in the zipper of his dirty jacket. "Are you going to the Poppy service?"

"No, I have to work."

"Aw. That's a shame." He fluttered his eyelashes again and Nora edged back. "Nora. Can you lend me two quid?"

"No."

"One quid?"

"No."

"Fifty pence."

"NO!"

His shoulders drooped.

"Okay. Well, I'd better go." He suddenly waved frantically in her face so that Nora edged back even further, almost falling off of her chair. "Bye-bye, Nora. Bye-bye. Eeeep."

"Bye." Nora said warily and watched him head towards the door. As he stepped up, someone pushed the door open to come in and White-Lightning Joe staggered back.

"Whooops. Eeeeeeep. Ha-ha. After you, Madam." He said with a low bow and the woman hurried past with a repulsed look at him.

White-Lightning Joe closed the door and set off up the road, brandishing his poppy with a smirk at the woman with a boxful who was approaching him.

"Hello." Nora greeted the new customer.

"Your shop in Walltown told me that you sell books on tissue craft." The woman said.

Nora stared at her.

"Where?"

"Walltown!" She repeated .

Nora decided not to point out that they didn't have a shop in Walltown so smiled politely.

"Well we have a section on crafts so if we specifically had tissue crafts then that's where they'd be, on the next floor." Nora explained.

The woman looked around.

"Where are the stairs?" She frowned.

"Back there." Nora indicated.

"Can't you check your computer and see?"

"We don't have our books listed I'm afraid." Nora explained.

"Oh, don't you? How silly of you." She headed for the stairs, shaking her head. "You really should you know."

Nora watched her go and sighed.

"Now there's an idea." She muttered and set about polishing the till with much beeping.

Five minutes later an extremely plump woman and a very skinny child entered The Secondhand Bookworm and the child ran up to the counter.

"Where's the Poppy-Man?" The lady asked, leaving the door wide open so that an empty crisp packet blew in.

"The Poppy-Man!" The skinny child echoed, looking as windswept as a scarecrow.

Nora stared at them.

"There were some people outside selling poppies earlier, about three of them." She explained.

"No, the Poppy-Man! The large poppy!" The woman corrected insistently.

Nora blinked.

"Pardon?"

"He's a big poppy." The skinny girl explained as if it was obvious.

"Oh! I didn't know about a large Poppy-Man, do you mean someone dressed as a poppy?" She asked.

"Yes, yes, the Poppy-Man!" The child exclaimed.

"I'm afraid I haven't seen him." Nora assured them, wishing she had.

"He's not in here then?" The plump woman asked, scanning the room.

"No, I definitely didn't see a giant poppy walk in."

"Fine! We'll go and look outside for him then!" The woman said shortly and with a glare at Nora she took hold of the girl's arm and stomped back out of the shop.

While Nora stared, a sudden voice sounded from under the cash book.

"Nora. Where do Isaac Asimov paperbacks go? They look like crime...oh no, of course not, what was I thinking, they're sci-fi, never mind. Thank you." Roger said and the walkie-talkie beeped.

Nora saw a flash on the monitor as a Skype message from the Seatown branch popped up. She clicked on it and read:

'We found two customers trapped behind our wall of boxes!'

Nora's shoulders shook with laughter and she began to reply when the door opened, letting in another small pile of leaves that swirled in a perfect circle and settled on the mat.

A man marched into the room.

"It's warm in here!" He said, fanning the air before his face.

Nora watched him head determinedly through to the back of the shop.

"Door." She sighed, seeing that it had been left wide open.

She stood up, stepped around the counter and was about to walk over and close it when the space was filled by a looming dark shadow, like an eclipse of the sun. An enormous man in a long green raincoat and a furious expression on his face stomped loudly on the leaves on the mat and then on the flagstones, leaving the door wide open behind him, too.

Nora smiled warily.

"Hello. Can I help?" She asked, feeling the warm air began to drift out onto the street.

"I'm looking for a newspaper." The man said.

"There's a newsagents on the corner." Nora explained.

"You don't sell newspapers?"

"I'm afraid not."

"What are you? A library?" He scowled.

"No, we're a bookshop." Nora said, heading back around the front of the desk for protection.

"And you don't sell newspapers?"

"No, sorry." Nora assured.

"They've got some coupons in The Sun today and knowing my luck they've all sold out." He scowled, turning around. "There are leaves on the floor by the way. You might think about hoovering."

Nora blinked, watching him go where he left the door wide open so that an empty *Peperami* wrapper plopped onto the mat. She was about to go and pick it up when a large Poppy appeared in the doorway.

"Good morning." It said.

"Good morning." She stared.

The Poppy was a man in a dodgy black spandex body suit. He wore huge black shoes, had gigantic black foam hands and an enormous red foam poppy costume that covered his entire head and a radius of about two foot above it, his shoulders and torso, and reached down to his knees. The black middle circle of the poppy was located in the centre of his chest and his face was behind some thick red gauze that blended into one of the petals of the poppy shaped foam.

He attempted to enter through the doorway but got wedged between the frames. Nora watched him struggle for a while, large hands flailing comically about and bony knees thrashing for momentum until he gave up. He remained outside, presumably staring into the shop.

"Can I help?" Nora asked, supressing the urge to laugh as she walked over to him.

"Na, don't worry. Seems like the only way I'd get in is to remove this costume and what I'm wearing underneath don't leave much to the imagination." He said in a muffled tone.

"Oh, okay." Nora tried not to look.

"Unless you know your entire stock?" He seemed to shrug.

"Are you looking for a specific book?" Nora asked, bending down and picking up the Peperoni packet and some leaves.

"Yeah, '*The Gruffalo*', it's about a mouse walking through a forest or something." The giant poppy said.

"Oh yes, that's a lovely book! We don't have it at the moment; we get asked for it a lot." Nora explained.

"Ah well, thanks, it's for my son so I ask whenever I see a bookshop. Thanks, luv." He waved a large hand, turned and headed off up the street.

Nora watched him go, smiling to herself.

She returned behind the counter, dropped the rubbish into the bin and then watched as the door blew open by itself and about fifteen leaves sailed in. With a groan, Nora flopped into her seat, wondering if she should invest in a large net.

It was almost eleven o'clock and Roger stood tidying the Cole section which had had a good rummage through over the weekend. His time in the paperback room had been going well until a large group of walkers had arrived. When his hand had been crushed by a heavy walking boot for the third time he had returned downstairs and was now waiting for the clock to approach eleven so they could observe the national one minute silence for the war dead.

Nora was writing down her last sale in the cash book; three postcards showing the view of the town with the keep from the castle ruins in the background. As she picked up a yellow highlighter to draw a bright yellow line over the sale for Georgina to notice the retailing of postcards easily, Nora wondered if the Duke of Cole would have a whole range of new postcards taken when his castle renovations had been built. She was happily picturing a large Disney castle behind the shop, with her standing on a balcony beside the Duke wearing a diamond crown on her head, surrounded by glittering stars and fluttering blue birds, when Roger cursing and muttering because several books wouldn't fit back on the shelves drew her back to reality.

Clearing her throat, Nora ran the yellow highlighter across the page and looked up and into the town square through the window.

Many people had been emerging from their houses or shops in the tempest to gather on the cobbles near the war memorial, where several solemn looking clergymen were loitering with the giant Poppy-Man. Nora stared at the odd scene, slightly bemused. Her amusement then vanished when she recognised two ladies standing on the fringe of the crowd.

"Glory!" Nora whispered.

One of the ladies was squat and plump and had a huge red puffy duffle coat wrapped around her, bare legs, white knee high socks and white plimsolls with a tan coloured fishing hat. The woman beside her was taller and had a giant knitted bobble hat, a thick pink scarf wrapped several times around her neck, a thick blue coat, luminous yellow trousers and similar white plimsolls to her mother's. Several bags surrounded them on the floor.

"I spy the Ravens." Roger said glumly.

He was now looking through the glass in the door at the gathering, having abandoned sorting out the Cole section.

"Hmm. Indeed. I was hoping I was imagining that." Nora grimaced, throwing down the highlighter to join him.

The wind rattled the hinges and then opened the door so that it pushed Roger into Nora and Nora into one of the postcard spinners.

"It's a sign." Nora said as Roger steadied himself and checked his watch.

He gave her an ironic look, stepping up onto the doorstep. Nora stepped up with him and they stood in the doorway being buffeted by the wind as the minute hand almost reached eleven o'clock.

Other shopkeepers were in their doorways and Philip and Alice waved at them from the delicatessen. Nora waved back, Roger frowned at them and then an ear-splitting 'BOOM' shook the windows of the shop, vibrating through both Nora and Roger.

"Wow." Nora breathed, clutching her chest.

The canon that marked the strike of eleven o'clock had been fired from the castle ruins behind them. Several people had ducked at the sound and the Anglican vicar's hat had blown off, but Nora supposed that was because of the wind. Trying not to smile, she closed her eyes and gathered her thoughts as Castletown observed the minute's silence.

A second ear splitting 'BOOM!!!" sounded throughout the town to indicate the end of the minute's silence. A woman dropped her bag of apples so that all the apples rolled into the road and about the square and the feet of the gathered clergy.

"Oh dear." Roger said as he watched everyone hastily try to pick them up and two people bang heads.

Nora swallowed back a laugh which became a groan.

"Incoming!" She whispered hard, eyes riveted on the Ravens.

Although the Catholic priest was intoning prayers for the war dead, the Ravens had decided to shuffle through the crowd, eyes fixed upon the bookshop.

"It's too early to close up isn't it?" Roger frowned, turning Nora around and ushering her back into the shop.

"I'm afraid so." She smirked and he closed the door behind her as she hurried around the counter.

"Now is the perfect time to visit the men's room." Roger said and grabbed the keys off the desk.

"The ladies room." Nora corrected.

"I'll leave you to it." He smiled.

"Traitor." Nora glowered playfully as the door opened and Nora heard the familiar rustle of plastic bags.

When she looked up and smiled politely, her brows lifted curiously to see that it was only Mrs Raven entering the shop.

"Good morning." Nora greeted her cheerfully.

Mrs Raven shuffled into the room, her eyes fixed on the front of the desk. Nora watched as she stretched out her arms, which had a bag hanging from each elbow, and approached her slowly. For a moment Nora wondered if Mrs Raven was sleep-walking. Her hands reached for a pile of leaflets that advertised The Secondhand Bookworm in Seatown and Mrs Raven determinedly took up the entire pile.

"I'll…just…take…these." She whispered breathlessly and stared at Nora.

"Oh. Okay."

"Thank you." She whispered and Nora watched her turn away and shuffle back towards the door. Wondering why Mrs Raven would need the entire pile Nora's gaze was drawn to the window and met with the piercing blue pair of eyes belonging to Miss Raven who was staring at her from outside.

Nora gave a hesitant wave. She then turned to the computer monitor which was flashing a Skype message.

'Do you have anything about the Pre-Raphaelites? Customer waiting.'

Nora blinked and walked over to the art section to have a look. She could only find a standard hardback about the Pre-Raphaelites by Essential Art with an introduction by Dr Juliet Hacking, priced at £10 so she Skyped the information through and watched the pen begin to move a moment later.

'Got that here. Thought we'd be short, they're popular. Thank you though.'

"*No worries.*' Nora typed and then added. *'Did you employ the Ravens for advertising?'*

Mrs Raven was now handing out leaflets to people who were walking away from the eleven o'clock service. Miss Raven was holding the flaps of her deerstalker hat against her head while the gales battered them both.

The sound of footsteps from the back room then startled her as she hadn't realised there had been a customer there.

He approached the counter and seemed engrossed in a book he was holding. Nora noticed that he had a large hearing aid in each ear.

She smiled when he looked up and wiggled the tome at her.

"George Eliot's 'Silas Marner'." He said almost whimsically. "Makes Jane Austen look like Pulp Fiction.

Jane Austen found a theme; it wasn't broke so she didn't fix it. Have you read any?"

"Oh, of George Eliot?"

"Hmm."

"Yes, I read 'Middlemarch' some years ago." Nora nodded.

"Read them *all*, young lady, read them all and you'll see what I mean. Now, how much do I owe you for this?" He asked, putting it on the top of the message pad.

Nora opened the front cover to read the price.

"That's two pounds fifty please." She said.

"That's a good price. Is it new?" The man took out a little purse and shook it, peering inside for coins.

"Yes, all the Wordsworth Classics are ordered in new." Nora explained.

As the man paid, the door opened to admit two people who were wearing matching raincoats and who immediately headed for the window.

Nora ran the George Eliot sale through the till as the man picked a book off the shelf and passed it to the woman.

"Do you need a bag?" Nora offered her customer.

She looked around her when she heard the sound of high pitched whistling.

"Eh? Hold up, my ear-wiggy's playing up." He twisted his hearing aid and the whistling changed pitch several times before it stopped.

Nora smiled with understanding.

"Do you need a bag?" Nora repeated.

"No, no, no." The man took up the book and squashed it unceremoniously into his pocket. "Save the planet and all that."

Nora watched him head off, her attention returning to the new customers.

The man in the raincoat was studying the book and the woman in the raincoat with him was looking around, her nose crinkled up disdainfully. She took the book from the man.

"Can we go? The smell." She said.

The man watched her put the book back.

"I didn't notice a smell."

"It's because they don't clean the damn place." The woman said. "They just shove sprays around."

Nora stared in astonishment.

"Oh. I didn't notice." The man shrugged and they both left.

Nora sniffed warily, wondering if there was a slight damp smell she was immune to. The bookshop had been flooded several months before but the dehumidifier from Humphrey's boat seemed to have taken care of that.

She turned back to the computer monitor and saw that Georgina had replied to her question about the Ravens.

'Don't be daft!'

Nora's lips twitched and then she sat pondering the reason why Mrs Raven would require their entire stack of Seatown Bookworm leaflets. The Ravens seemed to have gone now. Several leaflets were sailing about in the wind.

Suddenly, Nora felt her iPhone buzz, indicating that she had received a text message. Nora dug it out of her jeans, swiped the screen and saw Humphrey's handsome face smiling up at her. Glad of the distraction from her bookworms, Nora tapped the message to read it.

'On my way home from Tiny Town. Stuck in traffic and finally have a signal. Did the canon blow out your eardrums? Xx' Humphrey had sent.

Nora chuckled.

'Almost. How did you know x' She sent back.

'I remember it from last year. Any sign of the new Duke, then? xx'

'Not that I noticed. He might not be here but in one of his other stately properties. He's a very busy man x'

'Do I have reason to be jealous? xx'

Nora rolled her eyes.

'Of me and the Duke. In my dreams x' Nora sent back.

'Word is that he's book mad like you. I'll have to flex my muscles xx' Humphrey decided.

Nora giggled.

'Ten paces in the town square?' She joked.

'If that's what it takes. I'll be over soon xx'

'Humphrey! We're still just friends, remember!'

'Traffic is moving. See you in a bit xx'

Nora sighed and popped her phone back into her pocket, imagining Humphrey duelling with the Duke over her on the cobbles and deciding she quite liked that idea.

The sound of keys tinkling preceded the return of Roger followed by the large group of walkers.

"...and we observed the minute's silence in your attic room, I hope you don't mind. It was a bit bizarre us all standing there facing each other while surrounded by six thousand paperbacks but Mavis said a prayer for the war dead." One man was saying loudly.

"And also for Hetty who almost had a heart attack because of that cannon going off." Another man said with a laugh.

"Yes, it was rather loud." Roger agreed.

They entered the front of the shop and Roger looked at Nora warily.

"Why are you sniffing?"

"Does this shop smell?" She asked him as he walked behind her and hung up the keys.

"Yes. Of musty old books." He replied.

"I must be immune to it." Nora smiled politely at the group of walkers who were talking loudly amongst themselves, two of them holding a handful of books each.

"Are all your books secondhand?" A man with three paperbacks asked Nora.

"Mostly." She opened the top paperback and put the price into the till. "We have a few new ones."

"Such as?" He dug in his rucksack for his wallet.

"Well, those books about the art of '*Eric Ravilious'* are new because there is an exhibition of his work in Seatown and we have been getting a lot of requests for books about him. Also some local history books that we are able to order through a local publishing company."

"And the Wordsworth classics." Roger added.

"Would you like a bag for these, sir?"

"Ah yes please, a bag would be good." The man nodded and slapped a twenty pound note on the desk. "But the majority of your books here are secondhand?"

Both Nora and Roger nodded. Roger unhooked a bright blue bag and began to put the paperbacks inside. Once Nora had given the customer his change one of the ladies with him placed her pile of books onto the counter. She opened her bag and a handful of used tissues fell all over the counter.

Nora reached for the top book, trying not to think about old lady bogies. When she saw the price written inside she showed the lady.

"This one is eight pounds fifty." Nora said.

"What?" The lady leaned in and pointed to the unclipped price tag on the dust wrapper. "It says its three pounds ninety nine."

"That's not our price I'm afraid." Nora explained.

"But your price is more expensive than the original price when the book was new."

"That's inflation, Mavis." The man with her said.

"In a secondhand bookshop?"

"Some books do increase in value, especially if they go out of print." Nora explained.

The other two walkers were talking together behind them, the man kicking mud off his boots against the edge of a bookcase.

Nora saw Roger turn to glare at him. She bit back a smile.

"Well, I'll leave that one then." Mavis decided.

"Sorry, but we buy all of our books in and prices do change." Nora said.

"Yes, yes, I'm sure that's the case." Mavis sighed, rummaging around her purse.

Nora ran the other book prices through the till and took a ten pound note from Mavis.

"Would you like a bag?" Roger asked.

"Yes, please." Mavis smiled with a nod.

Roger bagged up the books and Nora handed back the change. They watched the group of walkers leave loudly.

The door closed behind them and Nora was distracted by the black blur of a biretta soaring past the window, closely followed by a clergyman in a fur edged vestment running after it with his hand stretched out, trailed by White-Lightning Joe and a woman with a box of poppies hanging around her neck and a red collection tin in her hand.

"This town is odd." Nora chuckled and flopped into the chair.

Roger checked his watch.

"Would you like a cake?" He decided. "My treat."

"Oh that would be lovely." Nora accepted.

"They do some nice Victoria Sponge cake in the deli." He said, heading for the narrow corridor behind the counter that led under the stairs.

"Thanks." Nora nodded. "I'll put the kettle on."

She dashed off to the kitchen quickly, filled up the little kettle and dashed back to see Roger emerge wrapped in a scarf, thick coat and wearing his beanie hat and gloves. Nora stared.

"It's windy." He pointed out defensively, putting on some fluffy brown spotty earmuffs.

Nora giggled.

"Kettle's on."

"Back in a moment." He nodded, walking around the counter and out of the door.

Nora sat down, chuckling to herself as she watched him head towards the deli, stooped over against the wind, immediately pursued by a poppy seller.

2 MISS READ AND THE ROAD SWEEPER

Later that afternoon, while Roger was at lunch, Nora sat at the desk marking up some books that she had bought from a local woman who was moving to Nottinghamshire. A tottering pile of 'Miss Read' novels sat on the worn out wooden stool next to her. As Nora pencilled in the prices she added them so that the stool wobbled precariously.

She had just priced up a copy of 'Storm in the Village' when a large man with a red face stepped down into the shop.

"I'll stand here shall I? And mind the step?" He asked loudly, pointing to Nora's printed sign on the window.

Nora laughed politely and the man guffawed loudly.

"Bet you hear that one every day." He said, smirked and closed the door behind him. He cast a quick gaze around the shop and then walked up to Nora.

"Do you buy books?"

Nora nodded.

"Yes we do."

"I'm having a clear out. Ah, I'll take a card." He said, spotting the little business card holder on the desk and picking up one of the bright blue cards. "But I'm also after some books to buy. Do you have a section on dog psychology?"

Nora stared at him.

"Erm, not an entire section but we have a section on animals and a few shelves of books about dogs."

He slid the business card into his pocket.

"Where do I go?"

"The top room." Nora pointed upwards. "The stairs are through there."

"Oh, three floors of books!" He exclaimed, walking around the desk and heading for the back. "I may be some time."

Nora watched him go and then blinked in surprise to hear polite knocking at the door.

"Hello, hello, hello. It's that time of year again." A familiar voice sailed in as the door opened and a man named Paul stepped down into the shop followed by several crisp packets and a gust of wind.

Nora straightened up.

"Oh, hello. We only seem to see you once a year in here." Nora watched him cross to the counter with his clipboard.

He grimaced guiltily, flattening his hair which was wild from the wind.

"It's one of life's mysteries when you intend to go into the bookshop around the corner from your office and never seem to find the moment." He said with a sigh. "One day I will come in and browse around."

Nora peered at his clipboard.

"Christmas tree time?" She asked.

Paul nodded.

"They're sixty five pounds this year." He explained. "We'll be delivering them during the second week of

December, complete with lights which will be put on the steady setting. Last year the whole town was flashing through various sequences and it wasn't quite the sophisticated look we were hoping for in Castletown."

"I did notice that last Christmas." Nora chuckled.

He unclipped a sheet and handed it to her.

"I'll pass it on to Georgina." She promised.

"Thanks." He winked at Nora and then turned, leaving the shop while whistling cheerfully.

There was the sudden sound of a fanfare announcing that a message had arrived on Skype chat so Nora read it.

'Hello Nora, it's Betty. Georgina has gone to The Bank. Lovely weather here, how are you? Been asked out by a window cleaner. Made my Day. Pretend he wasn't JUST being polite. Betty.'

Nora chuckled and replied back while the door opened and Roger returned from lunch wrapped up like an Eskimo.

"If those poppy sellers had had their way I would have bought at least six on my break." He scowled in a muffled voice behind his scarf.

"Oh yes, they are rather eager." Nora laughed.

Roger muttered and mumbled moaningly to himself as he removed his layers of winter wear, finally emerging from under the stairs to stand and peer at the cash book.

"Have you been busy?"

Nora pointed to the stool.

"I bought those."

"Oh." He picked up a Miss Read. "I've never read any of these."

"I think they're for old ladies."

"Sexist." He said.

Nora grinned, continuing to mark up the Miss Read books.

"Shall I make us an after-lunch cup of tea?" Roger suggested.

"At this rate I will look like a teapot." Nora pointed out. "And yes, please."

"We actually do need a teapot here." Roger mused, looking at Nora as though imagining her with a spout and handle.

"We don't." Nora laughed.

"Tea from a teapot tastes so much better. You're a very uncivilised young woman." He decided and headed off to make them a nice hot drink.

Nora continued to mark up the Miss Read novels she had bought. The weather outside was dark and gloomy and still very blustery so that a gust of wind swung the door open and a Twirl bar wrapper and a cigarette end dropped onto the mat.

Nora sighed, put down her book, stood up and grabbed the tall plastic broom and dustpan that was squashed next to the night storage heater behind the counter. She then set about sweeping up leaves and rubbish in the doorway, glancing into the square as the street cleaner walked past chatting on his mobile phone.

The street cleaner was a new replacement in the town and was talkative with the shop owners and residents as he went about with his cart and sometimes his motorised sweeper. His name was Hugh and he was in his late twenties.

Hugh wore his hair in a 1950's pompadour style and had jagged teeth. Usually he sported a thick white duffle coat with a dirty luminous yellow bib squashed over the top and high-vis yellow trousers. The entire look was finished off with wellington boots and thick mud-caked, holey gloves which Nora had decided must once have been white.

Despite his willingness to chat, Hugh was fiercely protective of the pavements and was often seen flying past picking up rubbish behind people and glaring. The glaring had also been aimed at Nora that very morning when she had walked through his pile of swept up leaves resulting in a scowl from him.

Hugh was currently speaking about the public toilets with a woman whose head was wrapped in a headscarf decorated with large brightly coloured butterflies. Nora grimaced as a gust of wind blew the leaves off her dustpan and back onto the carpet.

"Any books on ambulances?"

Nora jumped at the sound of a voice near her ear. She turned to see a man who had been in the shop the whole time.

"Sorry." He apologised.

"Erm…ambulances? No. I'm pretty sure we don't see many books specifically on ambulances." Nora said, scooping up the fresh leaves quickly, followed by a crisp packet and the cigarette end.

"Can you check your computer?" He asked.

Nora walked across the shop and stood behind the counter shaking her head.

"We don't list our books I'm afraid." She said.

"Really? Well, I suppose there are quite a lot here."

"There are." She nodded happily, pleased he understood.

"But you could use a barcode system." He suggested.

"They're mostly secondhand." She explained, pouring the leaves and other rubbish into the bin behind the desk.

"Yes, it should be quite easy to set up."

Nora smiled politely.

"I'll mention it to the owner." She said.

"Oh, isn't this your shop?"

"No, my friend's."

"Would he know if you had any books about ambulances?"

Nora smiled.

"He's not here, I'm afraid." She said, deciding not to correct him as to Georgina's gender. "Did you look in the motoring section?"

"I did." He nodded. "It doesn't surprise me as there aren't many around. I probably already have them all."

He picked up one of the display books from the top of the counter, read the title and then replaced it, turning around and leaving. Nora dropped the broom and dustpan to the side and returned to marking up the last of the Miss Read books.

"The Village School." Nora read the title. "Number one of the Fairacre series."

She placed it on her pile and then made a grab at the stack as it began to slide off the stool towards the floor. Standing up, Nora gathered the books in her arms and placed them onto the carpet.

She decided to add up the takings of the day so far and had just grabbed the calculator when she noticed a figure walking past the shop window and towards the doorway of The Secondhand Bookworm.

Nora stared in surprise.

One of her regular customers had arrived with his usual black flowing coat, but instead of his signature white shoulder length hair he sported a short back and sides.

"Hello Nora." Spencer Brown smiled, stepping into the shop and closing the door behind him. "Anything new for me?"

Nora stared at Spencer, trying to process his new image.

As if reading her mind, Spencer reached up and ran a hand through his tiny fringe.

"Sal made me have a haircut, said it was getting a bit too wild and I was looking like a woman." He explained.

Nora bit back a smile.

"Oh. It looks very nice."

"What a terrible liar you are." Spencer grinned, looking pointedly behind the counter at the rare and antiquarian books. "Anything new in by Aleister Crowley?"

"No." Nora said flatly.

She was still staring at Spencer's hair.

"I'm enjoying devouring Crowley's '777' that Georgina got for me." Spencer's blue eyes glittered. "What an evil book. Signed by the man himself."

"Don't you mean the *beast* himself?" Nora muttered and Spencer chuckled.

"I'm pretty sure it's signed in blood you know." He said half seriously.

"How terrible."

"It's all research, Nora." He said, heading for the room behind her. "It's all research. I'll go and check upstairs." He decided. "See if anything new has come in."

Nora watched him go and was about to gather up the pens all over the desk when the duffled figure of Mrs Raven loomed up to the door. Nora watched silently as Mrs Raven glided in, leaving the door open behind her. She walked up to the counter, scanning for more leaflets about the Seatown shop. When she reached the counter, Nora smiled.

"Hello."

Mrs Raven stared at Nora through her large glasses.

"We're looking for…looking for…Lemony Snickets." She whispered breathlessly.

"Oh. Yes, if we have any they would be upstairs." Nora nodded.

Mrs Raven stared at Nora for what seemed like ages before she moved around the desk towards the walkway into the back of the shop and the stairwell. Nora's eyes followed her and then stopped as Mrs Raven paused, slowly turned her head and fixed Nora with a long stare.

"Are…you…on…your…own?" She whispered sinisterly.

"Yes." Nora replied.

Without saying another word Mrs Raven continued walking and Nora heard her creaking up the stairs.

Nora wondered where Miss Raven was and then jumped when she met Miss Raven's blue stare peering in through the window again. Smiling uncomfortably, Nora was pleased to see Roger return from the kitchen with two mugs of tea.

"I'm glad you're back." Nora whispered. "I think the Ravens are planning to murder me."

"You'll be taken back to Raven Manor and chopped up into a thousand pieces and used to fill up their great stash of our Bookworm bags that they have collected over the last several years." Roger said.

"Don't say that!"

Roger chuckled, passing her a cup of tea.

"Georgina has sent a message about you going on calls on Thursday." Roger said, gesturing to the monitor with a loud slurp of his tea.

"Oh. Hmm what delights will that behold I wonder." She said, wheeling herself in the swivel chair to in front of the keyboard. She read the message:

'Nora - on Thursday can I pick you up from the train station so I can drop you back home after the last call which is around the corner from you?'

'Yes, that's fine.' Nora skyped back.

'I have asked Cara to come to my house tomorrow morning to pick up some transfers and price a few books I have there so she will be a bit late to you.' Georgina wrote.

'Okay!'

'DOWNPOUR heading your way!!' Georgina's next message warned.

"Oh dear." Nora peered through the windows into the street. "Rain warning."

"Eh?" Roger looked up sharply. "Well, most of the stuff is already in because of the wind." Roger said, pondering the postcard spinners and the box of free maps that was the bane of Nora's life. The black boxes that held a selection of paperbacks for fifty pence each were still outside, clipped against the wall.

"I just hope the road doesn't flood again." Nora grimaced, remembering the last time that heavy rain had deluged the town.

"Let's not talk about that." Roger frowned.

Nora stood up, took a sip of hot tea and cracked her knuckles.

"Sandbags at the ready." Nora decided.

"I'll move them outside." Roger said, putting down his mug. "I can't expect a lady to drag sandbags onto the street while I sit watching."

"You're a rare breed, Roger." Nora chuckled as he walked over to where they were now kept stacked behind the door.

Roger had just bent down to drag the first one out when Mrs Raven stomped through into the front room, walked past Nora without looking at her, pulled open the door and almost flattened Roger against the wall.

Nora covered her mouth as Roger straightened up with a scowl.

"Excuse…me…" Mrs Raven whispered hard and stepped out into the street to join Miss Raven, who for some reason had decided not to come in that day.

Roger threw Nora a look so she smiled sympathetically. Shaking his head he hauled up the first bag and placed it against the wall outside next to the cheap paperback boxes, pondering the road.

"How is it out there?" Nora asked, joining him by the door and they peered out into the street.

"Gloomy." Roger frowned.

The skies were dark and it was starting to drizzle. The town was empty except for the Ravens, who were now climbing into a taxi on the cobbles, and a seagull attacking a discarded sandwich on the pavement outside Lady Lane's Antiques.

"I thought we were getting a drain put in the road outside?" Roger glowered. "If we have a repeat of before I shan't be amused."

"Yes we are at some point. The road hasn't flooded since but it does go like a lake still and being prepared with sandbags now will stop the shop getting submerged." Nora explained.

The street cleaner walked past with his broom and stared at Roger and Nora peering out into the town.

"He's weird." Roger muttered.

Smirking, Nora turned as Spencer Brown reappeared carrying a small pile of books.

"Alien invasion?" He asked hopefully, seeing them standing looking out into the street.

Nora headed back to the counter.

"No, it's starting to rain."

Spencer grimaced.

"I'd better get back. Can you keep these by for me Nora? I can't remember if I have these already, can you just write the titles down for me?"

"Of course." Nora grabbed some post-its, wrote out the titles for Spencer, and then bagged up the books as he dashed out into the rain which was getting heavier.

The phone rang so Roger answered it while Nora placed the books under the counter. She then looked towards the window in shock at the sudden sound of immensely heavy rain. While Roger dealt with the customer on the telephone, Nora ran to the door and watched.

As had happened before, the rain began to gather at the kerb and the puddle in the road grew rapidly. The water that poured down from the top of the hill added to the mini lake outside The Secondhand Bookworm, which grew until the level was almost at the kerb. Nora stood poised, ready to drag the sandbags in front of the door if it rose any higher.

A couple of people were running screaming and laughing across the square under newspapers. As the rain began to ease off again into a drizzle, a man came out of the delicatessen and stepped into the road, his foot sinking almost to his shin. Muttering he ran through the lake to the bookshop side of the street and headed off down the road.

"Blimey. Close call." Roger said, joining her at the door.

"Luckily there's no traffic." Nora agreed.

The street cleaner came along and stopped, staring at the puddle. He turned and looked at them.

"That's crap!" Hugh said, pointing and shaking his head. "They need to put a drain there."

"They do indeed." Nora nodded.

The sound of a car coming down the hill caught her attention.

"Erm, you had better move out of the way." She told Hugh quickly.

Hugh stared at her.

"Wha'?"

"That car going through that puddle will cause a tidal wave. You'll get soaked." Nora explained.

Hugh turned and watched the approaching car.

"Oi!" He yelled threateningly at it as it neared the narrow part of the road just before them.

Nora covered her mouth to suppress a laugh as the old woman driving the car slammed on her brakes when she saw Hugh pointing and waving frantically at the puddle. It didn't help that his wet hair was flat against his head and face.

The car drove slowly through the water so that it lapped the kerb gently and the old woman stared at Hugh as she passed him with a look of astonishment.

Hugh glared after the car and when it had gone he attempted to sweep the water around the corner with his largest broom.

Swallowing back a laugh, Nora watched Hugh come back shaking his head.

"All of the drains are blocked up." He said.

"Yes, they're all pretty old. It does flood here." Nora agreed.

"Really? What, in there?" He peered into the shop past Nora.

"It flooded right to the back of the room once. Which is why we have sandbags." Roger explained glumly.

Hugh rubbed his chin, pondering the lake that was slowly dispersing.

"All of the drains around 'ere are crap." He said. "They really need to sort it out."

"Hmm well the Indian restaurant has been part of the problem. They've been pouring oil down their sinks for about twenty five years." Nora shared, still pondering the puddle. "They're still doing it; even though they have a new owner called Max who assured us he wouldn't let them. I don't think he can control them."

Hugh stared at Nora.

"We'll just have to see what happens." She concluded with a frown at the puddle and sighed, hoping that there wouldn't be any more flooding into the bookshop.

"You need a cone." Hugh said, scratching his head.

"We do have one actually." Nora remembered.

"Well, shove it just there and the cars should slow down." He pointed.

"Good idea." She said and went back into the shop, leaving Hugh examining the puddle with Roger who was no doubt reminiscing about the last time the shop had flooded.

Nora grabbed the shop keys and hurried into the kitchen. She unlocked the back door to the yard which was currently covered in weeds and moss, spotted the red cone next to one of the small drains near the back door, put one foot onto the moss covered floor, leaned forward and picked it up.

She screamed as a big spider ran away once she had lifted it. Holding the cone away from her at arm's length, Nora shut the door, locked it and walked back through the shop, meeting Roger who was waiting for her.

"We just had a Skype message from Seatown. Mrs Jones of Piertown is looking for a Clive Cussler. Mind if I go and check?" He asked, frowning at the sight of Nora holding the cone at arm's length in front of her.

"Sure, go ahead. I'm just going to put this in the road. Do you have a walkie-talkie?" She nodded.

"No." Roger said sardonically and Nora heard him climbing the stairs as she pulled open the door. Hugh was no longer about so Nora dropped the cone in the road, noting that the water was dissipating.

"That should help." She decided happily and returned into the shop.

She stood for a moment watching the traffic slow down noticeably and drive through the puddle with minimum wave-effect. Pleased, Nora turned and was suddenly aware of a man standing at the counter.

"Oh, hello. Can I help?" She asked, brushing the dust from her hands.

"Would you have a phone number for a holiday park in Dorset?" The man asked.

For a moment Nora just stared at him.

"Pardon?"

"In all these here books? A phone number for a holiday park in Dorset? Or a travel book on Dorset with caravan sites in it?" He asked.

"I'm pretty sure that we don't." Nora decided. "You could check in the newsagents?"

"Never mind." He said and turned around, leaving the shop.

Nora was just about to take a sip of tea when a man threw open the door and remained on the doorstep.

"Hallow! Hallow there! Do you have any framed maps?" The man shouted into the room.

Nora wiped some spilt tea from her chin.

"No." She replied. "We only have maps to use. Walking maps." She explained.

She watched as a dog obviously belonging to him squashed past his legs to come into the shop. He was a black and white collie and kept his nose to the ground. The man flinched.

"Bertie! Get back here." He shouted but remained standing on the doorstep. "Ah that's a shame. Thanks anyway." He said to Nora.

"No worries."

Nora then almost dropped her tea when she saw the dog sit down on the carpet and scoot its behind from one side of the room to the other.

"Oi! Bertie! Out now!" The man shouted, clicking his fingers.

The dog jumped up and looking delighted, ran out of the shop. The man closed the door and Nora remained staring at the carpet for a long moment. She then leaned forward, placed her forehead on the desk and closed her eyes, her shoulders shaking with silent laughter.

It was dark when Roger set the alarm and Nora waited on the step behind the sandbags. Two large sacks of sand had been placed in front of the door in case it rained overnight. There was also now a wooden board that slipped down in front of the door too and stood six inches high, made by Georgina's uncle as an added defence against any water.

As the alarm beeped, Roger strolled to the door, stepped over the board and the bags while grumbling and closed it behind him for Nora to lock up. Roger had picked Nora up that morning from Little Cove as they took it in turns to car share whenever they worked a day together.

"Hi Nora. You didn't get flooded again then?" Billy from the Antiques Centre called across the square.

Nora waved, shaking her head.

"It'll be good when they get that new drain in." Roger glowered, looking at the road while they walked past the barber shop.

"I'm not really convinced that it will make much of a difference." Nora said. "I'm sure it's the entire system that backs up and that's all down to the restaurants pouring oil continuously down there."

She cast a dark look back at the Indian Restaurant.

"Max has been avoiding Georgina. I think he's put his uncle in charge." She added.

"Typical." Roger said glumly.

They stopped at the corner shop and Roger bought himself a Lion bar and Nora a Curly Wurly. They chatted about books all the way to where his small white Nissan Micra was parked not far from the castle gates, climbed in, he pulled the automatic gearstick towards him and they set off as it started to drizzle.

Roger drove hair-raisingly fast over the bridge until they joined a little queue of traffic at the roundabout.

Once clear he put his foot down and Nora wondered if her cheeks were experiencing g-force. They arrived at Little Cove in less than ten minutes, pulling up before the front gate of Nora's house.

"Thanks for the lift." Nora gasped, opening the door and climbing out a little unsteadily. "My turn next time."

"I don't think we're down to work together until next week." Roger said.

"Until then!" Nora saluted, slung her bag over her shoulder and stepped back as he screeched away, quickly becoming a shrinking dot in the distance. With a slight smile she turned around to head indoors, hoping that the next day in The Secondhand Bookworm would bring with it less rain.

3 THE CHIHUAHUA IN A BIRDCAGE

It all seemed normal in the square as Nora peered out of the window of The Secondhand Bookworm the next morning while she ate a chocolate croissant. A car was driving the wrong way up the one way street; an elderly man was parking his electric mobility scooter in the middle of the road; a woman's twin pushchair was empty of the twins who were in the process of pulling handfuls of lettuces out of the grocers' boxes and throwing them in the air; a dog was letting out a continuous howl where it was tied up outside the butcher shop; two cars were abandoned illegally on the cobbles where the traffic warden was writing tickets, and three people were gathered around the free map box, twisting, turning, unfolding and folding a large sheet of paper.

Nora was watching the latter, chewing grimly in expectation.

"Any second now, any second now." She said as she munched.

Less than a moment later the door flew open and the man holding the map stood on the threshold.

"Excuse me, Miss."

Nora swallowed her mouthful quickly.

"Hello." She greeted, stepping over a large pile of yellow soft cover Wisden Almanacs on the floor.

"You're out of Castletown maps. This one just has Seatown on it."

"If you open it out that way, in the right hand bottom corner is a map of Castletown." She explained patiently.

The man's eyes narrowed incredulously.

"Wha'?"

Over his shoulder two grey heads appeared.

"Do they have a Castletown map?" A lady asked.

"They only have Seatown maps out here." Said the other.

"Hold up." The man unfolded the map, held it close to his face and then lowered it with a jolt, shaking his head. "That little thing! What a con!"

Nora arched an eyebrow, watching him fold it up and push through his two grey-headed companions.

"It is FREEEEEE!" Nora called but the door slammed, drowning out her voice.

She went back to the little round stool by the window which was surrounded by blue foldout boxes and stacks of books that Georgina had delivered on her way back from Seatown the evening before. For most of the morning since opening an hour and a half ago, Nora had been pricing up the new stock, waiting for Cara to arrive. It had been relatively quiet but now people were arriving in the town.

Nora brushed the croissant crumbs from her trousers and looked up upon hearing the door open again. She saw a tall man wearing a vibrant purple shirt, black chinos and pointed shiny black shoes. He noticed Nora and winked at her.

"Hello down there." He greeted cheerfully.

"Good morning." Nora smiled.

"Do you have any cookery books?" He looked around the shop.

"Yes." She said. "Just through there and next to the staircase."

"I shall go through just through there." He said, winked again and set off.

The door opened again and a woman appeared on the doorstep.

"Hello. Can I bring my dog into your shop? He won't poop." The woman said.

"Er…sure."

"Long shot. But do you sell sticky back paper?"

"Erm…no sorry."

"Okay. I saw that you sell postcards. Do you have a birthday card that says, 'You'll always be my friend because you know too much.'?" She next asked.

"Erm…"

The dog sniffed around by the Folio Society books, tugging at its lead until it got bored and made a lunge for the door.

"Argh." The woman was almost pulled over and so continued towards the door. "Thanks anyway."

The door was left open and the sound of a conversation that two women were having floated in.

"Did you see the programme last night about how one journalist's grandfather could never forget and forgive?" One woman was asking.

"They show that every year." The other woman said.

"Do you think they have a postcard of the view down the hill as you come into town?" The first woman pondered.

"I can't see that they do."

"Well. Where can I get one?"

"Why don't you ask inside?" The second woman suggested.

At that precise moment the wind blew the door closed and Nora looked up, laughing.

"Oh dear. And it's only eleven fifteen." She sighed, stood up and carried a pile of priced books to the counter. She had just placed them neatly in front of the antiquarian shelves when the door opened yet again and bashed against the wall,

Nora flinched and stared at her colleague Cara who had arrived. Cara's short blond hair was wild from the wind and her expression was a combination of amusement and despair. She stepped quickly down into the shop, leaving the door open as she carried a large box in her arms.

"Nora!" She exclaimed. "Did you see the oriental woman with the Chihuahua in a birdcage?"

"Whaaaaaaat?!"

Nora watched Cara pause and move aside a stack of Shire guides with her foot, stopping by the windows to peer out into the street.

"Blast, she must have gone. Well, it was a while ago!" Cara said.

"Did you say 'the oriental woman with a Chihuahua in a birdcage'?" Nora repeated warily.

Cara looked back and nodded, walking towards the desk with the box.

"I'm not making it up!" She exclaimed. "It's true. Look, I should have been here about ten minutes ago but I was walking from the train station and saw her crossing the road, her hair was piled up high on her head and she was wearing these blue platforms as high as this box," she dropped the box on the stool, "and I saw that she was carrying this pink antique birdcage and then I saw it: the face of a Chihuahua peering out at me."

Nora gasped with laughter but Cara continued talking, opening the box she had placed on the stool.

"I was so distracted that I tripped on the kerb and dropped the entire contents of the box across the pavements. It was so embarrassing." Cara concluded. "Thankfully the pavements are dry and everything was okay. There was only one old man around and he doubled the time it took for me to pick everything up by trying to help!"

"Oh that it is the funniest thing I've heard." Nora laughed, sitting down in the swivel chair with a thud. She leaned forward, giggling and snorting with laughter until Cara chuckled and then sighed, beginning to take out the books from inside the box.

"I didn't even have breakfast this morning so I bought this." She held up a microwave burger.

Nora was still chuckling about the Chihuahua in the birdcage. She picked up the box of tissues from under the counter, pulled one out and wiped her eyes and then blew her nose.

"Go and cook it." Nora nodded with a chuckle.

"Thanks." Cara smiled, left Nora with the box and headed off for the kitchen.

Nora picked up the book on the top.

"Making Walking Sticks for a Hobby." She read aloud.

"A bestseller." Cara's voice sailed back and Nora smirked.

Nora flicked through it, distracted by a man outside who was perusing the postcards in the spinner by the window.

"None on the castle, none on the castle. Ah! Just one on the castle. None on the castle, none on the castle. Ah! Just one on the castle." He was saying to himself.

Nora thought about closing the door when two customers arrived. One was a large woman in an enormous purple mac; the other was an equally large man about Nora's age.

"Can I use your toilet?" The man asked.

"Erm…no, I'm sorry but we can't allow customers to use our toilets because of health and safety." Nora replied.

"Because of health and what?"

"Safety. We keep bleaches in there. We wouldn't want to be sued if someone washed their hands in bleach instead of soap." She explained lamely.

The man shrugged, turning away.

"Oh, he's always liked his toilets." The woman laughed. "Even as a nipper he would go into people's houses and into shops and say, can I use your toilet? He was like the toilet inspector." She said and chortled loudly.

Nora smiled warily.

"Well, there are some public toilets just over there." She indicated.

"Thank you dear." The woman said and they headed off, closing the door behind them.

Cara came back in, eating.

"Nora. I have a plan for this afternoon." She said in a muffled voice through her mouthful of burger.

Nora got up from the chair, heading back to the small stool where she could continue pricing.

"Hmmm?" She replied suspiciously, taking up her pencil.

Cara dropped into the seat, picked up a pen and pondered the message pad.

"We have an influx of cookery books and shelf space in the room above us, with excess aircraft books on the floor in the back room. I think we should move the entire cookery section upstairs and the aircraft through to the stairwell." She explained, drawing a diagram as she spoke through her burger.

"Sounds good." Nora agreed.

"That would be a start. We have a load of war books to come over so getting those sections moved today would be really good." Cara said.

"Okay, well I'll take all these children's books up and there are some paperbacks that need to go away at some point. But there's no rush for those. People seem to like a rummage through the piles up there."

"I also want to label the entire needlecraft section at some point. It needs new labels since it was moved." Cara added, licking tomato sauce off her fingers.

A woman stepped into the shop, her coat covered in poppies pinned in various places.

"Good morning." Cara greeted, placing her half-eaten burger onto her diagram and quickly wiping her hands with a wet wipe. "Can I help?"

"Do you have any information about the new castle that is being built?" The woman asked.

"Oh. Nora?" Cara invited, shrugging when the woman turned to look at Nora.

"There's nothing available yet." Nora explained. "We have a lot of books about the castle ruins, but the building of the new castle by the new Duke of Cole is a brand new project. It was on the news about a month ago."

"Yes, I know. But I would like any information available about it."

"Have you tried the tourist information office?" Nora asked.

"The tourist information office is closed." The woman said.

Nora frowned at the clock.

"Is it? They're usually open at this time of day."

"It is closed…permanently." The woman elaborated.

Nora blinked.

"Permanently? Are you sure?"

"That is what their sign says on their door." The woman replied. '*As of November 3rd we will be closing.*'

Nora glanced at the Cara who was absorbed replying to a Skype message on the computer as she finished off her burger.

"Oh. I didn't know about that. Oh dear. That's strange."

"Yes." The woman agreed. "So do *you* have any information that you could give me? On hearsay perhaps?"

Nora thought about what she had heard about the project over the last couple of months.

"Well, the local word is that they are finishing the new castle behind the castle ruins that was started by the last Duke of Cole in the late Nineteenth Century. This is because the present Duke of Cole, who inherited the property last year when his relative died, plans to move in and live here in Castletown. A Duke hasn't lived here for a long time so that's big news. The historical ruins and the new castle will finally be open to the public next year, sometime in the summer. The Duke is going to live in part of the new castle, I think his apartments will be like a stately home architecturally part of the new castle, so he will live there while the whole property is open to the public, but then he will live in the whole thing when it is closed to the public which I heard will be from October to April every year. The new castle incorporates a lot of the restored old buildings so it has about a thousand years of history." Nora explained. "I believe it will all be opened to the public from April to October each year and will be fully furnished and decorated in an historical style with lots of authentic furniture and objects and heirlooms that the Duke will be bringing from his current home."

"There now." The woman said happily. "You should write your own free leaflet for visitors like me. Or ask your town council to put up a sign by the castle ruins to explain exactly what is happening."

"Isn't there one there then?" Nora asked, feeling sure that she had seen one.

"Not as interesting and informative as you." The woman smiled. "Goodbye."

Nora felt secretly pleased at being called interesting and informative. She looked at Cara who had eaten her burger and finished typing.

"Did you know that the tourist information office has closed?" Nora asked her.

"Yes." Cara nodded. "I was here on Sunday with Georgina when the woman came in. They sold Georgina all their town guides so we'll be getting a delivery next week of about two thousand."

"Two thousand!" Nora gulped.

"A good profit on them though." Cara explained. "She said that when they arrive to store them in the bathroom."

"Okay." Nora grinned. "Not to use as toilet paper though?"

"No!" Cara laughed.

Nora picked up her pencil, determined to get the new stock marked up and glanced out of the window to see that the town was suddenly full of French students all holding clipboards and all wearing matching bright yellow caps and white plastic rainproof ponchos.

The students were gathering together and scribbling down notes, disappearing inside shops and also grabbing people who were walking through the square. Nora then saw a small group of students looking towards the bookshop.

"Uh-oh, what's this?" She said.

Cara looked up from scribbling down some book request from Seatown.

"Students." She grimaced.

"In November?" Nora sighed.

Four French students gathered around the postcard spinners on the pavement, speaking loudly in French and examining the cards.

"Seatown are asking for a list of our Robert Ludlum novels. There's no rush so I should probably wait to deal with the students." Cara decided.

"Thanks." Nora appreciated, casting a wary look at them as they all entered the shop and surged for the counter, waving their clipboards.

"Essss-cuse me." A tall girl with long blond hair in plaits said.

"Yes?"

"Can we ask you zome…er…some…questions?"

"Is for a zchool procket…ah, project." A boy added, trying his best to speak English.

"Erm. I suppose so." Cara said, throwing Nora a look.

The students all looked at their clipboards and poised their pens, conferred in French and then the first girl, who obviously spoke English the best, spoke.

"Ah….errr….What is ze oldest part of the castle?"

"The Keep." Cara replied.

They all looked at her and then at one another.

"Keep? Keep. Keep." They chorused and wrote it down.

"Quezzzzztion deux…ah, two…How long is ze the river?"

Cara looked at Nora and shrugged.

"Google?" Nora suggested with a small smile.

Cara turned to the computer.

"How are they supposed to find this all out without Google?" She muttered.

"Ah, 'ere we are. Twenty Five miles." Cara said, suddenly imitating their accent.

"Twenty five miles?" They all chorused, conferred with one another and wrote it down on their sheet.

"It's also the fastest flowing river in England." Cara read out but the students looked blank a moment and then went onto the next question.

Nora chuckled, continuing to price her pile of books.

"Ah, number trois, what are the people ooo are er….born…born? Oui, born… in Castletown known as?" The blond girl with the plaits asked.

"LAMPREYS!" Nora replied so loudly that the French students jumped and turned to look at her, clutching their clipboards.

"Sorry." Nora apologised. "I know that answer. I read about it once. The people who are born in Castletown are called Lampreys."

Cara smirked.

"Lamp…lamp?..." The students chorused, nonplussed.

"L...A…M…P…R…E…Y…S." Nora spelt out carefully so that the students took her word for it and wrote it down.

"Lampreys are rare blood sucking fish found down river past the castle. They're freaky little things but really ancient, like some of the people in this town." She chuckled. "Apparently during the middle ages lampreys were eaten by the upper classes throughout Europe. I read once that a 'surfeit of Lampreys' has been blamed for the deaths of King Henry I and King John who overindulged in them. The old Dukes of Castletown were renowned for serving lampreys." She explained keenly.

The French Students were staring at Nora non-comprehendingly.

"Any more questions?" Cara asked them with a grin.

"Oui, ah…last one….er….Oooo destroyed ze original Castle?"

"Oliver Cromwell's troops in 1643 during the Civil War." Nora volunteered eagerly.

The French Students all turned to her again.

"I read about that too." She shrugged with a smirk.

The students finished scribbling and then all began to wave their postcards.

"Thank you, thank you. Merci." They said. "And zeeees."

"Please, these and stamps?" One of the boys said, brandishing a handful of cards.

"Er…nine postcards and nine stamps?" Cara said in a French accent.

Nora arched an eyebrow.

"Er..." The boy winced. "Er…"

"Yes." The spokes-girl answered for him.

"Yes." He repeated.

Cara ran the prices through the till.

"Seven pounds and seventy nine pence." She said, still with a French accent.

Nora got up from her stool and joined Cara behind the counter, grabbing a brown paper bag that was hanging up for the postcards and stamps.

"You're speaking with an accent." She pointed out in a whisper.

"Am I?" Cara gasped. "I do that sometimes with foreigners. I can't help it."

Nora smirked. Meanwhile, the boy brandished a twenty pound note and Cara gave him his change and then two packs of worldwide postcard stamps and then she cut out a single stamp from another pack of four.

This was repeated for all of the students who wanted varying amounts of cards and 'stamps!' until they left and Cara shut the till.

"Reminds me of summer." Nora sighed, thinking of the endless tourists demanding stamps.

"Hmm. Stamps! Stamps! Stamps!" Cara agreed.

"Why did Georgina decide to stock stamps?" Nora wondered aloud, almost ruefully.

"We're always getting asked so it shuts them up." Cara grinned.

"I need a cup of tea after that."

"I agree." Cara nodded.

With a smile Nora set off for the kitchen to put the kettle on, thinking about blood sucking fish and Oliver Cromwell and wondering if their day would be besieged by more French students.

4 IN THE ANTIQUES SHOP

Lunchtime arrived quickly and Nora had to wade her way through a sea of freshly arrived French students on her way to the delicatessen. She bought a sandwich, crisps, bottle of elderflower and lemonade and a wedge of cherry and chocolate brownie which were all placed in a little bag. She then decided to visit the antique shops.

Nora's brother Seymour had acquired a rundown theatre on the edge of Little Cove. He had been working on renovating it for six months and was due to open its doors for the first time at Christmas. Nora had been tasked with finding interesting items for props, a job she enjoyed, and so she set off to have a browse around 'Passageway Collectibles' which was down a long winding passage between the bank and a jewellery shop.

The passage was lined with large statues of Buddha, stone fountains, an enormous golden lion and numerous statues. The door to the building stood open so Nora walked in and down a long hallway that was lined either side with tall glass cases, all alarmed and filled with various treasures. There were ornaments, glassware, statues and small items, some with tags bearing large prices.

Usually Nora would turn left and enter the huge room that had a rickety staircase in it and was surrounded by large items such as four poster beds, hansom cabs, great wooden chests with carved figures and units but today she noticed a door open ahead of her and a room full of newly displayed items.

Curious, Nora walked down the corridor, glancing at a case with a stuffed squirrel inside. The new room was different from the rest of the shop and Nora entered quietly. It was full of large cabinets with little walkways between them. There was the distant sound of oriental music and in the cases were fascinating items such as swords, numerous pairs of vases, some Shi-Shi dogs, daggers, religious idols, carved wooden boxes and other trinkets. A bookcase filled with violent-looking 18 rated DVDs caused her to pause warily. In the far corner was a desk with a glass top and a till. Nora wandered around and stopped when a pair of cobra candlesticks caught her eye.

"Hello." A smooth female voice spoke.

Nora turned quickly towards the desk.

A woman now stood behind it, stroking something that she was holding in her arms.

"Oh. Hello." Nora replied, glancing at a large black Chinese screen which she assumed the lady had been behind. The woman moved forwards and Nora took in her appearance quickly.

She was Asian with a very beautiful face. Her thick black hair was piled high up onto the top of her head in a fascinating style. She wore tall blue wedge sandals, tight blue silk leggings and an oriental patterned silk blouse with a black jacket that had shoulder pads and looked two sizes too big for her. Nora saw that she was carrying a Chihuahua in her arm and remembered with a small smile Cara's story about seeing a Chihuahua in a birdcage.

"You like?" The woman asked, picking up one of the cobra candles.

Nora looked at it.

"Oh. Oh yes, I do."

"Twenty pounds for the two." The woman said.

Nora nodded.

"Hmmm. That's a very good price."

"Yes." The woman agreed.

Nora looked at her curiously as a long tapered finger stroked the top of the cobra's head.

"It bring you luck." The woman smiled, half teasingly.

"My brother owns a theatre." Nora explained. "I think they would be good in one of his sets. They are unusual."

"Ah, yes." The woman agreed, setting the candle down and pondering Nora.

The Chihuahua made a slight struggle in the woman's arm so she began to stroke it so that the dog closed its eyes contentedly.

Nora gave the room another scan.

"Do you mind if I use my mobile?" She asked.

The woman smiled.

"No. Of course not." She said smoothly.

As Nora drew it out there was the sound of heavy footsteps on the floor above them. They both looked up. The woman's eyes narrowed and she muttered something in Chinese, smiled at Nora and turned away, going back to her desk.

While Nora swiped the screen of her iPhone and scrolled down her list of contacts for Seymour's name and number, she heard the heavy footsteps reaching the stairs and stomping down.

"Jiao? JIAO?" The voice of Billy called. He was the owner of Passageway Collectibles as well as having rooms in the Antiques Centre in the town.

The woman turned slowly and sighed, looking unimpressed.

Nora spun around as she pressed 'dial' and saw Billy marching down the corridor towards the room. The woman named Jiao remained where she was.

"Hello Nora." Billy greeted, his large stomach preceding him.

He weaved his way through the cases and reached Jiao who addressed him in a harsh whisper.

"Hey Nora." Seymour's voice filled Nora's ear so loudly that she jumped and held the phone slightly away.

"Hello. Are you busy?" Nora asked in a slightly hushed tone.

"I'm on stage at the moment." Seymour whispered back.

"Performing?!" Nora was alarmed.

Seymour's laugh filled her head.

"No, working on lighting with Hallam." He said, referring to their cousin. "The theatre doesn't open until Christmas, remember?" He chuckled.

"Well, I'm in one of the antique shops and I've found a pair of cobra candlesticks." Nora explained, picking one up and realising that they were heavy and made of metal.

"Cobra wha'?" Seymour asked. "Hallam, use this."

"Candlesticks." Nora said.

"Sounds good." Seymour replied.

There was the sound of hammering and Hallam's voice in the background.

"I kind of like them myself. They're beautiful and strange, but I thought they would be good in one of your stage sets. You'd like them."

"How much?" Seymour asked.

"Twenty pounds."

"Only twenty quid? Get them, Nora, and I'll pay you back. If they're no good then you can have them in your room if you like them anyway." Seymour said with a strained voice. "Here, Hallam, this bolt is really stuck."

"You're not up a ladder or anything are you?" Nora asked suspiciously.

"No."

"What are you doing?"

"Hanging from the ceiling." He admitted.

"You're what?! Seymour, don't answer the phone when you're hanging from the ceiling!" Nora warned him loudly.

Jiao and Billy glanced at her.

Seymour laughed.

"I'm fine." He assured, his voice strained again followed by the sound of hammering close to her ear. "Thanks Hallam." He said, distracted slightly.

Nora picked up both candlesticks with one hand and moved towards for the counter.

"I'll get these for you and bring them home tonight." She said.

"Excellent. Thanks. Bye."

"Bye." Nora replied and hung up, slipped the phone in her pocket and drew out her purse.

Nora placed the cobras onto the counter and smiled at Billy who was staring at Jiao.

"Ah, you having the cobras. Good luck for your plays yes?" She said, leaning forward for some tissue paper to wrap them in.

Nora grinned, taking out a twenty pound note.

"You an actress, Nora?" Billy asked, looking at her.

"No." Nora laughed. "My brother has a theatre in Little Cove."

"Ah." Billy nodded. "Well if he wants to borrow any of my stuff then tell him he's welcome."

"Really?" Nora stared at him.

He shrugged.

"Sure. He'd have to bring his own truck or van to collect it but any of the bigger stuff he can use."

"That's really nice of you. Thanks. I'll tell him." Nora said, pleased.

Billy nodded, pondering Jiao who wrapped up the cobras and slipped them into a paper bag. Nora handed her the money.

"You need a receipt?" Jiao asked.

"That would be good, thanks." Nora replied.

She glanced at Billy who was staring at Jiao intensely and sensed a fiery atmosphere between them.

"What's the theatre called?" Billy asked Nora without looking at her.

"The Jolly Theatre." Nora said. "Jolly is our family surname."

"I've heard of it." Billy nodded. "There's a great expectation about it in a couple of papers for opening night at Christmas. It's your brother's you say?"

"Yes."

"I may bring Jiao along when it opens." He decided.

"Well if you do then be sure to tell them who you are at the door. I'll leave your name at the ticket booth and you'll get a discount." Nora promised.

He smiled.

"Thanks Nora."

"Thank you, Nora." Jiao said smoothly, passing her the bag of cobra candlesticks.

Nora said goodbye and made her way out as Billy and Jiao began a rapid and slightly volatile conversation.

Nora decided to go back to the shop and eat her lunch in the kitchen of The Secondhand Bookworm. She ran down the street, almost bumping into Imogen from the greengrocers who was carrying a large box of vegetables, said a laughing hello and then reached the bookshop which looked as though it was teeming with business.

Once inside, Nora saw that the front of the shop was full of French students. Cara was leaning on her right hand which was propping up her chin, looking bored, while she held up an A4 sheet of paper with her other hand. On it the answers to the French students' questions were written in large letters so Nora smirked to herself and squeezed through the young people.

"I'm going to eat in the kitchen. I won't be long." Nora told Cara, leaning behind her and putting the bag of cobras under the stairs.

"What's in that?"

"Snakes." Nora replied.

Cara arched an eyebrow.

With a grin, Nora turned her back on the students who were reading out the answers on her sheet and writing them down, and headed off to eat.

When Nora returned from the kitchen ten minutes later, Cara was taping her answer sheet to the window of the door beneath the 'OPEN' sign.

Nora laughed.

"I really can't take any more students piling in. Even if they do buy a few stamps and postcards." She said. "But I think even Georgina would agree that the carpet and our sanity is more important."

"What's happened to the…oh…yuk." Nora leaned over the desk and saw the muddy trail that was darkening the cream carpet from the French students.

"Hmmm." Cara glowered and walked back to the counter with the sellotape holder, dropped it onto the desk and headed for her coat and bag.

"By the way, I discovered where the Chihuahua in the birdcage lives!" Nora said.

Cara looked at her sharply.

"Then it wasn't a hallucination?" She sighed, pleased.

"No. The owner is a woman who now has a room in 'Passageway Collectables'. Her name is Jiao." Nora explained.

"Well we'll be seeing more of the Chihuahua about the town then."

Nora nodded as she tidied up her hair.

"I hope so. It's so cute."

Cara chuckled and headed off for her lunch, announcing that she was going to order a jacket potato. As she left, the phone began to ring so Nora made a grab for it.

"Good afternoon, The Secondhand Bookworm." She greeted.

"Sorry Nora it's only me." Betty's distinct and slightly husky voice said, calling from the Seatown shop.

"Oh hello!" Nora sat down.

"Sorry to be a pain but there you are, that's me all over. I've got a lady here interested in a second edition copy of 'The Hobbit', and very lovely it is too." Betty explained. "It says inside that it's a second edition sixth impression. What does that mean? I would ask Roger but he's gone down into the town to get some change. Lovely." Betty said in her usual dry but humour-filled tone.

"I'm pretty sure that it means the sixth print run. So it's a second edition but the sixth run of printing." Nora replied thoughtfully.

"Ah thank you ever so Nora, we thought that's what it meant." Betty said gratefully.

"That's okay."

"Look forward to working with you tomorrow Nora. Goodbye." Betty said and Nora bade her goodbye and hung up, pleased that Seatown sounded busy and that they were having some good sales.

A man stepped into the shop wearing a leather jacket with leather biker's trousers, boots and carrying a helmet. He had a bushy black beard and greying hair and twinkling blue eyes which scanned the interior of the shop.

"Good afternoon." He said and headed off for the motoring section which he had obviously already visited before.

Nora greeted him and cast her gaze upon two more people who entered. The door was left ajar so that the sound of the approaching motorised street sweeper could be heard, pushed determinedly by Hugh. The newcomers were a man and a woman and the man put down a large umbrella which was dotted with raindrops.

Noticing it, Nora glanced out of the window and saw that it had started spitting so she leapt up. The woman stood before the topography section.

Nora opened the door and stuck her hand out. Drops of rain fell onto her arm so she brought the postcards inside first, followed by the box of free maps. It wasn't heavy rain so she left the black boxes of paperbacks clipped to the wall either side of the door.

"Blast this weather." A voice sailed past her and Nora only just caught a glimpse of Tobey from the Bank running past. "Hi, Nora." He hailed and disappeared around the corner.

Nora pulled the door closed, heading back for the counter, hearing it click shut behind her. The door had only been closed half a second when it was cast open with a crash.

Nora flinched and the woman browsing through the topography section stepped back in alarm. A large pink dressing table stool heralded Cara's entrance as Cara stepped down and carried it into the front of the shop.

"What have you got there?!" Nora exclaimed, standing up.

"Isn't it brilliant? It's just what I need. It was in the charity shop." Cara said, walking it around to behind the counter.

"Didn't you get the train into work this morning?" Nora asked her, wondering how on earth Cara was intending to get the stool home.

"Yes." Cara replied distractedly, her attention focused fondly upon her new stool. "It was only eight pounds."

Nora watched, bemused, as Cara stroked the top of the stool lovingly.

"I'll drop you home with it. You can put it in the boot of my car…or the back seat, the boot of my car is so tiny it only fits a pair of shoes in it…"

"No it's ok." Cara shook her head. "I'll take it on the train. Believe me I've taken just about anything on the train. Even my wardrobe."

"What?"

"Really." Cara nodded. She checked the clock. "My lunch is probably done in five minutes. I ordered it and went to the charity shop and saw this. Back in a bit." She said and hurried off again.

Nora looked at the stool and then reached for the paper towels, noticing that the stool was a bit wet because of the rain. She placed the towels over the top and patted them down, then turned to deal with a customer who had arrived.

He was in a beige suit with a black shirt and dark green tie and was staring at Nora patiently.

"Hello." Nora greeted.

"Do you have a poet's corner?" He asked gravely.

"A what, sorry?" Nora asked.

"Poet's corner…..poetry books." He said, suddenly looking a little embarrassed.

"We have a poetry section at the top of the stairs." Nora nodded.

He started away, going a bit red in the face.

"Up the stairs?" He asked.

"Just through there and up the top of the first staircase." Nora indicated.

He nodded and walked away as a Skype message sounded on the computer monitor.

Nora sat down to read it.

'Do you have any Nicholas Sparks novels pl? This is Georgina. Am here now.'

'Oh hi! Sorry, I can't get upstairs to look. Cara is on lunch at the moment.' Nora typed back.

'We would like a copy of 'A message in a bottle', paperback when you get a chance to look. Someone was asking for it because of the film.'

'I think we have it. I remember seeing Kevin Costner's huge face on the front.' Nora wrote.

'Wonderful. Do you have anything on Fra Angelico pl? Early Italian Renaissance artist. If you do please send any over for stock,' was the next message.

Nora stood up to check the art section and pulled one out.

'I've got 'Fra Angelico', Temporis Collection, large hardcover priced at £20."

"Pl send over for stock. Busy here!" Georgina replied.

Nora popped it into the transfer box and then picked up a book on the side of the counter that had been placed there while Nora had been on lunch just as the telephone began to ring.

"The Secondhand Bookworm." Nora greeted the caller cheerfully.

"Oh hello. I'm sorry to be a nuisance but can you tell me how to spell Art Nouveau?" The voice of an old woman asked.

Nora paused.

"Erm...okay?" She replied hesitantly.

"Oh thank you dear." The woman replied.

"A-R-T N-O-U-V-E-A-U." Nora spelt warily.

The woman repeated it.

"Thank you ever so much, my dear." She said and hung up.

Nora replaced her receiver and stared ahead a moment.

Cara returned with her jacket potato and informed Nora that the coach containing the French students was last seen driving out of town so they could have a bit of peace as they set about moving the cookery and aircraft sections that afternoon.

Near closing time, Nora noticed that it had stopped raining but the roads were full of puddles and the sky looked dark and cloudy. There was the sound of voices coming from outside the delicatessen and then a couple of flashes which Nora thought at first were lightning. She then noticed the owner, Philip, standing in the road on the cobbles with a camera.

She followed the direction to where the camera was pointed and saw his colleague Alice holding a large leg of pork with a long slim carving knife. She was posing for photographs but then she grinned and pretended to play the pig's leg with the knife like a violin, making Philip laugh and photograph that shot too.

Chuckling, Nora then watched as a large woman in a big fluffy pink cardigan covered in Betty Boop badges opened the door of The Secondhand Bookworm and stood on the step, staring into the room.

"Hello" Cara greeted brightly from behind the counter, arriving back from sorting out the last shelf in the new cookery section.

"D'you sell birthday candles luv?" The woman's booming voice asked.

Cara remained smiling, returned her walkie-talkie to its stand and sat down.

"I'm sorry I'm afraid we don't." She replied.

"Oh." The woman was disappointed.

"They might do them next door." Cara then suggested.

"Oh. Well I'll check in there then. Thanks, luv."

"You're welcome." Cara smiled.

When the lady had gone, Cara screwed up her face.

"Birthday candles? Why do people assume we're a haberdashery?"

Nora chuckled, picking up the last of the books she had priced to carry upstairs and pop on the shelves in the travel section.

"I did suggest to Georgina that we sell fridge magnets, but she keeps refusing." She said.

Cara laughed, stifling a yawn.

"I think we may have overdone it, moving those sections." Nora decided.

"Yes but it looks so good now." Cara said.

Nora agreed and headed for the back room, just as a customer was heard stomping down the stairs.

"Perhaps I'll leave these a moment." She decided, heading back to the front again.

Cara turned expectantly but as Nora placed her pile of books back on the floor she was distracted by Hugh the street sweeper walking past the window shouting into his mobile phone. They could hear his voice as he said: "Yeah the bog's blocked in the short term car park. There was a really big *you-know-what*!" in a really loud voice.

A man walking across the cobbles dropped his bag, staring at Hugh who just continued walking. Nora would have laughed but the customer reached the counter and faced Cara.

"Hello, sir." Cara greeted.

"Look here." The man said, opening the book that he was holding and jabbing the price that was written in pencil on the front paper. "This is overpriced."

Cara leaned forward to see it.

"Eight pounds." She read aloud and shook her head. "I'm afraid that's the price sir. All of our prices are fair."

"I disagree. It's not worth more than five pounds to me." He said.

"I'm afraid I can't change the prices in the books, sir." Cara replied and then turned to the monitor.

"Good luck selling it." The man said, closed the book and left it on the counter, turning away.

Nora watched him go and once the door was closed Cara shook her head.

"That's a rip off!! Soooo expensive. A fortune!" She said sarcastically and stuck her tongue out at the door.

She then gasped when she saw the man looking through the window as he marched off muttering. Both Nora and Cara watched until he had gone completely and then they looked at each other.

"Hope he didn't notice me doing that." Cara said.

Nora laughed, heading towards the back with the travel books. She popped the books away quickly and then wheeled the Henry hoover into the front from the kitchen, plugged it in and sped around with the nozzle over the front carpet, in the corners, the mat and also above the door when she noticed a couple of cobwebs, managing to clean most of the front of the shop while Cara counted all of the change in the till.

Once Henry was back in the kitchen, Nora sat down with a sigh on Cara's dressing table stool, looking up as a young man opened the door.

"Are you still open?" He asked hopefully.

"For another ten minutes." Cara nodded, dropping the ten pence pieces back into their section with a crash.

The young man walked in, pleased, and scanned the room. He stood examining the art books as another customer came downstairs, scratching his head.

"No luck." He told Cara sadly.

"Oh, I'm sorry sir." Cara sympathised. "As I said I can order you a new copy."

"Thank you but no." He declined. "I like looking in the film sections for it anyway; you have some good books up there. A great section on directors. Thanks anyway. Cheerio."

The young man glanced at him and smiled as the customer left.

"What was he after?" Nora asked Cara.

"The screenplay for 'In Bruges'." She replied.

"Never heard of it." Nora said.

"In Bruges is an amazing film!" The young man joined in. "And a great place for a holiday."

"Yes, but Ralph Fiennes is lovely and he was a baddy in it." Cara told him.

Nora screwed up her nose.

"Wasn't he Lord Voldemort?" She asked.

Cara smirked and the customer gasped.

"I can't believe you said that." He laughed.

The man who had exited had left the door ajar and a car suddenly pulled up outside the shop just as a woman with a little Jack Russell was strolling past.

"Excuse me!" The woman behind the steering wheel called through the open passenger window. "I was on the train! And I saw your dog eating something, hahahahaha!"

"Yeah. First time she'd caught a rabbit." The woman with the dog replied.

"Hahahaha." The woman in the car roared, until the car behind her beeped and she sped away.

Cara and Nora looked at one another and the young man sniggered into his coat.

Nora stood up from the dressing table stool to run upstairs and check that all of the customers were out of the shop. She leaned through the doorway in the back room, which was empty, and then sped up the stairs onto the next floor. Someone had pulled a battered brown box that held oboe music off the shelf onto the floor in the music section, so Nora hoisted it back, pushed a row of gardening books deeper into their shelf, gently kicked a little stool to the side and then continued on to check the next rooms.

The whole shop was empty so Nora ran down, turned off the lights and met the young man at the foot of the stairs.

"Ah, right, you're closing. I'll have to come back again." He said, turning towards the front.

Nora followed him and he glanced back at her.

"What time do you open tomorrow?" He asked.

"Ten o'clock."

"Great. Well thanks for letting me look." He smiled at Cara and headed off.

Nora still followed him to the door and when he had stepped out she lugged the black boxes of cheap paperbacks in. It was still raining and the town was empty so she turned the 'OPEN' sign to 'CLOSED' and shut the door.

"Are you sure you don't want me to drive you and the pink dressing table stool home, or at least to the train station?" Nora asked as she walked around to grab her keys so as to lock up.

Cara shook her head, pressing the code into the PDQ machine to finish the end of day banking.

"I just got a text from my uncle. He's in the pub and he has his van parked over the road. He said he'd give me a lift back to my flat." Cara said, ticking off the credit card slips in the cash book.

"Ah well that's good then."

"Yeah, I have to have a drink with him first though." Cara sighed.

"A nice refreshing glass of lemonade." Nora suggested.

"Cola." Cara had already decided and looked at the computer monitor.

Nora locked the front door to stop anyone pushing their way into the shop and Cara threw the little money bags into the cash tin.

'Have a nice evening.' Cara read as she typed a farewell to the Seatown shop on the Skype messenger.

She then closed the computer down, turned off the till and did the last calculations in the cash book while Nora shrugged into her coat and tugged her beanie hat over her hair, making sure that she had the cobra candlesticks with her.

"So I'm with Betty in the afternoon tomorrow." Nora said as Cara twisted a large green scarf around her neck and picked up her bag and some transfers, including a copy of 'A message in a bottle' with Kevin Costner's huge face on the front.

"I'm in Seatown."

"Shall I take your stool?" She offered but Cara shook her head.

"I can manage." She assured her.

Nora ran and opened the door and Cara punched in the alarm code, turned off the light and picked up her stool, walking around the desk and across the carpet to the front while the alarm beeped loudly preparing to set once the door was shut.

"Hurry, hurry, hurry!" Nora said, always fearing that the alarm would go off if they weren't quick.

"I'm trying." Cara squashed herself through the door with the stool, but with the weight of her many bags she leaned backwards and stepped back into the shop.

Nora grabbed her scarf and helped pull her through the door and Cara's laugh was thick and painful as the scarf strangled her.

"I'm sorry!" Nora gasped, helping her through quickly.

Cara plonked the stool onto the pavement, startling Albert from the Print Shop who was hurrying past.

"Good evening." He greeted, casting bemused looks at the stool.

"Hello." Cara loosened her scarf as Nora slammed the door and sighed, sticking her key in the lock.

"Phew." She breathed.

Cara sat down heavily on her stool, causing Nora to laugh at the image of her on the pavement sitting comfortably on a big pink dressing table seat watching the traffic go past.

"What?" Cara asked innocently.

Nora grinned, turned the key in the lock, made sure the door was secure and listened to make sure that the alarm had set.

A car beeped at Cara as it went past, the driver and passengers amused to see her sitting there and Nora laughed, dragging the sandbags in front of the door.

"I'm going home," she said, dropping the black board in front and straightening up.

Cara remained sitting, looking comfortable.

When she heard a sound, she looked sharply at Nora and saw that Nora had taken a photograph of her.

"I'll be doing some tagging on Facebook tonight." Nora teased.

Cara laughed, shrugging.

"I don't mind." She said and heaved up the stool, eyes set across the square at 'The Black Unicorn' pub a little up the road on the opposite side where her uncle would be.

"Well, enjoy your cola." Nora smiled, walking with her.

"Where are you parked?" Cara asked.

"Up the hill by the church." Nora nodded.

"You fancy a cola too?" Cara offered.

"Ah that would be nice but I have to get back." Nora declined.

They crossed the road quickly and walked past the delicatessen, the butcher and then crossed again to Lady Lane's where Mr Sykes from the Antique Centre was talking to Geraldine Lane, who was placing some necklaces into her window display. The door next to her shop had had a 'To Let' sign in it for a couple of months and Cara and Nora paused to read it, seeing that it had been changed and that there would be a new shop opening on Saturday above Lady Lane's.

"Wonder what that'll be." Nora mused, interested.

"More Antiques?" Cara suggested dryly.

They reached 'The Black Unicorn' and said their goodbyes and Nora continued up the hill.

"You would think…" Nora puffed to herself, "…that I would be…fitter….doing this almost every day." She finally saw her little blue car in the distance.

There was a small queue of traffic as she drove down the hill. Once it had dispersed, Nora joined the trickle of cars heading over the bridge and out of the town and made her way home to Little Cove.

5 THE ALMOST-FIGHT AND THE BOOK SIGNER

Wednesday morning was cold and foggy after it had rained heavily throughout the night. As she drove down the hill that led into the valley and towards Castletown and The Secondhand Bookworm, Nora saw that the entire town was immersed in cloud. The remaining turrets of the castle ruins, now incorporating scaffolding and cranes, gradually loomed into view as her car took her nearer. An eerie mist hovered over the river that wound under the bridge next to the railway station.

Nora passed over the waters and watched as the castle ruins gradually unveiled through the fog, standing on the rise that incorporated the ancient keep and parts of the famous structures that had remained intact over the centuries. The gift shop and the tea rooms were now positioned before the new outer walls but were currently closed for the season.

Nora was impressed with the size of the new castle that was being built and wondered what it would be like to live there. Nora was sure that it would do a lot of good for the town and that the medieval tournaments and fairs would be even more exciting with a working and living castle as a back drop rather than just the ruins. It was also thrilling to have a Duke move back into Castletown too.

The Duke of Cole was in his early thirties, one of the few Roman Catholic aristocratic families remaining in England since the Reformation. He had spent most of his life and a lot of his great wealth building churches and cathedrals and also castles and stately homes. The incorporation of the castle ruins into the last great baronial ancestral home in England was a grand project that interested many people and was beginning to put Castletown on the map once again. The mock medieval style combined with the Norman and Tudor rooms that had survived as the ruins of the castle brought history and charm to the estate.

Nora decided to park her car along the moat so she could have a look at the new castle which was rising fast and had an air of excitement about it. The tall elm trees that lined the street down to the Castletown petting zoo, model village and bird sanctuary were dripping with moisture. Nora reversed into an easy space, grabbed her bag and croissant and locked her car behind her.

There were ducks waddling alongside the water which was almost to the top of the moat due to all the rain that had fallen the past week and especially the night before. Mounds of soggy leaves covered the path and road. Nora hopped over the low posts and fencing that acted as a simple barrier between the path and the road, jumped onto the grass and then stepped onto the path and startled a moorhen which ran and dived off the bank and splashed into the moat.

She watched the castle come clear into view as the fog dispersed. There was a huge facade flagged with magnificent round turrets that stood about two hundred feet high. This now combined the new stately home and original Norman and medieval parts of the surviving castle. Arched windows of various sizes denoted rooms and halls within which were fast taking shape so that the whole castle stretched back to incorporate the Norman keep that was flanked with two of the old restored baileys.

There was a quadrangle that contained the Duke's main residential accommodation in the style of a gothic stately mansion and joined onto the other parts which would house the historical treasures of his ancient family line. A lot of the Duke's treasures were already connected to Castletown's history and many items would be coming home after several centuries spent in other parts of Great Britain. These items would be opened for public viewing once the new castle was complete and the Duke was in residence.

Nora had learned from Monica, a castle ruins tour guide, that there would be an armoury, a chapel, a grand hall, a picture gallery, dining rooms and drawing rooms, parlours, bedrooms and libraries. There were also gardens and stables and all of the ancient historical buildings such as the gatehouse tower, barbican, and of course the keep.

The Duke was renowned not only for building magnificent stately homes but for his great collections of artwork. As this new house was in the style of the ancient castle that had once stood in Castletown it would have a real sense of history about it, especially as it restored and incorporated ancient rooms, one of which Monica said was haunted. Nobody had seen the Duke yet but Nora had *Googled* him when the news had first been announced and thought he was a dish.

Nora eventually reached The Secondhand Bookworm. She glanced at the small puddle in the road outside, pushed her key into the lock and ran inside the shop, closing the door, locking it and running to the alarm. She punched in the code and then turned on the light, dropped her bag on the swivel chair and looked at the counter.

There was a message from Cara on the pad indicating that she had popped in with a delivery on her way through to Seatown. Cara's flat was close to Georgina's house so Georgina often asked Cara to take transfers to Castletown. It sometimes meant that Cara was able to drive the shop van which was much better at taking the steep hills to Castletown than her own small car, an unreliable vehicle that was currently in the garage for repairs.

Nora remembered that Betty was due in for the afternoon and so she read Cara's notes as she shrugged out of her jacket:

'Morning Nora! The sheet music needs to be priced; maybe Betty might enjoy doing that. I dropped in twenty new plastic tubs for the sheet music to be sorted into as the cardboard ones are falling apart. Also another project for Betty??? Please look for any books by Douglas Reeman for Mr Peggotty and can you telephone Mrs GROUTADGE to say that a copy of 'The Hundred Days' by Patrick O'Brian is now here and does she want it – it is under the counter? I think it would be best to leave moving the other sections around until we work together next week but you're the boss there so let me know what you think! Have a nice day, speak to you on SKYPE!

Smiling to herself, Nora turned around to hang up her coat and was faced with a wall of plastic tubs, some full of stock. She arched her eyebrows and decided to run the tubs up to the next floor ready for Betty to fill with the sheet music so that they would be able to move.

She dropped her jacket on the chair, pushed the button on the computer to turn it on and then picked up some of the tubs.

It only took Nora a few minutes to turn the lights on in the rest of the shop, run the whole pile of empty plastic tubs up into the room above and leave them in the music section in front of the window, but as she did so she gradually became aware of a strange smell. It was a rancid sharp odour, very faint in the air.

Thinking of the duck and dog poop that often covered the paths alongside the moat, Nora checked the bottom of her boots as she headed back down the stairs again but they were clean. She decided to grab the internal set of keys and investigate the kitchen for the pong when the telephone rang.

Nora rushed down the last few steps and raced into the front of the shop where she took up the receiver just in time.

"Good morning, The Secondhand Bookworm." She greeted, slightly breathless.

"Oh, yes, hello. Do you have any books written by 'Bob Copper' in stock?" A man's voice sounded from the end of the line.

"Oh, maybe." Nora replied with a thought. "I'll just have a look on our shelves for you."

"Thank you. Ah, Bob Copper. One of the greatest authors of all time to my reckoning. Damn shame his books are so hard to come by." The man said in Nora's ear while she took the phone with her to the topography section opposite the front door and scanned the shelves. He continued rambling on until she spotted the author's name on the spines of several books.

"We do have some!" She said when he finally took a breath and stopped talking. "We have three here by the looks of it."

"Oh!" The caller exclaimed, surprised. "What are the titles?"

"We have a hard back copy of 'Early to Rise' in an orange dust wrapper." Nora said and pulled it out, awkwardly opening the tome as she leaned the book against the others on the shelf. "It's priced at twelve pounds fifty. We also have 'Bob Copper's Sussex which is a soft cover binding and is priced at five pounds." She placed them across the row of books to pull out the last one which she also opened. "And we have 'Songs and Southern Breezes' in a brown dust wrapper that is slightly faded by the sun. This one is priced at ten pounds." She concluded.

"I'll take the lot!" The caller said, pleased. "Tell me, are you open on Sundays?"

"Yes." Nora said, gathering the volumes and taking them to the counter. "From eleven until four."

"Splendid! Would you be able to put them aside for me? I would be very interested in them." He asked.

"No problem." Nora nodded and picked up a pen. She shifted the receiver to her other ear. "Can I just jot down your name and telephone number and they'll be under the counter for you."

He gave Nora his details and then rambled on about his collection of Bob Copper books for another five minutes so that Nora leaned on her elbow until finally he said goodbye. Once she had hung up, Nora grabbed a reservation bag, popped the Bob Copper books into it with his reservation sheet and placed the whole package under the counter.

Nora then ran upstairs to check for any 'Douglas Reeman' books in the fiction section. On her way up she scanned the shop, which was tidy and appeared ready for the day's bookworms.

The cookery books looked nice in their new section. The whole category had been meticulously sorted by

Cara so that the different sections within it for chefs, healthy cooking, special diets, recipes, foreign dishes, cake making, spices and the like all appeared clear and easy to locate.

The few piles of books which Nora had taken up from the day before were neatly stacked out of the way before their topics and so Nora decided that organising the music would be the best priority when Betty arrived. The current brown boxes that contained the sheet music looked scruffy and in great need of their new plastic tubs and Nora knew that once the section was reorganised they would most probably have an increase in sheet music sales.

Up in the green paperback room, Nora scanned the numerous titles in the 'R' section for any 'Reeman' books, faintly aware of the rancid smell again. There weren't any novels by 'Douglas Reeman' currently on the shelf, so Nora stepped back and then sniffed the air, frowning.

"Maybe a new curry dish?" She pondered aloud and was about to head to the window to sniff in the direction of the Indian Restaurant, which faced her across the small yard, when she heard the phone ringing again in the distance.

"Argh. If that's you Mr Hill then I'll burn your books." She cried, referring to one of their regular customers. She ran down the stairs and ended at the bottom of the shop slightly dizzy.

Once in the front room, Nora made a grab for the telephone but it cut off as the answer machine got to it first.

"Fine." Nora sighed, sank into the swivel chair and then stood up again as she came in contact with her bag that was still on the seat.

Sighing, she gathered her things from the chair.

Under the stairs were two boxes on a small bookcase which also had a shelf for personal belongings. Nora popped her bag safely on the shelf and grabbed the cash tin. She glanced at the clock and realised that it was almost opening time so set about filling up the till.

Nora had just finished throwing the last of the cash into the till when a man loomed up to the door and pushed it. As it wouldn't budge, he glanced at the opening times on the glass and then checked his watch with a pointed glare in at Nora.

Nora closed the till, grabbed her keys and walked around the counter to unlock the door.

"Hello." She greeted, pulling the door open wide.

"Whatever." The man said gruffly, stepped down and headed quickly into the shop where he disappeared through to the back.

Nora turned around to ponder the weather outside. It was cool and damp and fog still hung in the air so she decided to just put out the black boxes, free maps and one of the postcard spinners under the blind, suspecting that it might well rain.

Once all of this was done and the postcards and maps were out on the street, she then went back inside.

"One four seven one." She said as she dialled the number on the telephone receiver to check who had called. The number had been withheld so Nora next dialled Mrs Groutdage's line.

Mrs Groutdage had a high pitched voice and was very excitable.

"Oh thank you dear, thank you, thank you!" She exclaimed. "I certainly would like the copy of 'A hundred days'. Can you put it by for me and I will be in next week to collect it?"

"Yes, I have your name and number so I'll pop it under the counter for you."

"Oh thank you dear, thank you, wonderful, thank you!" She shrieked and hung up happily.

Nora sat down in the swivel chair just as a man in grey suit with a large brown hat, flowery tie and battered old walking stick entered the shop. He was followed closely by a small wife who was wearing sunglasses and dressed in a similar grey suit to her husband.

"It is in the window Michael so you will have to ask the lady." She said.

"Oh it goes on and on." The man gasped and began walking off into the back room, mouth agape.

The woman ignored him and instead walked up to the counter before Nora.

"The Bradshaw's Handbook in the window." She said. "May I have a look please?"

Nora pointed to the one on the counter top.

"We have an exact copy here." Nora said and watched the woman glance down to where the fat brown book sat next to a pile of town guides. "They are facsimiles of the original 1863 edition."

"OH! You have one here. MICHAEL!!!!" She then shouted, making Nora jump.

"We have lots of them in at the moment." Nora explained.

"I bet you do." The woman nodded. "They are very popular what with the series being shown again on the television. Have you been watching it?"

"No." Nora admitted.

At that moment her husband arrived.

"Here, Michael!" The woman called to him. "They have one here."

Her husband paced back into the front. Nora watched him lean over the counter and open the front of the book. He began to scan through it, squinting and muttering so that Nora wondered if he would buy the copy as it had very tiny print.

He slammed the front shut.

"I'll take it!" He concluded and reached inside his jacket for his wallet.

His wife nudged him aside.

"I'll get it." She said, taking out her purse.

"No! Look, I'll get it." The man argued, nudging her back and already holding a ten pound note towards Nora.

Nora didn't move, sensing a fight brewing.

"No! I will get it!" The woman persisted severely and then glanced at Nora who was staring at them blankly. "We're going to have an argument now." She said with a forced laugh and slapped the man's hand away.

Nora turned to the till and punched the price of the book into the machine.

"I'll get it, look, here we are." The woman concluded as she fanned out a large pile of notes from her purse.

With a sigh the man walked off, defeated. He turned his back on his wife huffily and started to study the art books, but Nora could sense he was bristling because of being bullied. His wife meanwhile extended a ten pound note to Nora and smiled bossily.

"Thank you." Nora said.

"I just like to get rid of my money." The man said bitterly from before the art books and then stomped with his stick to the Cole section, prodding the carpet angrily with the wood.

"Would you like a bag?" Nora asked the woman, placing the ten pound note into the till.

"No we're going to the car." The woman shook her head.

Nora noticed that a laminated price was tacked to the book so managed to whip it off without the woman even noticing. She stuck it on the till while the woman shoved the book under her arm and joined her husband who ignored her.

'Bradshaw's Handbook' was a new project in The Secondhand Bookworm, one of a few new books that Georgina had decided to stock among her secondhand books. They usually kept a large amount on the shelves because it was proving popular and Nora was asked at least once a day about it and sold about three or four a week.

While the couple then walked out in silence, Nora jumped up and headed into the stairwell area behind her where several cases of railway books surrounded the first floor staircase. There were six duplicate copies of 'Bradshaw's Handbook' already in the railway section so Nora eased one out, carried it through to the front and popped it onto the counter, pressing the ten pound sticker onto it.

Nora then set about displaying the book replacement nicely, pausing to say hello to a customer who walked in and headed straight into the back room. She saw the Skype bar flashing orange at the bottom of the monitor and so clicked on it. It was a message from Seatown that just said:

'Morning, Nora.'

Nora Skyped a '*Good morning*' followed by a smiling sunshine emoticon. She then sniffed the air as the rancid smell invaded her nostrils once more.

"What *is* that?" She spoke to herself, just as the man came through from the back room and gave her a guilty look, his expression suspicious.

Nora watched him leave and sniffed the air, wincing at the horrid scent and deciding that maybe he was the cause all along. She grabbed the air freshener and grimaced as she sprayed it.

Nora then stood up and sprayed all around and was about to go into the back room to check out the kitchen in case there was something nasty festering in there when a man in a grey and yellow uniform, carrying a brown box, bounded into The Secondhand Bookworm.

"Good mor…." He began but got a lung full of air freshener and choked and gagged and began to cough loudly.

"Sorry." Nora apologised, watching him walk in.

"Flipping heck!!" The man spluttered, carrying the box around the counter.

"I had an erm…smelly customer." Nora said, watching him put the box down on the floor and straighten up while still coughing.

"Well I'll be a very fragrant delivery man." He coughed, blinking back the tears that sprang to his eyes. "Everyone else on my round will think I'm wearing perfume."

Nora smirked and watched him shake his head as though clearing his mind. He then picked up the stylus hanging from his electronic hand held device, squinted at it and prodded a few on screen icons.

"What's the surname?" He asked.

"Jolly." Nora replied.

He tapped it in and then handed it to Nora, fanning his hand before his face and letting out a few weak coughs.

Nora tried not to laugh.

"Just pop your squiggle there." He said.

Nora signed the screen and handed it back to him.

"Thanks, luv. Have a nice…" He coughed again as he headed off, "…day!"

"Thanks." Nora said, a little guiltily. She then turned and considered the box, deciding to unpack it straight away in case there were any customer orders lurking inside.

The box was opened easily and Nora laughed.

"More Bradshaw's Handbooks?" She chuckled and picked up the invoice sheet which listed fifteen copies.

As Nora counted them out and priced them in pencil she glanced out of the window, wondering where all the customers were. She noticed the 'Bradshaw's Handbook' man and woman walk past holding hands, with the 'Bradshaw's Handbook' still tucked neatly under the woman's arm. It looked as if they were speaking again after their argument over payment in the shop earlier.

Once the pricing of the new books was completed, Nora made a pile of the extra Bradshaw's Handbooks. As she did so she wondered why she had a nagging feeling in the back of her head that she had been meaning to do something all morning and had kept getting interrupted. She was about to head off to unlock the kitchen when Eugene Harvey entered The Secondhand Bookworm.

Eugene Harvey was a local author who looked more like a mad train spotter. He was dressed as usual in a long green anorak and a beanie hat. Eugene had written and self-published several books about local history and was obsessed with empty fields that once contained ancient structures. Nora had flicked through one of his thin tomes with great amusement to see that it contained at least fifty photographs of boring empty fields and information about where a windmill or a shed had once stood hundreds of years ago.

Nora watched him step down and completely ignore her, shuffling to the local section where he began to rummage through the village guides, pausing to put on a pair of glasses and then continue.

Suddenly Nora jumped as the fat address book burst out from between the folders under the counter and dropped to the floor followed by the telephone ringing. Ignoring the book at her feet, Nora picked up the receiver and heard a strange shuffling sound coming from the other end.

"Good morning, The Secondhand Bookworm." Nora greeted cheerfully, her gaze following Eugene as he walked really quickly across the room and headed towards the ordinance survey map section just through the doorway to the stairwell.

"Oh hello my dear, this is Mrs Pepper. Your colleague left a message for me that a copy of 'My Garden in autumn and winter' by Bowles has come in, but it is part of a set. He thought I would not want the set but I do, can you tell me if it is still there?"

"Yes of course, it would just be under the counter here." Nora replied and leaned back to check the reservation books.

A three volume set of hardback books with mustard colour dust jackets was neatly wrapped up next to a clear bag with three Tai Chi books on one side and what looked like nine or ten Rupert annuals on the other.

"Oh yes, they're here." Nora said, sliding them out.

"Oh lovely, are you open on Sundays?" Mrs Pepper asked.

"Yes we are. Eleven until four."

"Wonderful. I'll be in then. Thanks dear. Goodbye."

"Bye." Nora bade grimly, squashing the books back on the shelf which she needn't have taken off.

A tiny woman in a bright red cardigan stepped into the shop, looking at the floor from behind her large glasses and giggling. She came up to the counter and Nora saw that she was carrying some postcards from the spinner outside.

"Hello." Nora greeted, standing up.

The woman just giggled to herself and placed her camera and handbag onto the counter, muttering something while still smiling.

"Er. Just these?" Nora asked her but she still refused to speak, seemingly oblivious that Nora was even standing there.

Eugene came back into the front of the shop at that very moment. Nora watched him stop next to the postcard lady, ignoring Nora too. He picked up the Castletown guides which promptly absorbed his interest.

Nora counted the lady's postcards which amounted to six and ran the prices through the till.

"Thank you, that's one pound twenty for four and then thirty five pence each for the individual two, so one pound ninety please." Nora said.

The woman was distracted by Eugene and picked up a guide too.

"Oh that's nice." She said.

Nora watched them as they both stood looking through a copy of the town guide each.

'Hmm. They're quite suited.' Nora thought and smirked to herself.

Without looking up, the woman extended a folded five pound note towards Nora's hand so she took it, gave the lady her change and the woman returned the guide, as did Eugene who then shuffled quickly back to the local section.

Distracted by whimsical thoughts of matchmaking, Nora hadn't noticed that the woman walked away leaving her little camera on the counter.

When she looked down she saw the camera on the desk and looked up to see that the woman had vanished. There was no sign of her through the window either, so Nora picked up the camera and rushed around the counter.

"Could you watch the counter a second?" She said to Eugene who turned and stared at her, looking alarmed. "A lady has left her camera."

"Er…er….er…" He stuttered but Nora ignored him, picking up speed.

"The last thing we want is another object in the lost property box." She said and ran out of the shop onto the street.

Nora faintly registered that the fog had completely cleared and that the sun was attempting to shine over Castletown. The cobbles were empty so Nora peered up the hill where she spotted the woman's bright red cardigan and saw that she was almost half way up the road with a large man next to her.

It only took a quick sprint for Nora to reach them.

"Excuse me." Nora said so that the woman turned with a small soft scream.

"Oh!" She exclaimed.

"You left your camera in the bookshop." Nora said, handing it to her with a smile.

"Amber! Why did I marry you?! You've got a head like a sieve you have." Her husband rebuked.

Without waiting to be thanked, Nora ran back down the hill.

"Shame she's spoken for." Nora muttered with a grin, vaguely noticing Penny filling up her flower pots with windmills as usual. "Eugene would be a lot more suited to her."

Once Nora reached the shop she jumped back into The Secondhand Bookworm where Eugene was standing as if frozen, staring at the desk.

"Thanks." Nora said as he turned to her quickly. "There's no one around but just in case." She explained, walking back to the swivel seat and catching her breath.

Eugene grunted and turned back to the Cole books.

As Nora caught her breath she was aware of that same rancid smell in the air now that the spray freshener had cleared.

"What on earth is it?" She narrowed her eyes and stared out of the window.

Suddenly she was aware of Eugene standing at the counter.

"You have two copies of my book." He said, placing them on the desk.

Nora beheld him uncertainly.

"Oh. Yes." She said.

"Would you like me to sign them?" He offered.

Nora blinked.

"Erm. Yes okay, that would be great. Thanks." She said and rolled a pen towards him.

He smiled smugly as he bent over and opened the first page of the slim paper binding. He then scrawled his name across the title page in both books. Still smiling, he took them back to the shelf.

In a moment Eugene was back, standing before her once more and holding two more tomes.

"Some more of my books. Would you like me to sign them?" He offered.

"Go ahead." Nora smiled politely.

He concentrated in silence as he signed the title pages of each book and then grinning broadly took them back to the shelf.

Nora wondered if he would be back again shortly but when she stole a glance at him she noted that he was absorbed in a thick hardback book so that she could only see the top of his fluffy curly dark hair.

Nora heard the door open a few moments later and saw Eugene's lady friend Blanche come in. When Blanche saw Eugene at the Cole section she looked surprised.

"Oh I don't usually see you in glasses." Blanche told him.

"Mmmm. I've got this at home from the library." Eugene replied, holding up the book that he had been reading.

"What is it?" Blanche asked, adjusting her large pink quilted coat. "Watermills and windmills of Cole."

"Mmmm." Eugene nodded, almost dreamily.

"How much is it?" Blanche asked him.

"Fifteen pounds, but there is a painting in here by Constable." Eugene opened the book and held it up to her face.

"Oh." She sounded fascinated. "Have you seen his paintings in Wisteria House?"

"Yes, but did you know he painted that one the day before he died?" Eugene said.

"No I did not. Gosh, I'd be very interested to see that." Blanche said seriously. "And I have some friends who would also."

"Mmmm." Eugene put the book back and Blanche glanced around the shop, oblivious of Nora watching them curiously.

"No, I must go." She said and then smiled at Nora while Eugene took off his glasses. "It is easy to spend too much time in here. We must go. Bye."

"Bye." Nora smiled.

Once the door had closed behind them Nora sighed, wondering what other book-wormy delights the day ahead would hold.

6 Z FOR ZACHARIAH

It was almost ten thirty when Nora realised that she was gasping for tea and that she was getting a cold turkey headache from not having had a brew for a few hours. She unhooked the keys and was about to go into the kitchen when a woman cast open the door and remained on the threshold. She was tall and extremely thin. Nora had a fleeting thought that if the woman hadn't been wearing clothes Nora may have supposed the wind had blown the door open.

"Is he here?!" A crackling, sharp voice asked Nora.

"I'm sorry?" Nora replied.

"My husband." The woman snapped, peering inside the room.

Nora stared at her, bemused.

"I don't know I'm afraid." She apologised.

"He's missing again!" The woman glowered, drew the door closed and marched off up the street.

Nora turned, leaving the counter and heading for the kitchen to put the kettle on. Distracted by a pile of books on the top of the little step ladder she removed them and put them on the radiator cover instead. It wasn't until

Nora put the key in the lock of the kitchen door that she became aware of a putrid stink emanating from the kitchen.

She paused.

"Uh-oh." She breathed and then turned the key in the lock, tentatively opening the door.

The kitchen was just as she and Cara had left it the day before except that the awful smell inside was so sharp and malodorous that it made Nora contract her eyes and cover her mouth.

"Bleurgh! Ewww! What on earth is that then?" She spoke aloud.

All thoughts of tea forgotten, Nora edged into the tiny room and judged that the smell could either be something monstrous that Cara had left growing in the bin or perhaps something evil emanating from the sink.

As she made to step towards the sink she suddenly became aware of a haze of luminous yellow, glowing evilly through the frosted window of the door that led out into the little yard. Grimacing, Nora fumbled for the small key that opened the door, stuck it in the lock and pushed down the handle. The door flung open revealing the yard and Nora stifled a scream.

A wave of reeking spice and excrement washed over Nora. She covered her mouth and nose and stared wide-eyed at a fluorescent green and yellow sea of sewage that included toilet paper, water, diarrhoea and various sized bowel movements. Indeed, Nora counted at least twenty unspeakable objects gathered by the door and then she shrieked as the little drain close by began to bubble up.

"Oh. My. Gosh!" She spoke against her hand, reached out and pulled shut the door and then ran from the kitchen.

Back in the front room, Nora grabbed the telephone, heaving against her hand but telling herself to get control and remain calm.

"Calm. Calm. It's just a sea of turds." She said as an incantation and hastily rang the Seatown shop.

As the telephone rang at the other end, Nora remembered the last time she had had to telephone Georgina about a 'Bookworm Catastrophe' and that had been blocked drains at the front of the shop. At least on that occasion there had only been rain water.

"The Secondhand Bookworm." Georgina's merry voice rang out.

"George it's me." Nora said, and then uncovered her mouth so that Georgina would actually be able to understand what she was saying. "It's Nora."

"Hello Nora!" Georgina greeted cheerfully. "Roger and I were just talking about you."

Nora blinked but her mind was focused on the situation.

"I've got a bit of a problem!" She said and felt the insane urge to burst out laughing when she said so.

"Oh dear. I know that tone. Not another flood I hope." Georgina said calmly.

"Well…." Nora winced and imagined with horror the sea of poop washing into the shop.

"It hasn't flooded has it?" Georgina then groaned.

"No. Well, not yet. I really hope it doesn't." Nora grimaced.

"What doesn't?"

"Well…all morning I've been aware of this smell, ugh, like putrid putrescence lingering in the air, almost like rancid spice and decay…or a curse of evil pestilence and rot…"

"Nora!" Georgina interrupted.

Nora winced and shuddered.

"Did you swallow a thesaurus?" Georgina half laughed.

"I thought that a couple of the customers may have messed themselves." Nora explained, ignoring Georgina's sudden squeal of laughter. "Or there was a super villain in the town and his secret weapon was his unmentionable stench. But I finally made it out into the kitchen just now and…well…there's a sea….!"

"A sea of what?" Georgina asked, almost bemused.

"Turds?" Nora offered and blenched.

"What?!" Georgina exclaimed but there was amusement in her tone.

"The sewage drains are blocked again." Nora concluded drearily.

"Oh great! How lovely." Georgina groaned.

"It's worse than the other times. It's like Chernobyl." Nora said. "Eeeew, I don't know why it didn't register that it could have been blocked drains again, but Max was so nice when he bought the restaurant that I dismissed it from my mind. I bet his minions are still pouring oil and fat down the drains and it's all blocked up and is backing up into the yard. The shop reeks."

"Yes well Max can enjoy the pleasure of the fragrance." Georgina decided. "What you need to do is close up the shop and go round to the Indian restaurant and let him know what's happened. Get Max to come back with you and see for himself what it's like. And what his oil causes." Georgina added grimly. "Wait until there aren't any customers and then just go round to him. Meanwhile I'll give mum a call because she is out and about with my old uncle Orville…"

"Uncle Orville? As in Orville the Duck? From the Keith Harris show?" Nora giggled.

"Yes he gets that all the time." Georgina smirked.

"Did you know that the original Orville puppet is insured for one hundred thousand pounds? A bit of useless Seymour information." Nora said.

Georgina laughed.

"No I didn't. How ridiculous! Anyway! To the situation at hand!"

"Oh yes." Nora winced.

"I'll get them to drop in and uncle Orville can have a look and see if he can unblock it before we call Dynorod. I do hope we don't have to call Dynorod as it'll cost us nearly two hundred pounds again." Georgina sighed.

Nora suspected that they would have to, but didn't say so, holding out hope that uncle Orville might work a miracle out there.

"The shop's empty at the moment. I'll go to the restaurant now." Nora decided.

"Okay. Good luck!" Georgina said.

Once they had hung up, Nora made a quick scribbled note for the door that said 'Poop Emergency', stuck it on the window facing outward and closed and locked the door.

She ran up and down the stairs to check that she wasn't about to traumatise anyone by locking them inside The Secondhand Bookworm and then stepped out into the street and breathed in the fresh air as she locked the door behind her.

It was a little chilly outside and felt like it might rain so Nora glared up at the sky, willing the clouds to disperse. She decided to drag the postcard spinner back inside when she returned and so left it where it was while she set off on the short distance to the corner of the street.

Nora turned into 'Tree Lane', paced past 'Adelia's Photography Studio', which was a new shop located above the Estate Agents, and was immediately standing outside the newly named 'Castle India'.

'Castle India' was closed and looked dark and deserted inside. Nora peered through the window, unnerved slightly by the huge golden dragon staring at her from its place before the entrance booth.

She knocked loudly and waited, reading the menu which looked tempting, and then knocked again. There was a shadow of movement from deep within the restaurant and a young man in a black shirt and black trousers came hurrying along.

"We. Closed." He said, pointing to the sign.

"I'm from the bookshop." Nora said against the window and pointed past him. "Next door."

He stared at her, suspiciously.

"I need to speak to Max. Now." She called.

The man continued to stare at her.

"Why?" He asked.

"The drains are blocked up. *Your* drains are blocked up." She accentuated with narrowed eyes.

The man continued to stare and then tipped his chin up slightly in an acquiescing gesture.

"Max not here. But his uncle run restaurant now. He be here one hour. I tell him to come." He said.

Nora studied him thoughtfully and then imitated his gesture.

"One hour." She said, lifted her chin in the air and turned away.

She then broke into a run and legged it back to The Secondhand Bookworm, where a man was peering into the shop through the door window.

"Hello!" Nora greeted cheerfully.

"Oh." He looked her up and down and noticed her key. "Was it you with the 'Poop Emergency?"

"Pardon?"

He pointed to the door.

"Oh! I meant to write 'Drain Emergency'" She said and tore it off the window once inside.

The man smirked at her, following her into the shop.

Once Nora had grabbed hold of the postcard spinner and dragged it in, the man glanced around.

"Where's your section on clocks and clock making?" The man asked.

"In the room above." Nora said, leaving the door open. "I apologise for the smell. The drains are blocked."

He glanced at her but didn't say anything and headed off.

Nora sat down in the swivel chair thoughtfully.

So it appeared that Max had handed the restaurant over to his uncle who was obviously carrying on the previous owner's tradition of pouring oil down the drains. She Skyped a message to Georgina to tell her and explain that Max's uncle would be around in about an hour.

'Good!' Georgina replied. *'Mum and Orville are on their way.'*

Nora smiled with relief and scanned the town beyond the windows. It was empty so she grabbed the keys and sped up the stairs to the toilet that was located on the next floor in the children's book room.

Hastily unlocking it, Nora leaned in and flushed the chain. She then locked it up and flew back down the stairs to the kitchen whereupon she covered her face with her sweater, threw open the yard door and looked out.

Where the manhole cover was located, hidden now beneath a sea of rancid excrement and curry, the water began to bubble up fiercely in a perfect rectangular area.

Nora shook her head, closed the door and walked back into the front of the shop, understanding that once again, the entire system was completely blocked.

She returned to the desk, musing over the probability that with the large amount of rain that had fallen over the last few weeks, including the flooded road a few months before, it must have added to the crisis of the drain blockage.

She no longer had a desire for tea, or even to place anything near her mouth so she sat down and stared at the door as a large woman in a tent-like dress loomed up to the window, pressed her nose against the glass and peered into the room. When she saw Nora she gave a start, pushed open the door and stood there.

"Have you seen my husband?" She asked loudly.

Nora looked around.

"Well…there is a man in here." She remembered.

"Is he fat, bald and ugly, 'cause that would be him?" The woman asked, puffing down the step while holding onto the door handle.

Nora thought it best not to confirm that he was fat, bald and ugly so searched her mind for an answer.

"You can call for him if you like." She offered lamely.

"Yeah, I'll holler for him else he'll never come out. He's avoiding taking me to the chiropodists to have my corns done." The woman said, stalking across the carpet.

"Sorry about the smell." Nora said.

"Eh? I don't smell nuffin!" The woman stated and made her way deeper into the shop.

Nora cringed to hear her screeching up the stairs for her husband who promptly stepped out of the back room and yelled at her for shouting up the stairs for him.

Nora pretended to be busy sorting out the desk as they retreated from the back while arguing, continuing the dispute as they headed out. The man ignored Nora so she grimaced to herself, glanced up as they left and then quickly stood up to reopen the door and let some fresh air in.

She didn't have any more customers in the twenty minutes that it took for a large Volkswagen to arrive and pull up on the cobbles in the square, heralding the arrival of Georgina's mother.

Nora was tidying up the shelf of reserved books, wishing she had a peg for her nose, when a man stepped into the shop, humming happily to himself, closely followed by Mrs Pickering. Nora realised that the man was uncle Orville.

Uncle Orville was a little man with pure white hair and enormous glasses that caused his eyes to look like an owl's. He was in a white sweater, grey cords and great big fishermen's boots that even covered his thighs so that Nora stared at them. In his thickly gloved hands was a long, thin metal pole.

"Hmmm hmmm hmmm." He sung happily as he walked quickly into the shop, trailed by Georgina's mother.

"Hello, Nora." Mrs Pickering greeted.

"Hello." Nora replied.

Mrs Pickering was a tall, austere looking lady in her early eighties, with elegant white hair tied up into a flawless chiffon, a pink angora jumper and cream jeans with neat little heeled boots. She was carrying a gold clutch bag and her lips were pursed in disdain.

"What a marvellous situation." She said drily. "This is uncle Orville. He has no sense of smell and he's a little deaf. The perfect candidate for inspecting sewage problems according to my daughter."

"Eh?" Uncle Orville beamed, blinking repetitively and stopping next to Nora.

Nora smiled.

"Now where's this problem young lady?" He asked loudly in a light raspy voice.

"You take him and show him dear." Mrs Pickering ordered. "I'll mind the counter."

"Okay." Nora nodded. "It's through here." She indicated to uncle Orville.

When he put his head to the side and leaned closer to her with his ear pointing in her direction, Nora repeated it loudly.

"Lead the way. Hmmmm, hmmmm, hmmmm." He hummed.

Nora eased down the sleeve of her sweater on her left arm and covered her mouth and nose, taking uncle Orville towards the kitchen.

Oblivious to the smell, he followed her and then took the lead when she stopped outside the little room and gestured inside. Without batting so much as an eyelid, uncle Orville stomped straight into the nuclear spillage and hunted around for the manhole cover.

Nora peered through the shelves of books on war which had the windows into the yard set behind them. She watched through the dusty and cobwebbed glass as uncle Orville stuck his metal rod in several places and then violently eased up the manhole cover.

Unable to take the stench any longer, Nora closed the kitchen door and headed back to the front only to be confronted by a tall man in a long white silk kurta that reached down to his knees and a white silk churidas. Over the top of this he had an expensive ivory Sherwani with gold buttons which were all undone. He was imposing with thick black trimmed hair, very dark eyes and a solemn expression.

"Ah Nora dear. This is Mr....?" Mrs Pickering indicated and paused for him to say his name.

"Duleepsinhji." He said, touching his hands together. "Namaste." He greeted politely but his dark eyes were narrowed. "I am Max's uncle. You have problem?"

"Erm....yes." Nora said. "If you would be so kind as to follow me."

She turned and after a hesitation Mr Duleepsinhji walked behind her. Nora sensed he wasn't too happy about this.

In the kitchen they met uncle Orville who was placing each foot of his wellington boots into a bucket of cold water. He looked up and blinked at Nora with his massive owl-like eyes.

"It's all blocked up, Nora." He said, humming cheerfully as he cleaned off his boots. "Georgina will have to call Dynorod."

"Oh dear." Nora said and then turned to Mr Duleepsinhji. "We only use a small drain for our shop in the yard but all of your drains from the flats and your restaurant flow past here. I have personally seen large vats of fat being poured down the drain through that window there." Nora pointed.

Mr Duleepsinhji shook his head.

"It not us." He said flatly.

Nora just stared at him as he leaned out of the door.

After a moment he pointed.

"You put your books down toilet. Look at the paper. It your fault." He said, uninterested.

Nora gaped at him.

"That's actually toilet paper." She said, amazed at the ludicrous accusation.

"It not my problem." He said curtly, leaned back in and before Nora knew it he had pushed past her and was heading away.

Uncle Orville stared at her.

"What was that?" He asked, cupping a hand around his ear.

Nora just stared back.

She then turned quickly and followed Mr Duleepsinhji who was almost half way across the front room towards the front door.

Mrs Pickering looked up from the crime novel that she was reading. Her eyes darted to Nora.

"Excuse me sir, but the drains are blocked again because the chefs in your kitchen continuously pour oil down the sinks and drains, even though they have been told by…"

He whirled around to face her.

"You flush books down the toilet." He interrupted. "It not my problem."

"It's toilet paper! Books wouldn't fit down there!" Nora gasped.

"It not my problem." He concluded, turned and left the shop, leaving Nora and Mrs Pickering gaping.

As the two women stood staring at the door, a lady appeared in place of Mr Duleepsinhji. She was wearing a large hat which had several giant brooches of fruit pinned over it. The sight of it distracted Nora momentarily.

"Have you seen my husband?" She asked loudly. "What the heck is that smell?"

"Georgina will not allow that man to evade responsibility for his misdemeanours." Mrs Pickering said to Nora, completely ignoring the woman in the doorway.

Nora glanced at her.

"Er. No she won't." Nora agreed.

"Excuse me!" The lady in the doorway prompted.

"Sorry madam but I don't know who your husband is. The smell is blocked drains." Nora told her and went to turn to the Skype to let Georgina know when the woman continued.

"How much are the postcards?" She asked.

Mrs Pickering turned her nose up at the lady and lifted her crime novel higher, continuing to read as she awaited uncle Orville.

"They are thirty five pence each or four for one pound twenty." Nora explained. She then turned and began to relate what had passed to Georgina, typing so fast that both the lady and Mrs Pickering stared at her.

"Do you sell stamps?" The lady in the doorway next asked.

"Yes." Nora replied, casting her a quick polite smile.

"Hmmm. Is my husband in here do you know?" She persisted.

"I don't know I'm afraid. I don't know who your husband is." Nora shrugged off the question, concentrating on relaying everything to Georgina so that she would give the go ahead to call the drain people.

Uncle Orville walked through, his wellington boots sparkling clean, his gloves in a bag and his rod washed too.

"I can't do much with that. Not much point us hanging around here." He said loudly.

Mrs Pickering clicked her tongue and shook her head, closing her crime novel and dropping it into her clutch bag.

"He's wearing a brown mac and has grey hair." The lady in the doorway then called.

"Madam! I suggest you call the missing people bureau if you have misplaced your husband!" Mrs Pickering declared, standing up and fixing her with a withering look.

Nora glanced from the monitor and pressed send as she looked from Mrs Pickering to the lady in the doorway.

The silence was broken only by uncle Orwell's humming. The lady opened her mouth to speak when a man in a brown mac with greying hair materialized behind her.

"There you are, Kate." He said wearily.

The woman gave a start, turned to him and drew in her breath.

"Where have you been? I thought you said you'd be in the bookshop." She demanded.

He went to speak but the woman ushered him away.

"Well it's too late now. The bus is due and there is a problem with drains in there." She concluded.

Nora watched them leave, wanting to laugh and then turned to Mrs Pickering who smiled.

"Goodbye, Nora dear." Mrs Pickering bade, tapping her fondly on the arm.

"Thank you for coming." Nora appreciated. "Thank you." She said to uncle Orwell who was already beginning away.

He didn't hear her and made for the door.

"Georgina and I will be at your brother's theatre for the opening performance at Christmas." Mrs Pickering then said. "I trust it will be good?"

"It sounds as though it will be." Nora nodded.

"I assume that you will be attending." Mrs Pickering added, pausing to look at her.

Nora nodded.

"Then I will see you there if not before. Dress smartly young lady. I hear a rumour that my son is pursuing you and I expect he will be your date." Mrs Pickering said, her eyes twinkling.

Nora grinned.

"I'll make sure I look my best for him." She assured.

"As will I make sure he looks his best for you." She promised, winked and left with uncle Orwell, just as a Skype message arrived from Seatown.

'Phone DYNOROD!'

Nora sighed, pleased, drew out the Yellow Pages and with her nose screwed up because of the relentless odour, set out calling the professionals.

It was almost twelve o'clock when a large orange Dynorod van pulled up in the square. Nora was bagging some books for a customer who was giving her information on the weather forecast for the rest of the week and as a tall skinny man in a blue boiler suit bounded into The Secondhand Bookworm, the customer left.

"Hi there. You have some blocked drains?" The man asked cheerfully.

Nora hung up a load of blue carriers that had dropped and slid over the carpet as she had unhooked one for the customer.

"That is an understatement." She said and he smiled. "Through here."

She glanced around to check that no one was entering the shop and then led the man to the kitchen. He stood on the step of the back door and scanned the area which was at that moment bubbling up like a bog.

"Lovely. Where do these drains go?" He asked, examining it without even wincing at the stench.

"Through that door. It's bolted." Nora spoke through her sleeve. "It leads out into the alley where the sewer pipe from the Indian Restaurant and the flats flow past and goes out into Main Street. It must be blocked through there and backing up again."

"Yes I saw on our records that we have been here a few times before. They're still pouring oil down into the system then." He shook his head. "I'll have to have a look into the drains once it's all unblocked and if I see it is a build-up of oil and fat I'll make sure I write it in my report."

"Thanks." Nora gagged.

"I'll go this way out and work from the alley. Save me treading muck through your shop." He decided and stepped into the yard with a squelch and a slosh. A large poop floated past his boots.

Nora gasped and then left him splodging through the yard, shut the kitchen door behind her and headed back into the front of the shop just as the telephone rang.

"The Secondhand Bookworm." Nora greeted, still speaking in a muffled way as she screwed up her nose.

"Hello. Can I speak to the person in charge of the catering and kitchen facilities?" An enthusiastic voice asked.

"What is it about?" Nora asked, wondering if someone was aware of the catastrophe taking place out the back and offering to come and clean the kitchen for her.

"Good afternoon madam, how are you today? I'm calling from 'Ardour Kitchens' with some great offers only available for the rest of…"

"We already have a kitchen here thanks." Nora interrupted. "Even though it is covered in sewage."

There was a silence.

"You don't want one at home either then?" The caller asked, ignoring her last comment.

"No, thank you." Nora replied.

"Thank you for your time; you have a nice day now. Goodbye." He said and hung up as an old man with bright white hair in a checked shirt and cream trousers walked in.

He had his hands in his back pockets, was wearing sunglasses with the shades turned up and was chewing loudly on what looked like an imperial mint.

"Rare sight." He said, the mint clicking against his teeth and then swirling around his tongue as he scanned the room.

Nora looked at him, trying to hide her disgust.

"Secondhand bookshop." He clarified, clicking and then sucking the mint. "Long may you continue. Got any railway stuff?"

Nora indicated with her hand.

"Just through there and on the left." She directed.

"Through the arch?" He said and walked through, dragging his feet and sucking the mint.

Nora glanced at the walkway. It wasn't an arch but she didn't argue with him, instead she saw a message from Georgina on the computer asking Nora to telephone their Environmental Health contact for the area and tell him what was occurring with the drains.

Nora had his number in the phone book and did so, speaking with him for about five minutes until he said he would go and visit the Indian Restaurant on Friday and pop in and speak to her afterwards.

Nora hung up, watching the Dynorod man heading backwards and forwards across the square from his van to the alleyway with long iron rods and a machine that he would connect to the taps in the kitchen sink.

A woman carrying a large recyclable bag full of vegetables walked into the shop, smiled blandly at Nora and peered around.

"Do you have a Cookery section?" She asked.

"Yes. It's…oh hang on, we moved it yesterday…it's now in the room above us." Nora remembered.

"Thanks."

She went to walk through and then said thank you to someone in front of her, hurrying through the walkway and disappearing. The person who had let her by was a nice looking young man in a white t-shirt and jeans. He was holding three books from the history room, his eyes blinking quickly and his face grimacing slightly because of the smell.

"Sorry about the stink." Nora apologised.

"No worries." He said, placing the books onto the counter.

"The drains are blocked because of the Indian Restaurant pouring fat down the drains for years." She explained, deciding to make everyone aware due to Mr Duleepsinhji's bad attitude.

The young man looked disgusted.

"I hope they're paying for the clean out."

"They will do." Nora said in a threatening tone, drawing a book about the Incas towards her.

She ran the prices of his books through the till.

"Eighteen pounds please. Do you need a bag?"

"No I'll pop them in here." He said, passing Nora a twenty pound note and indicating his satchel.

She smiled and gave him two pounds change and then wrote down the sale in the cash book while he tried to stuff the books into his satchel and finally gave up.

"On second thoughts can I have a bag?" He asked.

"Sure." Nora nodded and unhooked a blue carrier.

He slid the books inside it.

"Do you keep an eye out for books for people?" He then asked Nora.

"Erm...I could make a note of any titles needed and make the owner of the shop aware." Nora offered, picking up a pen.

"Well it's not a title it's a thing." He said.

"Oh. What is it?"

"Nahuatl." The boy replied.

Nora blinked at him.

"Okay well how do you spell that?" She asked and he smiled and spelt it out for her.

"What subject is it?" Nora asked, doubting that they had such a thing.

"It's a language system." He explained. "It's very ancient and books on it are very rare. I have people everywhere keeping an eye out for me."

"Okay well I'll make the owner aware and if she ever comes across anyone selling any then she'll know she has a customer for it and we in turn can let you know." Nora explained.

"Great. Thanks." He grinned, giving her his name and number.

He drew the strap of the satchel over his chest, gave a courteous nod of his head and left.

Nora watched him thoughtfully, liking it when customers were interesting and also well-mannered. She then saw the woman who had asked for cookery books walk back into the front of the shop.

"You would think with what's going on this year there would be a lot of books on party food and canapés. You would think someone had...." She looked at Nora prompting her to finish her sentence.

"Erm…published one?" Nora offered.

"Yes. But we've looked in Waterstones and W.H. Smith's and there's nothing."

"Oh dear. Would you like me to check and see if our Seatown branch has one for you?" Nora asked, reaching for the mouse.

"No, no we're not from around here." The woman shook her head and looked up as the man with the mint in his mouth (which had thankfully been crunched or sucked up and swallowed) stomped through.

"Have you looked for long enough?" The woman asked him.

"Yes, yes. Cheerio." He bade Nora, popped down the shades of his glasses and both he and the cookery woman left.

Nora glanced at the clock, remembering that Betty was due in at half past one and realising that she was getting hungry. She hadn't wanted to eat anything after discovering the Nuclear Disaster and so was planning to buy something fresh and neutral from the deli and eat it in the Secret Garden. She would also buy a nice steaming cup of coffee, she decided.

'Any books on Tin-Tin?'

A message from Seatown flashed on the screen.

'Nora, I know you can't look yet. Please look when Betty comes and let me know. Cara.'

'Will do' Nora typed and then jumped as a large woman walked heavily across the carpet and straight up to the counter.

"Have you seen my husband?" She asked through a hairy upper lip.

Nora stared at her and then tried not to look at the moustache.

"Erm…" She frowned in bafflement, realising that it was probably the third time she had been asked that already that morning. "I don't think that anyone is in at the moment. Everyone seems to have lost their husband today."

The woman didn't smile but her upper lip bristled.

"Maybe it's an epidemic." She growled. She cast a dark look around. "So he's not in here then?"

Nora couldn't be bothered to go through the whole 'I don't know who your husband is!!' charade so shook her head.

"No. I don't believe he is." She said.

"Gimme one of them then." The woman told her, slapping a palm upon the town guides on the counter.

"Oh. Okay, that's two pounds please." Nora said, pressing the buttons on the till.

The woman with the hairy lip dug into the pocket of her trousers and finally dropped a two pound coin onto the counter.

"I don't need a bag. Just a husband beacon." She muttered and left.

Nora wondered how the Dynorod man was doing in the yard so left the empty front of the shop to have a look. There was a loud suction sound like a hoover coming from outside and she opened the door to see a yellow pipe attached to the cold tap.

The smell was still horrible and Nora peeked out to see several manholes uncovered around the little bricked yard. Most of the water had gone but there was a lot of tissue paper and large poops all over the floor. Shuddering, Nora left the man to it and returned to the counter, giving the front room another liberal dose of air freshener.

After about forty minutes, while Nora was browsing through the NASA website on the computer, the Dynorod man walked into the shop.

Nora slowly rose from the seat and stared him up and down, resisting covering her mouth. His blue boiler suit was covered in excrement. It was flicked over his face and his hands and when Nora looked down she saw in horror that he was leaving large sloppy brown footprints over the clean cream carpet.

Deciding not to say anything due to the fact that he had kindly unblocked the drains, Nora forced a polite smile as he walked up to the counter reading a sheet of paper that he had filled in.

"Right then." He started with a thoughtful frown. "I've gawped down the drains and can tell you for certain it is a build-up of cooking fat and oil. The drain is about this wide now." He made a small circle with his thumb and forefinger. "I would recommend alerting Southern Water and the Environmental Health. Southern Water is going to have to professionally clean out the drains. I've written it all down on this sheet so you can try and get your money back from the Indian Restaurant. If you could just sign here." He offered Nora the poo-splattered pen which, after a hesitation, she took tentatively and, holding the pen at the top with the tips of her fingers, as well as avoiding the brown splashes over the paper, she signed on the dotted line as best she could.

The Dynorod man was oblivious and whistled as he took the pen and paper back. Nora tried not to wince as he tore off the top sheet and gave it to her.

"How much do we owe you?" She asked him, almost heaving.

He pointed to the sheet.

"One hundred and seventy five pounds and fifty three pence." He said.

Nora bit the side of her lip.

"We should have it in cash in the till for you." She said and pressed a button so that the till drawer flew open.

Nora counted out the amount and handed it to him.

"Thanks. Good luck." He said seriously, dropping the pen into the top pocket of his boiler suit.

"Thank you. And thanks for that." She indicated back towards the kitchen, screwing up her nose.

"No problem." He grinned and headed off.

Nora looked in dismay at the footprints left on the carpet and the putrid smell of sewage left behind. Then she sighed, relieved that the drains were at least all unblocked.

"I'll arrange to take Max to court." Georgina said when Nora had telephoned Seatown to let her know that everything was sorted.

"I think you'll get your money back." Nora decided.

"I would like it all back. I've had Roger hunting out all of the past Dynorod receipts and it amounts to about eight hundred pounds! Seeing as it isn't our fault in the slightest then it is unjust that I should foot the bill for their environmental destruction. I'll telephone Southern Water and make them aware. I am sure the Environmental Health contact will have a field day with them on Friday. I look forward to seeing him." Georgina concluded. "Are you okay though, Nora, after having to deal with *that*?"

"Yes, but I feel like Ann Burden, believing she is the last survivor after a nuclear war." Nora sighed, remembering a significant and disturbing post-apocalyptic book she had once been made to read in school by Robert C. O'Brien and often went on about. It had been so disturbing that it had recently been made into a movie.

Georgina chuckled.

"Don't start on about that book again."

Nora smirked.

"Once Betty is here and I've had something to eat I'll wash out the yard with buckets of hot soapy water." Nora decided.

"Thank you, Nora. I'll arrange for the whole yard to be jet hosed at some point too." Georgina concluded.

Once they had hung up, Nora sat down with a sigh, shaking her head and deciding to tackle the carpet with hot soapy water and a thick pair of marigolds!

7 HAVE YOU GOT MY KNICKERS?!

Betty arrived just before one thirty to find the shop quiet, pleasingly fragrant and several wet patches all over the carpet. Once Nora had explained the morning's happenings to Betty while Betty hung up her cream puffy gilet, she basked in her colleague's sympathy.

"Oh. Nora. How terrible for you." Betty commiserated. "Listen, you go and have your lunch and I'll mind the fort here. Get some fresh air and put the whole episode from your mind."

Nora smiled gratefully.

"Thanks, Betty. Do you need anything before I go?"

"No dear. You run along, Nora." Betty said, standing before the till and looking at the cash book over the top of her glasses.

"Thanks." Nora appreciated, slipping into her coat and taking up her bag.

She headed off with a fond glance back at Betty. A petite lady in her seventies, Betty was very down to earth and motherly to all the members of staff, with a fiery temper and a sharp wit, willing to assist anyone and with a great love of books.

Betty and Nora hadn't work together much in the two months Betty had been employed, but when they did Nora always had an amusing story to tell her sister and brothers at the end of the day.

Ever since Nora's landlady had thrown Nora out of her flat because the building had started subsiding, Nora had been living back at her family home with her mother, father, two brothers and sister, dogs, guinea pigs, fish, and a ghost that haunted the attic. She had one other brother, Wilbur, who was older than she but he had his own house so didn't have to endure the cramped and chaotic daily living in the Jolly household. Nora was currently on the lookout for a nice, new, *quiet* place of her own.

Wondering what the afternoon would have in store now that Betty had arrived, Nora carried out her plan of a delicious fresh lunch from the delicatessen and a walk down Riverside Road to the Secret Garden.

Past the jewellery shops, a traditional sweet shop, clothes shop and a furniture shop, there was a turning that led past a small car park and the old converted salt factories which had been in use back when Castletown was a port. The Secret Garden was currently in hibernation with the shrubs and trees bare and the large magnolia tree looking as though it was dead.

There was a familiar form sitting on the circle of empty benches that surrounded more bushes and trees. Nora also noticed a lady wrapped in an expensive caramel coloured coat, holding a glass of wine and reading a book on a bench up the steps overlooking the river.

Nora opened the gate and the figure on the circle of seats turned. His pleasant face broke into a grin and he popped the last piece of his sandwich into his mouth, checking his watch.

"Nora. You're late." Charles said, tapping the wrist watch and shaking his head. "I've got to get back to the office."

Nora chuckled, walking around and joining him on the seats.

"You wouldn't believe the morning I've had." She assured him, dropping down onto the bench with a sigh.

"Yes I would." He argued, watching Nora take out her sandwich. "I really must come in at some point. I need a new book to read."

"We have some interesting editions of late nineteenth century novels in at the moment." She nodded, knowing the books that Charles liked. "I found this scruffy old black book in the boot of a woman's car last week. She practically forced me to have it else she said she would throw it in the bin. I gave her a few pounds for it and it turned out to be a very early copy of 'Jane Eyre'."

Charles' mouth fell open.

"Put it by for me?" He asked, gathering his things and checking his watch once more. "Darn it, I have to get back." He regretted.

Nora laughed.

"I've already put it under the counter for you for when you next pop in." She told him.

Charles was almost visibly drooling.

"I'll convince my wife she could do with another smelly old scruffy book in the house." He promised. "How much is it priced at?"

"Fifty pounds." Nora replied, taking a bite of her sausage sandwich and trying not to think of the yard.

"I just love reading them in their early editions." He said, squashing all of his rubbish into his lunch bag and standing up. "I'm sure I'll have it. I quite like the idea of reading 'Jane Eyre'. Would you believe I've never read it?"

Nora almost choked on her food.

"Haven't you?! It's one I would have definitely thought you'd have read."

"I just haven't gotten around to it." He admitted. "But I'll change that. I'll be in either this week or the next. Thanks, Nora."

"Bye Charles." Nora grinned and watched him head off back to his office, checking his watch once more and then giving her a wave.

Once Charles had disappeared beyond the old salt factories, Nora secretly took out her Kindle, casting a look about her in case any Secondhand Bookworm customers were lurking about and saw that she had one. The streets were empty, so Nora settled down to read a novel that she had downloaded onto the little machine while the elegant woman with her glass of wine on the bench by the river shot her an aloof look and turned the page of her paperback.

When Nora returned to The Secondhand Bookworm she couldn't see Betty behind the counter because of a horde of German tourists surrounding the desk.

"Stamp!" She heard repeated over and over. "Stamp! Stamp!"

When she walked further in she saw Betty concentrating hard on cutting out stamps from a grey book of 'World Postcard Stamps'. There were little brown postcard bags over the desk and the green handled scissors were shaking violently as Betty snipped around a blue airmail sticker.

"I wanted four packs!" A woman stated in a harsh German accent. "Four packs of stamps! To Germany. You only give me three!"

"Four postcards and three stamps to Germany!" Another woman was demanding, banging the counter.

"Yes. Yes." Betty nodded, placing the stamps she had just cut out into a brown bag with some postcards.

Thinking that Betty seemed quite calm and had everything under control, Nora dropped her bag under the stairs and went into the kitchen to give it a quick scrub and disinfectant, pop on the kettle, wash out two mugs and prepare a cup of tea each for her and Betty.

She swept the floor of the little room and washed it as well as the step, wiped down all the handles and the taps and when it was all clean she left the kettle boiling while she went to ask Betty what she would like to drink. When she reached the front room the last of the Germans was leaving the shop stompingly. Betty closed the till and sat down, red in the face.

"Oh Nora." Betty wailed. "I want to cry!"

"Why?" Nora gasped, alarmed.

"Those people! They were *evil*! They must have been part of an SS tour bus. Oh they were so rotten and rude." Betty said and scowled fiercely. "I felt like jabbing them." She made a jabbing motion with the scissors. "Right in the jugulars."

Nora bit her bottom lip, imaging the scene with a slight smile.

"Oh sorry, Betty. I thought you were quite happy dealing with them. I thought you were handling them marvellously."

"NO!" Betty shrieked. "It was awful. I hope I wrote all the sales down." She stood up and peered at the cash book. "I'll have to go through and look through the whole till roll and make sure. Damned stamps!"

"I'll make you a nice cup of tea." Nora said. "And I bought some cake."

Betty looked at her.

"Oh Nora. You shouldn't have. How much do I owe you?" She reached for her purse.

"No it's my treat!" Nora said firmly, shaking her head. "And I think you deserve it after dealing with that."

"Oh, thank you Nora." Betty smiled.

"What a day!" Nora exclaimed as she headed back into the kitchen to make the tea.

Deciding to leave the floor of the yard until they had had their tea and cake, Nora closed the back door, pleased that the entire kitchen was now poop-free and spotless.

She retrieved two small plates from one of the cupboards while their tea brewed, placed a paper towel over the middle of each plate and then positioned a slice of plum cake on top with a fork.

The plum cake was a great wedge of thick delicious fruit and sponge dusted with icing sugar and smelt delicious. Nora then put a dash of milk into each mug, squeezed out the teabags, dropped them into the bin and carefully took up the handles of the mugs in one hand and the little plates with the other.

When Nora reached the counter back in the front of the shop, Betty was speaking to a man who had bought a little pile of local books.

"…and so I was brought up in that area and my lovely father used to take me to see the spitfires, but enough of that, I shouldn't admit it or you'll know how old I am, and I'm terribly old."

"Madam, you look as though you are much younger than me I can assure you." The man said, reaching out for his change.

"Oh how kind of you." Betty laughed. "That's five and ten and two is one." She said counting the money into his palm. "Now, I'll put those into a bag for you."

Betty turned and winked at Nora as Nora placed the tea and cake onto the counter by the monitor.

"Lovely talking to you." The man said once Betty had handed him his blue carrier bag of books.

"Aw, now you have a lovely day at the museum. You can't miss it, it's tucked away down the side of the road and it's near the model railway shop." Betty said.

"Yes. Thank you." The man bowed his head and left.

Nora smirked, taking a sip of her tea.

"Aw what a lovely man. I'm old enough to be his mother." Betty said.

Nora laughed.

"Georgina said that there was a lovely gentleman in Seatown the other day whom she said was very interested in you." Nora then remembered.

Betty gasped in disgust.

"Oh that was that awful old man who buys annuals each Thursday and only likes to deal with me. Oh he is so OLD, Nora. I said to Georgina, 'Georgina I'm fed up not hard up'. She's just like my daughter is Georgina. She thinks I'll settle for any old codger just because I got excited at being leered at by a drunk on Monday. Oh Nora, I'm sorry about that blasted beeping on my phone, it keeps saying that I don't have a signal and I can't stop it. Why it tells me a thousand times a day I don't know!"

Nora sat down on the brown stool, laughing into her tea cup.

"Oh!" Betty gasped as her mobile, which was tucked in the pocket of her jeans, began to ring. "Who's that phoning me?! They know I'm at work. Oh it's my daughter, April. Do you mind if I answer it, Nora. I don't usually but poor April is going through a terrible time with that no good partner of hers."

"No, go ahead." Nora said and took up her piece of plum cake.

"Hello." Betty spoke into the phone. "What? Oh that's lovely, April. Where are you going? Oh I do need some things in Seatown, yes. Can you go into Marks and get me some knickers? You know the ones I like. I measured them the other night. Yes that's right. They're so comfortable. Yes two packs of knickers. Thank you, sweetie. Bye."

Nora was trying not to giggle as she chewed her cake.

Betty turned and looked at her as she hung up.

"I do hope no one is in the shop as I said all of that, Nora." Betty smirked, her brown eyes twinkling.

At that moment, two new customers walked in through the opened front doorway.

"Hello." Nora greeted.

"Hello. The book in your window. The Complete Angler. I'm interested in it." The man said.

"You don't fish!" The woman next to him said as Nora got up.

"It's not about fishing. It does talk about all makes of fish but its more about the contemplation of fishing." The man replied.

Betty gave Nora a look and she shrugged, walking to the window. She moved a few books aside, shuffled along a set of Jane Austen novels and reached into the front for the book.

"Thanks." The man appreciated and opened it up.

Meanwhile, the woman with him scrutinized the Folio Edition section and Nora walked back to the counter, running her finger along the top of the till and showing Betty a lump of dust with a wince.

"What a lovely door handle." The voice of a man exclaimed.

Nora turned and saw another couple entering the shop.

"It's only an ordinary brass one!" The woman with him exclaimed.

She was dressed in a woollen poncho, jeans and fur-lined boots.

The man remained silent and looked at the topography section next to the door.

"Your set of Bronte novels in the window. How much are they?" The poncho woman asked, stepping down and almost stumbling.

"Oooh!" Betty gasped but the woman ignored her and fixed Nora with an expectant stare.

"It's forty pounds." Nora replied.

The woman repeated the answer slowly and thoughtfully.

"Yes. I'd like it I think. For my daughter. They'd make a good Christmas present." The woman decided.

"Of course." Nora nodded, heading for the window.

The man with 'The Complete Angler' walked up to Betty and decided to purchase the book. Nora left them deep in conversation as she grabbed the box set.

"Would you like a bag for it?"

"Yes, please." The woman nodded.

Nora popped the set into a blue carrier bag and processed the transaction.

When the customers had all finally left, Nora wrote the sale down in the cash book and then wondered what to place in the window gap.

"Nora. What shall I do to make myself useful?" Betty asked, finishing her cake just as a message came through from Seatown.

Betty leaned forward to read it aloud.

"How's the poo?"

Nora laughed.

"I expect that's Cara." She said.

Betty clicked on the emoticons. She chose a smiley face blowing a kiss and sent that back.

"LOL." She read out Cara's reply. "Oh the pen is moving." She said as Cara continued to type from the other shop. "Nora. Did you get all of my messages?" Betty read the message.

Nora nodded so Betty wrote that she had.

"Coolio." Betty said, reading Cara's reply. "Have you done the music?" She read. She looked at Nora.

"Oh. We have a lot of new tubs in the music section if you want to have a look at those?"

"Oh Nora, that's my forte." Betty said excitedly. "I love doing the music section."

"Well I think the different categories need to be moved into the new tubs and then there is a pile of sheet music that needs marking up too."

"Oh if you don't mind me doing all of that, Nora I would love to?" Betty said.

"It'd be really good if you did it as you know the most about music." Nora assured her.

"Oh thank you, Nora." Betty enthused.

Nora replied to Cara that she had been a bit distracted with the poo-festival but they were getting onto it now, when a woman stepped into the shop.

"Excuse me. Is my husband in here?"

Nora gaped at her and Betty arched her eyebrows.

"I don't think we have anyone in here at the moment." Betty said and glanced at Nora. "I'll just consult my crystal ball." She muttered.

Nora was exasperated at the trend of missing husbands all day but she smirked at Betty's comment.

The woman left, looking up and down the street while Betty drank her tea.

"This tea is lovely, Nora. And the cake was delicious. Thank you." Betty said appreciatively.

"You're welcome." Nora said, popping the last of her cake into her mouth.

They had a few more customers as they finished their tea and also looked for a couple of crime novels for a customer in Seatown, to no avail.

Betty then headed off upstairs to arrange the music, clipping one of the walkie-talkies to her belt as she went. She had only been gone a moment when a man came into the shop.

"Am I allowed to come in? Just to get an idea?" He asked.

"Er, yes of course." Nora nodded, wondering what idea he was hoping to get.

He paced around the front room in interest, looking up when Betty came down the stairs and showed Nora a sign that had been sellotaped to the front of one of the old messy cardboard boxes.

"This is torn, Nora."

"Shall I make you a load of new signs?" Nora offered.

"Would you, Nora? That would be so wonderful. It's really muddled up there. There are vocal scores in with saxophone music and organ music in with wind instruments. I'll sort it out as I fill up and replace the boxes."

Nora agreed and Betty headed off once more to continue.

She returned a few minutes later.

"Sorry Nora. Another sign. Can I have four copies of this one please?" She asked, laying a crumpled sign on the mouse mat.

"Yes, sure." Nora nodded, bringing up the Word programme on the computer.

Betty glanced at the screen and then gasped.

"Oh fish!" She exclaimed.

Nora looked at her.

"Oh fish, fish, fish!" She reached for her mobile in her pocket, shaking her head. "Sorry Nora, do you mind if I phone my daughter? I hope she hasn't got my knickers and left Seatown yet."

Nora glanced at the customers in the Cole section, repressing her urge to laugh. They were staring at Betty who was concentrating on her phone.

"I want a copy of Bradshaw's." Betty said.

"Well we sell it." Nora pointed out.

"I know but…" She lowered her voice. "Even with my staff discount here I can get it cheaper from Waterstones in Seatown. I really want a copy for Bill." She admitted, referring to her man friend. "I'm seeing him tonight and I said I would get him a copy. Oh I don't want to spend more than I have to on him. Aren't I wicked?" She smirked as Nora chuckled behind her hands. "He says he loves me but he's so OLD, Nora."

Nora laughed.

"Have you got my knickers?!! It's me! Have you got my KNICKERS?!" Betty shouted loudly down the phone, ignoring Nora who was suddenly in silent hysterical laughter.

A man hobbled into the shop and when Betty repeated the question he stopped dead and stared at her. Betty turned around and bent over.

"April, I'm at work. Oh you have got my KNICKERS! Oh are you still in Seatown?" She asked a little less loudly into the receiver. "Oh fish! Well, I wanted a book but never mind. He'll just have to wait. I'll pick it up the next time I'm working there. That's if he's still alive. Bye sweetie."

Nora was desperately trying to control her expression and greet the customer politely.

"Er…yes. Do you have any books about Chinese Medicine? Ancient Chinese Medicine? At least, I'm not interested in British Medicine. I am a registered invalid so I can't go upstairs." The customer said loudly over Betty who hung up on her mobile and turned around with a glamorous smile.

"Well. I could check upstairs for you." Nora offered.

"Hold up. Are these all secondhand?" The man asked.

"Yes. We have a few new books but…"

"I only want new books!" He snapped and began to turn around.

"I can have a look on the internet and can always order…"

"NO!" The man snapped, hobbling away.

Betty and Nora regarded one another and then Betty made a rude gesture behind his back while mouthing insults at him that included the word 'old' several times.

When the man and woman from the Cole section approached the counter, Betty fixed them with a dazzling smile, although she winced slightly and looked a little self-conscious of her teeth.

"This please." The man said warily, dropping the book onto the cash book.

Nora opened the front while Betty unhooked a bag for the book.

"Twenty Five pounds please." Nora said, noticing that it was a new book specifically about Seatown.

He handed her two twenty pound notes and she gave him his change.

"Lovely book." Betty smiled, handing the bag to him.

"Mmm." The man said without smiling, snatched the bag and left with the woman, bickering with her as they headed off down the street.

"What a pig." Betty glowered. "Oh it's probably my teeth. Frightening the customers. I'll be glad when I have the lower plate fitted on Tuesday week but it's costing me."

"Do your teeth hurt?" Nora asked her.

"Yes. Oh Nora I've got to have these three out, Tuesday week and a plate fitted. When I went there last Wednesday and had this one out because I had an abscess, the nurse was trying to get me to have ANOTHER set for the top, these are false." She said, tapping her nice front teeth. "I was shouting at her, telling her I can't have another set when I can't afford it and I could be dead next year. What's the point of having TWO sets of top teeth when I could be dead next year?! I was laying in the chair with my mouth numb trying to shout at her and she said 'why do you not want new teeth?' so I shouted back," (Betty pretended that her mouth was numb) "It was different before, I had some money from my husband, but now I can't afford it as I'm trying to buy a house." She said, doing a numb face impression. Nora tried her best not to laugh as Betty continued. "The last set I had fitted was wonky. I've got small bottom teeth and large top teeth and he made them too small. So I'm going back on Tuesday to have them fitted and hopefully they'll be comfortable. I'm sorry about the food left in the kitchen. My daughters make me lunch and I have to throw it away because they give me food I can't eat and I daren't take it home or they'll tell me off."

Nora was desperately trying to keep a straight face and Betty smirked.

"Well, hopefully it will all work out alright." Nora finally said.

"Thank you, Nora." Betty appreciated and set off to continue with the music, leaving Nora chuckling about Betty's humorous way of telling a story.

The rest of the afternoon passed by quickly, with Nora printing and cutting out signs for the new plastic music tubs, Betty sticking them on with sellotape and filling the tubs up with the neatly sorted sheet music, several customers buying and selling books, a few telephone calls, another round of tea, and Nora throwing endless buckets of hot soapy water over the floor of the yard until it was time to close up the shop.

They had run out of time to price the remaining new stock of sheet music so Nora left it aside in the walkway under the stairs with a note for Cara to price it the following day if she got a chance.

Once the lights were off, the windows secure, the internal doors locked, the money counted, the PDQ banked, the computer shut down, coats on and bags organised, Betty and Nora set the alarm, turned off the last of the lights and stood at the door talking as they locked up.

"Have a nice evening, Nora. It was lovely to work with you." Betty said, zipping up her gilet.

"You too. When are we next working together?" Nora asked.

"Oh probably not for ages. I'm hardly ever put with you." Betty said miserably.

"We'll speak on the Skype." Nora decided. "And I'll check the roster on Friday and see when we're next together. I'm on calls tomorrow."

"Oh lovely Nora. Where are you parked?"

"Alongside the moat." Nora replied.

Betty pulled a face.

"I'm up the hill. I had to reverse into a really awkward place. I was lucky to get it because I pulled alongside it and this car behind me beeped so I stopped and waved them around, indicating to the space. It was some grey-head who pulled around me and gave me a filthy look as he went past. I just hope I can get out of it. Oh that's my phone. I'll see you soon. Bye Nora." She said and blew a kiss as she dug about her jeans for her mobile.

"Bye, Betty." Nora grinned, heading down the street towards her car.

She popped into the corner shop and bought a bottle of Evian which she opened and sipped from as she watched the mallards and moorhens running across her path or looking at her expecting food. After pausing for a while to read the sign about the new castle being built she finally reached her car, deciding that it really was turning out to be a typical bookworm week.

8 THE UNIVERSE OF BOOKS

Thursday morning arrived with a spattering of rain and then dull sunshine that crept over the houses and cottages of Little Cove. The sea was rough and could be heard from Nora's home and she listened to it as she sipped her coffee in the doorway of the Jolly house, overlooking the back gardens and the winding paths to the little cliffs.

Seymour dropped Nora at Little Cove railway station in time for her to catch the eight forty train to Piertown where Georgina lived. Nora watched the scenery pass by from her seat, yawning behind her hand and then replying to a text message from Humphrey that he had sent the evening before.

The station at Piertown was bustling and Nora scanned the road for The Secondhand Bookworm van as she jogged down the steps outside the station building. She spotted it and sprinted to the passenger side, drew open the door and waited for Georgina to clear her handbag, the black calls file, gym bag and flask off the seat before Nora slid into it.

"Morning, Nora!" Georgina greeted cheerfully and thrust the Tom-Tom into her hands.

"Morning." Nora replied, blinking at the satnav.

"It fell off." Georgina said, revving the engine and putting it in gear. She pulled away and a car beeped as the van careened in front of it. "Sorry." Georgina called.

Nora licked her fingers and wiped the spittle on the little sucker, pressing it to the windscreen and unzipping the calls file at the same time as putting her seatbelt on as she almost fell into Georgina who took a corner at top speed.

"We're in Piertown first. I know where the house is so don't worry about putting the address into the Tom-Tom. I'm glad you dressed up warm because we're going to your favourite place. The Mushroom Farm." Georgina said.

Nora looked at her quickly.

"We're not are we?!" Nora whined and then bit her tongue when Georgina glanced at her.

"No complaining today." Georgina warned. "I'm sure it will be a day of *maddos* as well. But I am in such a good mood after the weekend that I think I can deal with the mushrooms and the *maddos*."

Nora regarded her curiously.

"And what happened at the weekend?" She asked.

Georgina smiled, almost smugly.

"I went to Sandalwood House. To the vintage fashion and car revival fair. On a date." She said.

"Really?" Nora was interested.

"Hmmm, and he was wonderful. I'm seeing him again this weekend. He's an American and incredibly wealthy. He promised to rescue me from mother." Georgina said and they both laughed.

"What's his name?" Nora asked.

"Troy." Georgina replied, clearly dazzled by him.

"Oooh, so love is in the air." Nora grinned.

"Not quite yet but I'm definitely on cloud nine." Georgina confessed and then proceeded to tell Nora all that had occurred, which included a chocolate indulgence dinner, a nineteen fifties catwalk show, champagne and dancing.

The van soon pulled up outside the house of the first call and Georgina drove up a drive alongside the long façade.

Immediately there was a blur of movement followed by loud yapping and four dogs bounded around the corner of the abode.

"Uh-oh." Nora muttered, unclipping her seatbelt.

"Lovely." Georgina said with bright sarcasm.

A man walked around the corner, staring at the van and then smiling in welcome while the front door of the house opened and a woman flew out of the door.

"Wally! Teddy! All of you shut up! Get indoors or go around the back!" She shouted.

Georgina opened the van door and got out only to be almost bowled over by an Airedale terrier.

"Sorry! They're rescue dogs. Very friendly but a bit excitable. Silence Wally!" The woman cried and grabbed the collar of a scruffy black Cairn terrier.

The dog didn't stop barking. The two larger ones ran off when the man whistled but the Airedale called Teddy and the Cairn called Wally remained.

"It's no problem." Georgina smiled.

Nora got out of the car and looked around, wedging the calls file under her arm.

"I'm Georgina and this is my colleague, Nora." Georgina said.

"Thank you for coming." The woman said, jerking as Wally pulled at her repetitively while barking.

"You're a funny little thing aren't you." Georgina said to Wally, stroking him and seemingly oblivious to the fact that he tried to nip her. She looked around expectantly. “We’re here to see some books?” She prompted.

“Oh yes, sorry. Wally shush. They’re in the den.” She let go of Wally and he ran at Georgina’s ankles but she was wearing boots so paid no attention, following the woman as they made their way towards the house.

Nora greeted Teddy who was friendly and let her stroke him.

“Aw you’re just like my dogs.” She said and he licked her hand.

Nora trailed after Georgina, smirking at Wally who bounced level with Georgina while barking at her continuously. Teddy ran off and peed up against the wheel of the van and then skipped back to Nora.

The house was long and veered off to the right through a rustic kitchen where a college-aged boy was sitting at a breakfast bar listening to his iPod. He looked up, surprised, chewing some crisps from a large bag on the counter.

“This is my son, Mil.” The woman said, glaring at Wally who careened off barking ahead of them.

Mil saluted nonchalantly and Nora arched an eyebrow.

“Short for Milton?” She asked him, still stroking Teddy, who walked alongside her.

Mil looked impressed.

“Yeah. Family name.” He grimaced.

“My youngest brother is a Milton. After a mad uncle on my father’s side.” Nora said, glancing at Teddy who bounded from her side towards a unit.

“Really?” He smiled. “Is he a Mil?”

“No, he uses his full name.” Nora said. “I like it.” She gave a small gasp as Teddy peed up against the unit and then came back to her as if proud of what he had done.

Mil ignored him, staring at Nora.

"This way, Nora." Georgina hinted.

Nora smirked and followed while there was a scraping of a chair and Mil was suddenly walking with them.

They passed through a dining room and then a lounge and through a door to a large messy den. There were two enormous bookcases full of books which included a lot of coffee table tomes, but on the floor were about eight or ten boxfuls.

"We've had a sort through and they're the ones we'd like to sell on." The woman explained, gesturing to the boxes.

Nora gazed around, spotting an upright piano, a few sofa chairs, a flat screen television hooked up to a computer console and various other items. Her attention was upon the books in the bookcases and she considered the shelves with interest until Georgina indicated to the books in the boxes.

"We'll just go through them and see what we can use. Oomph!" She staggered slightly to the side because of Wally lunging at her, still barking.

"WALLY! I am so sorry. That's it! Mil, would you please put him in a cage." The woman said and Nora looked alarmed.

She glanced at Mil who reached for the terrier.

"We have dog cages in the dining room. Just for while visitors are here." He told her, grabbing Wally's collar.

Nora nodded, stroking Teddy protectively who seemed to have designated Nora as his new best friend.

"It's no problem." Georgina smiled politely but Nora could see that she was irritated as they had a whole day ahead for calls, so Nora headed for the boxes and knelt down before one. Teddy joined her and sat himself down panting and giving her his paw.

The first box contained a selection of history books that included specific battles, biographies of kings and queens, and detailed tomes on various historical eras. They were bright and interesting so Nora pulled most of them out and made a large 'yes' pile. Georgina busied herself rummaging through a box of art and architecture books while explaining to the woman which ones would be saleable and which ones were too general to stock at The Secondhand Bookworm.

In the next box in front of Nora was a whole collection of classic novels in small hardback bindings with ribbons, and also classic paperback penguin editions. She pulled out authors such as Virginia Woolf, George Orwell, Henry James and Jane Austen. There were also some tomes of bird watching and local interest which continued on into the next box.

Among the whole collection of the books for sale there were college text books which Nora left, cookery and railway books, a good selection of philosophy books and some interesting theology. While Georgina counted through the ones that they had taken aside to buy, pricing them up so as to make an offer, Nora stroked Teddy while thumbing through a book about Walsingham, a village in Norfolk.

"Okay we're done." Georgina called to the woman who had disappeared into the lounge.

Mil was sitting in one of the den chairs, listening to his iPod and flicking through a book on deep sea fishing while observing Nora and Georgina.

The woman came back in and Georgina stood up.

"For this pile, these here, this pile and this pile, oh and also these, I would offer one hundred pounds." She said.

The woman scanned briefly over the ones set aside.

"One hundred pounds? Okay, yes. Thank you that would be acceptable." She decided happily.

"Nora, would you be able to get the boxes from the van please?" Georgina asked, holding the keys towards her.

Nora stood up and exchanged the keys for the calls file, which Georgina unzipped while asking if the lady would be happy with a cheque or would prefer cash.

"Need a hand?" Mil asked, jumping up when Nora and Teddy passed him.

Nora met his eager green eyes.

"Sure." She shrugged and he walked with her through the house.

When they passed Wally in his cage he made a fierce gremlin sound, bashing at the bars which made both Nora and Mil laugh. Teddy skipped ahead and peed against the boot scraper just outside the door, but seeing that Mil ignored him Nora said nothing.

"So, you buy lots of books from people's houses?" Mil asked as Nora opened the van and dragged a blue box that was full of five more folded blue boxes towards her.

Nora nodded, letting Mil grab it and lift it up.

"Yes. Books are also brought into the shops by customers as well but we have one or two calls days a week." She explained, picking up two more folded boxes and walking back to the house.

She left the van doors open but locked it because their bags were in the front.

"Cool." Mil said, letting her go first. "You read a lot?"

Nora smiled slightly.

"A variety." She admitted.

"Cool. I'm taking a degree in maths at the moment so reading is a nice relief from equations and theorems." He said.

Nora glanced at him, impressed, ignoring Wally.

"Wow. I'm useless at maths. It took me three attempts to get my GCSE." She said, moving aside to let Teddy bound past.

Mil shrugged.

"It comes easy to some people; some people have to work hard at it." He said. "I failed my English miserably."

Nora smiled.

"My cousin Felix is very good at maths. My brothers figured that he received my share of maths brain." She said and Mil laughed.

They reached Georgina who had handed the lady a cheque and then they proceeded to box up all of the books. Nora and Mil carried the packed boxes to the van until Georgina had filled the last one and walked with them carrying the last box while Mil and Nora hoisted a box each of their own.

"It's nice to see a young man lending a hand." Georgina said to Mil.

"No problem." He smiled.

As they passed Wally he ran at the cage barking and Georgina jumped with a small yelp so that Nora left the house laughing and Teddy began barking and peeing up against a mountain bike in the drive.

Once everything was loaded and the other two dogs had bounded back around from the other side of the house, Nora dived into the passenger seat and smiled a goodbye to Mil.

"Thank you. Goodbye." Georgina sang as she slid into the driver's seat. "Quickly let's get away from this mad house." She muttered to Nora and passed her the calls file.

Nora smirked and opened the file, finding the address of the next call and arching an eyebrow.

"We're going to Universe of Books?" Nora asked incredulously while Georgina reversed out of the drive.

"Yes. You don't need to put that into the Tom-Tom either. I know where it is." She said.

"Aren't they that large so-called charity book enterprise?" Nora pondered.

"Exactly!" Georgina replied and they set off along the main road. "I find it all a bit odd, but I've seen their vans around so many times I decided we should go and check them out. They get books donated to them and sell them on over the internet for charity they say. But their complex is enormous and I've only seen them listed on Amazon and AbeBooks. I thought we could help one another out so I'm going to see if we can speak to someone there."

"Sounds exciting." Nora agreed and took a sip from her bottle of water as they set out on their way.

Universe of Books was on an industrial estate not far from Little Cove railway station. It was a nice complex and Georgina drove past various units towards the largest one that was set at the back. It was an enormous modern building with three stories and a car park that was full. The van drove through the opening between two blue metal gates and Nora saw that high blue fences surrounded the whole facility. When they pulled up between a Bentley and a Jaguar, Nora and Georgina looked at one another.

"This is weird." Nora said.

"Odd isn't it." Georgina agreed. "Look. 'Recycling books for charity'." She read the large sign above the double doors that led into the front of the building.

"I think it's a front for the Little Cove mafia." Nora decided.

Georgina laughed and they climbed out of the van.

"Well. Let's go and see what they have to say," she said and led the way.

Inside the building, Nora and Georgina climbed a modern staircase that wound up to the first floor. The top opened out onto a huge area which was carpeted. Ahead of them was a wall that stretched for at least one hundred feet left and right and contained a long row of about fifteen doors. The area seemed empty but both Georgina and Nora looked to their right and saw three desks in the middle of the vast room.

Three women were seated, one at each desk, with a telephone and a computer. The woman nearest to Georgina and Nora glanced up and stared at them. She then flashed them a bright smile and stood.

"Hello. Can I help?" She asked with over-enthusiastic cheerfulness.

Nora noticed the woman at the next desk pick up the phone and press a button while staring directly at her.

"Yes. Hello. My name is Georgina Pickering and I am from The Secondhand Bookworm. I'm just here to make contact really in the hope that we can help one another. Is your superior available?"

At that moment a red door opened and a tall thin man in a grey suit hurried out. He looked a little alarmed but smiled brightly as he approached Georgina who turned.

"Good morning. I'm Geoff Nightingale." He said, holding out his arm to shake Georgina's hand.

"Oh." Georgina edged back slightly when he reached her at top speed and then shook his hand. "Georgina Pickering."

"I am the General Manager here at Universe of Books. How can I help?" He said and glanced at Nora.

Nora smiled uneasily and then scanned the area.

At that moment a blue door opened and a man in a dark red boiler suit stepped out. When he noticed Nora he paused, stepped back inside and shut the door quickly.

Nora glanced sharply at Geoff Nightingale who was staring at her darkly. He then smiled as Georgina introduced Nora but he did not shake her hand.

"Basically I thought we could help one another. I run two secondhand and antiquarian book shops in the general area and am offered a large amount of books throughout the week. A lot of times people want to unload whole collections which I certainly can't accommodate. I thought that if I was to pass them onto you then you could collect what was left?" Georgina explained.

"And what would you like in return?" Geoff Nightingale asked.

Georgina stared at him and smiled a little uncomfortably.

"Well. Any books that you think may be beyond the general run of the mill recyclable category you could make me aware of and I could make an offer on them?" She suggested. "That to begin with."

Geoff Nightingale pondered Georgina a moment.

"If it is rarer and more interesting then you need to speak to Mickey Lonardo. He is our pre-ISBN guy." Geoff said.

He indicated to his left and both Georgina and Nora jumped. Standing silently next to Nora was a plump Italian-looking man, in his mid-thirties, wearing a black shirt, black chinos and a black tie.

"Oh. Hello." Georgina said and gave Nora a look.

Nora glanced back with an expression that said '*Definitely Mafia*!'

"Hello." Mickey returned politely but his dark eyes appraised them unnervingly.

"I will leave you in Mickey's hands but here is my card should you need to speak to me further." Geoff Nightingale said and shook Georgina's hand once more. "I think that an arrangement could be made. Let me think over it. If you'll excuse me." He turned and headed back for the red door and both Georgina and Nora watched in surprise.

"If you would follow me." Mickey Lonardo said, making Nora and Georgina jump again.

"Where to?" Georgina asked sharply.

"Over here." Mickey said and indicated to the left of the room.

Nora and Georgina followed his direction and saw a single desk in the middle of a vast space surrounded with large columns of books and boxes. Their new host began walking and so Georgina and Nora followed.

"This is where I work." Mickey explained slowly. "These are books donated which have no ISBN numbers. I list them for sale on AbeBooks and catalogue them here."

Georgina stared around.

"That's quite a task." She said.

"Yes it is." Mickey agreed.

He watched as Georgina scanned his piles of books, turned her nose up and looked baffled. His eyes narrowed slightly and so Nora cleared her throat.

"Well, thank you for showing us what you do." She said politely.

"If you are looking to send us contacts in return for some possible good items for your shop then I would be the person you would deal with." Mickey said slowly, picking a business card from a little silver holder on his desk and holding it out towards Georgina. She took it and added it to Geoff Nightingale's. "Mr Nightingale is very busy so it would be better to come through me." He concluded and then stared at them.

"Well. Yes. Erm. Thank you very much for your time." Georgina said, handing the cards to Nora.

"Good bye." Mickey hinted.

Nora turned and Georgina followed and as they began down the stairs Nora looked back to see Geoff Nightingale staring at her from the doorway of the red room. She picked up her pace and soon Georgina and Nora were hurrying from the building to the van of The Secondhand Bookworm, jumping into the seats and starting the engine.

"I bet we have a hit on us now!" Nora said half-jokingly, staring up at the imposing façade.

"Don't say that!" Georgina gasped.

"What on earth do they do in there?" Nora wondered.

"It was very suspicious." Georgina agreed.

"It really must be a front. Mickey Lonardo." Nora said and laughed sceptically. "Also known as Mickey 'Mad Eyes' Lonardo."

"Nora." Georgina laughed.

Nora shrugged, examining the business cards and then popping them into the calls file.

"He might have thought you were from a rival crime family. '*We can help each other*'." She said in a deep Italian accent.

"Well we shall see what happens." Georgina laughed and shook her head. "It does all seem rather strange though. Hmm. I think we'll be off. Where too?"

Nora wrote '*Mafia front*' next to Universe of Books on the calls sheet and then read out the next call.

"Oh yes. Mr Dawkins. He's a little bit eccentric." Georgina said while Nora punched the address into the Tom-Tom.

"Aren't they always?" Nora grimaced.

"But it sounded like his books could be interesting." Georgina said, pulling out of Universe of Books.

Nora wasn't convinced and sighed, watching the Universe of Books complex grow smaller in the side mirror and imagining what else, other than donated books, could possibly be behind the many coloured doors.

She looked back down at the calls sheet and frowned.

"Is this who I think it is?" Nora then said.

"What have I written?" Georgina asked, joining the main road out of Little Cove. "Oh wait, I remember. *Percival's house*. I'm afraid so, Nora. We're popping in there to look at some of his books; he wants some advice from me before he takes a selection to a London auction. Ridiculous if you ask me, but his wife does a lot of work for charity and Percival has a ton left over from the thousands he has purchased from me. We won't be taking any of the books I've been putting aside for him though. He said his wife would have a fit if she saw the amount he is intending to buy."

"Hmm." Nora closed the calls file as Georgina pointed the van north. "I can't wait."

"I've never been to his house so I think we'll enjoy it. He's not one for allowing many visitors." Georgina tried to encourage with a small smile.

Percival Faversham was one of Georgina's more 'exclusive' customers. He only dealt with her and then only after hours, when he didn't have to converse with her 'minions'. He had once owned a brick making company that he inherited from his father but had sold it and retired on several million pounds into the countryside. His wife was a former ballet dancer whom Nora had never seen. Sometimes she encountered Percival if Georgina met him at the shop after closing time, but he never acknowledged her.

"There's another call after Percival, not too far from his house, which is the only reason I agreed to go." Georgina added.

"Hmm." Nora said again and Georgina smiled.

"Actually, it makes more sense if we go there before Mr Dawkins. All of them were flexible about times so it doesn't matter in what order we do them." Georgina decided.

"Yes, let's get him over with." Nora agreed, smirking.

"I know where Percival lives, he's told me the location enough times, so just turn down the Tom-Tom or she'll be shouting at us the whole time about making a U-turn back to Mr Dawkins."

"Okay." Nora grinned and fiddled about with the satnav as Georgina veered sharply right onto the dual carriageway and almost squashed a rabbit.

After a twenty minute drive in the country, Georgina's Bookworm van turned down a lane and then into a drive with an automatic gate. The drive was lined either side with odd stones in large shapes. There was a fountain with a stone ball in the centre, a wide driveway before an enormous wood and glass house and two other buildings close by.

Percival was walking to meet Georgina as she and Nora stepped out of the van. He was in his early sixties with a head of thick grey hair. He wore a burgundy pullover with dark blue corduroy trousers.

"You got here alright bypassing those blasted roadworks then." Percival greeted.

"Yes, no problem at all." Georgina lied, having forgotten Percival's warning about 'roadworks' near his area, so spending an extra half an hour staring at a small traffic light plonked in the middle of an empty road while two men drank tea around a tiny hole.

"Good, good." He gave Nora a brief glance before he walked around to the back of the van. "Pick up anything for me today?"

"No, just some general shop stock." Georgina said.

"Come and see my library. Sylvia makes me keep most of my books in here and the auction books are there too. This way." He said grandly, indicating to one of the large buildings nearby.

"Do you keep your train books in it?"

"Of course. The library has state of the art security, humidity and temperature control and twenty-four hour surveillance."

Nora walked a little behind them, looking about her with interest. Georgina glanced back with a small smirk. Nora grinned.

They entered a building and Percival turned on the lights. Rows and rows of heavy oak bookcases housed endless books inside. Nora's eyes popped.

"Where do you keep your trains?" Georgina asked, looking around her, impressed.

"In the next building." Percival answered, leading her over to a special area of books.

"Percival has the country's leading collection of Hornby trains and train sets." Georgina explained to Nora. "Whenever they want to release a new Hornby train book, they come and photograph his collections. Almost all of the trains in all of the Hornby books are Percival's."

"Really?" Nora was mildly impressed.

"Now these are the books I am taking to the auction. Tell me what you think." Percival said, indicating to a table.

Nora watched as Georgina stood before it and peered over the tomes. She nodded, picking one up.

"Oh yes, I remember selling this one to you. This will fetch about one hundred pounds I should think."

She took up another, a large brown folio book of maps titled 'A New Atlas and Gazetteer of the Isle of Man' by James Wood.

"Oh, you're auctioning this?"

"I wanted to put a gem in the collection to make it interesting." He nodded. "And I have another copy as you know."

"Did you see this one when it came into the shop, Nora?"

Nora joined Georgina at the table as she opened the large book.

"No, I think I missed that one." Nora admitted, not recognising the dull brown binding.

"There are seventeen beautiful maps and this has them all complete and in very fine condition. It is worth about a thousand pounds."

"More now since I restored the spine." Percival said.

"Oh, yes. Very nice, a very fine job." Georgina admired. "Percival does some excellent restoration work."

Percival smiled smugly. Nora bit back a smirk, suspecting that Georgina kept him sweet because he obsessively spent so much every couple of months on a lot of her best finds.

They stood in Percival's library for half an hour and he gave them a tour of his bookcases, especially his special collections on train books and map books, before he took them into the large bright foyer of his main house to collect a small box of books that Georgina had promised to value for him. Nora gawped around in amazement. The house was very modern and very large. There was a huge wooden staircase that led up onto an open plan landing. A tall, slender woman with silver hair swept back into a bun glided down to meet them.

"Good morning, Georgina." The woman greeted smoothly.

"Oh hello, Sylvia." Georgina smiled.

"I hope you're not selling any more books to Percival. He already has too many."

"No, I'm just picking up a box of specials to value." Georgina nodded to the box she held.

"Hmm." Sylvia glanced between Georgina and Percival suspiciously.

"Oh this is my colleague, Nora. She runs my shop in Castletown."

Sylvia glanced briefly at Nora before regarding Georgina once more.

"Oh my dear, you must buy a ticket for the auction dinner in London next week." She told Georgina grandly. "All monies made on the night go to Guy's Hospital of which I am a patron."

"Sylvia is their main patron, aren't you darling." Percival said.

Sylvia smiled and Nora was reminded of a Siamese cat.

"Oh I would love to, but I'm afraid I don't have three hundred pounds to spare for a dinner ticket." Georgina stated.

Nora grinned to herself as Georgina ushered her towards the large double doors.

"Oh such a shame." Sylvia said although it didn't sound as though she meant it.

Percival opened the door and followed Georgina and Nora out.

"I hope it all goes well." Georgina called back to Sylvia.

"I am sure it will." She smiled.

"Have you seen the fountain?" Percival asked as they walked to the van.

"Yes. It's very nice." Georgina said.

Nora tripped slightly, feeling more and more like a bumbling peasant as Percival didn't even acknowledge her, even though he had noticed her tripping. She hurried into the van, leaving Georgina and Percival talking at the back while Georgina loaded his box of books inside.

Once Georgina had said goodbye, she jumped into the van and they sped quickly away.

"Hmph. I suppose he buys a lot from me but it is irritating to make house calls just to look at his books and collect a few so as to price them up for him. I don't know why he doesn't look them up himself on the internet." Georgina moaned.

"Or get his servants to." Nora said, typing the address for their next call into the satnav.

Georgina gave a snort of laughter.

"Where to next?"

"Mrs Dryden." Nora said. "She lives about five minutes away."

"Oh yes, just an ordinary call I expect." Georgina nodded. "She has a whole collection of topography and it sounded very straight-forward."

Nora looked at Georgina disbelievingly and they headed south, avoiding the tiny pot-hole roadworks.

Georgina had actually been right about Mrs Dryden, who had been a pleasant lady in a very flowery cottage with a single bookcase filled with good condition topography books. They were only there for fifteen minutes, bought two boxfuls, loaded up the van, waved goodbye and were heading back towards the coast and their next call at the home of Mr Dawkins in no time at all.

"Mr Dawkins." Nora said after she had put his address into the Tom-Tom again. "Why have you put two small question marks next to his name?"

"Oh." Georgina gave a weak smile. "An eccentric I'm afraid but he insisted I call around and I couldn't refuse."

"Why?"

"He was a bit scary." Georgina admitted.

"Oh dear. Do I need the shotgun?"

"No, he's not murderous, just eccentric." Georgina assured.

"Hmm. Okay." Nora winced and leaned back as the Tom-Tom ordered Georgina to take the third exit off the roundabout and she manoeuvred the van obediently.

To say that the next call was eccentric was an understatement. When the van pulled up outside the house, Nora and Georgina saw that it was more of an outbuilding than a place of residence. It was shabby and small and was practically attached to another lovely red bricked house with a 'FOR SALE' sign up in its garden. There was a howling dog in a sort of stable outside the shack/house with a fenced pen to prevent it getting out and when Mr Dawkins opened the door to them, the dog remained howling.

Mr Dawkins was a large scruffy man. His black greasy hair stood up on end so it looked like he had been strangled.

Inside the 'house', the two banana crates of books were on a heavily painted kitchen table. The house seemed to have only three rooms and the kitchen/diner/lounge was painted so thickly and so outrageously that Nora left Georgina to go through the books while she stared in astonishment, almost hypnotised at her surroundings.

The walls were painted in black and white stripes, the floor was coated in thick black tar, the ceiling was painted black and orange and there was hardly any lighting so it was almost hallucinogenic. It was also very warm. The kitchen cupboards and worktops were red and white diagonal stripes and there were saddles hanging up everywhere.

All throughout the visit the television was on very loudly, broadcasting an episode of 'Kojak', so scenes of murder and threat added to an already dodgy setting. The books for sale were rubbish and Nora was relieved when she and Georgina bade Mr Dawkins goodbye and were walking past the howling dog, climbing back into the van and heading off to find a pub and partake of a well needed early lunch before their afternoon of calls.

"I think we deserve a barrel of beer each too." Nora joked.

"So do I." Georgina agreed, put her foot down and sped away from Mr Dawkins, his psychedelic shed and his howling dog.

9 MUSHROOM FARMS, CHICKENS AND THE REMAINDER WAREHOUSE

The Mushroom Farm was located off a winding road in the middle of the South Downs on the edge of a forest. It was a large facility that was comprised of many murky buildings growing a grim horde of fungus and bacteria.

The Secondhand Bookworm van chugged across the whole complex towards what looked like a garage. It was close to a long low building that held staff facilities for the mushroom workers.

The garage was currently in use by 'The Piertown Lions', a charitable organisation that had regular book fairs and fetes to raise money for chosen charities. A man named Pip Green organised the collection of donated books to 'The Piertown Lions' which he stored on the Mushroom Farm.

A week before the book fair, he would telephone Georgina. She would then spend an hour or two skimming through the offerings and pulling out any books that could be sold on in her Bookworms. It usually meant filling up most of the van, getting frostbite even on a sunny day and running screaming from several thousand spiders.

Nora was already on edge as she had a fear of spiders but after an early tasty light pub lunch and two glasses of cream soda she felt able to face the terror. She saw that Mr Green was already there, that the garage door was up and that a wall of ugly crates was waiting just for them.

Mr Green smiled when he saw the van pull up beside his red Peugeot.

"Good afternoon!" He greeted them when they stepped out of the van.

"Hello, Pip." Georgina returned amiably. "Quite a lot here this time." She turned to Nora. "What time is the next call? Make sure you put the shop mobile in your pocket."

Nora launched herself back inside the van for the calls file while Georgina approached Mr Green and he showed her the crates that he thought would be worth going through.

"All of those ones contain sets of encyclopaedias, Reader's Digest, hard back fiction…"

"Yuk." Georgina grimaced.

"Exactly." Mr Green agreed. "So this whole side here has a whole variety of better ones."

"Okay, we'll get started." Georgina said, rolling up her sleeves.

"Can I get you a drink?" Mr Green offered, heading to his side of the garage where he was doing some sorting of his own.

"No thank you!" Georgina declined. "We just had lunch."

Nora entered the garage tentatively, looking up and seeing heavy black cobwebs above them.

"The next call is in Market Town at two thirty." Nora said.

"Good. That gives us an hour and a half. Don't look so horrified." She laughed at Nora.

"As long as there aren't any spiders this time." Nora winced.

"You might not want to go in that box then." Mr Green called over. He was stacking three heavy crates onto a towering pile next to him. "There's a whopper in there."

"Don't say that!" Georgina said.

Nora edged away.

"I'll start over here then." She decided and carefully opened the first box which looked like it contained a million ladybird books. When she showed Georgina, Georgina told her to take the lot as they were very good sellers and they could chuck away any rubbish ones back at base.

There was every kind of book in the garage. Georgina found some 'gems' which she placed in two separate boxes to be looked up on the computer once back at the shops and also to have the plates counted and checked. There were some lovely gardening books, three separate sets of Dickens novels which Nora counted against the list they always carried in the calls file, some antiquarian medicine books with fascinating engravings, some pristine editions of Classics Illustrated (Nora was distracted by an edition with 'Twenty Thousand Leagues Under the Sea' on the cover of one), a selection of cartography, archaeological books (especially Egyptology), various novels, digital visual art books, books on buttons, pins, firearms and weapons, a whole collection of reggae books, children's books, some signed Stephen Kings and many more.

Nora discovered a signed hardback copy of 'Sphere' by Michael Crichton and pondered the white dust wrapper which had a peculiar green circle thing on the front. Georgina whipped it from her and placed it in her special box.

The time passed slowly and Nora's hands gradually grew more and more numb from the damp and the cold. About an hour and a half into the sorting, and after three daddy longlegs scares, a sandwich van pulled up before the staff building and beeped a horn that sounded almost like a clown's hooter.

Nora laughed and glanced enviously at the people buying teas and coffees until Georgina told her to go and buy two hot chocolates which she willingly did.

While Georgina went through a box of historiography, Nora sipped her hot chocolate while sitting on a crate. A black spider ran over her foot so she screamed and spilt the rest of her drink on the dirty garage floor, much to Georgina's amusement.

"Quite a lot of books on ethnomusicology here." Nora called from in front of a box sometime later. "I think you need to look through these."

"Okay. That'll be the last of it." Georgina decided, heaving a crate of jazz books onto her 'yes' pile. "My hands are filthy, I'm cold and I've had enough."

"It's almost two." Nora said, checking her watch.

"Good." Georgina sang and stood before the ethnomusicology.

When the last of the boxes had been sorted so that a large stockpile was aside, Georgina haggled with Mr Green, wrote him a cheque and then worked with Nora to organise them and then fill up the van.

"That leaves us room for about six more boxes and then anything else will have to be placed around them and along the edges and up to the roof." Georgina said, chewing her lip thoughtfully.

"Great." Nora nodded.

They said goodbye to Mr Green and because the sandwich van was still there, Georgina let Nora buy another hot chocolate which she drank happily all the way to Market Town.

Chipping Court was on the edge of a bleak cul-de-sac in the middle of Market Town. Nora carried the calls file and looked sympathetic when Georgina explained that the customer, a Mrs Wright, was a retired piano teacher who was moving back into a house after having tried living in a flat but found it too terrifying.

"Well this is a scary place." Nora agreed, spotting a beaten up bike in the stairwell and sensing an overall atmosphere of menace.

At that moment a man with a skinhead and a tattoo covering half of his face stomped in and headed past Nora and Georgina. They glanced at one another and then stopped before door number two.

Georgina knocked and after a moment it was opened a fraction. Two beady eyes peered nervously out at them and Nora saw that a chain was across the slender gap between the door and the frame.

"Hello, Mrs Wright." Georgina greeted cheerfully. "We're from the bookshop."

"Hello, dears." Mrs Wright greeted in relief, closed the door, unchained it and opened up. She was a small, thin lady in a pink cardigan, white shirt and neat brown skirt.

"Do come in." Mrs Wright said at the same time the telephone in Nora's pocket began to ring.

Nora dug madly for it to answer it in time while they entered the flat and Mrs Wright led them into a small bedroom just off the hall. The books were spread neatly out on a flowery bedcover.

Nora saw that it was Castletown calling and swiped the screen.

"Hello!"

"Hallooooooooooooo." Cara's voice sung down the phone. "How's it going?"

"Okay." Nora replied, letting Mrs Wright squeeze by as she left the bedroom.

"Who is it?" Georgina asked, turning her nose up at the boring books on the bed.

"Cara." Nora replied. "We're in a flat at the moment." She explained to Cara.

"I have Mr Hill here." Cara said. "Wanting to know if Georgina will buy a set of 'The Decline and Fall of the Roman Empire' and a copy of 'King Charles II'?"

Nora was bemused.

"Okay, I'll ask Georgina." She relayed the message and Georgina groaned.

"Yes! Yes ok!" She said loudly, her tone one of frustration.

Nora smirked.

"I got that." Cara said with a grin in her voice. "Have a nice rest of the day."

"Thanks." Nora said and they rang off.

"These are all boring." Georgina said in a low voice.

"What about 'The Bowmen and other legends of the War' by Arthur Machen?" Nora spotted.

"Too tatty." Georgina said. "I suppose I could use the mushroom guides and the piano theory studies. Some of the sheet music is okay even though we have loads of it already. Okay." She eased them from the pile and muttered the prices as she thumbed across them. "Okay. Call her back." Georgina said and looked around the room, peering at a painting of a cat on the wall.

Nora found Mrs Wright sitting on the edge of a high backed winged chair in the little lounge, working on a cross-stitch hoop.

"Oh that's lovely." Nora said, noticing the delicate hummingbirds that the piano teacher was sewing.

Mrs Wright looked up with what Nora supposed was a perpetual look of nervousness.

"Erm. We've finished." Nora said and watched the lady set her cross-stich hoop aside, stand up and follow Nora to the bedroom, where Nora allowed her to go inside first.

"All done, Mrs Wright." Georgina said. "I could only use these ones I'm afraid and they're not worth vast sums of money to me. I could offer you five pounds for them."

"Five pounds?" Mrs Wright repeated.

There was a momentary pause and then she shook her little grey head.

"No thank you. Thank you for coming." She said simply and stood aside to let them out of the room.

"Oh." Georgina blinked and then glanced at Nora, starting forward.

Nora slipped out first and opened the flat door.

"Well…er…good luck with your move next week." Georgina said.

"In two weeks actually." Mrs Wright corrected.

Georgina stared at her and then smiled.

"Goodbye then." She said and followed Nora out into the hall where the door closed quietly behind them. "Well that was a blasted waste of time."

"Bit weird." Nora said, leading the way out.

They pulled open the main door and walked quickly from the Court to where the van was waiting.

"Okay, where to now?" Georgina asked.

"Park Town." Nora replied. "And you've written 'gatehouse' next to the address."

"Oh yes." Georgina brightened up. "It's the gatehouse on the edge of the big mansion estate called 'Cavendish Park'. Apparently the man there has inherited his late friend's library so it sounds quite nice."

"Oh good." Nora nodded and they jumped into the car and set off for Park Town.

Park Town was situated five miles from Market Town and five miles from Little Cove. It was so named for the large area of parkland in the centre of the town and also the grounds of the Cavendish Estate, where fallow deer roamed the ancient landscape and the public was allowed to walk throughout.

"We've got one more call in Little Cove a few streets away from your house." Georgina remembered, driving along the clear country roads. "But at this rate we might be early for it so I thought we could pop into the 'Remainder Factory'."

"The what?!" Nora asked, her mouth full of Mars bar.

"Cara took a call from them yesterday." Georgina explained. "They're a new company that basically gets all of the new books which have had excessive print runs and stores them in a large factory warehouse. They invited us to go and have a look and pull out any we would like and buy them there and then. It saves us getting a rep coming along from a company and bringing samples and then us waiting for a week for the books to arrive at our shops. By the way, Julius Small is coming into Castletown tomorrow with his remainders. I'm working there with you for the morning, well until about three actually."

"Okay." Nora said, taking another bite of her Mars bar and watching the fields pass by.

Cavendish Park was a magnificent estate owned by Lady Emma Farewell-Minnings who sometimes popped into The Secondhand Bookworm branch at Castletown. Her head gardener lived in one of the gatehouses and he was waiting for the van when Georgina turned off the main road and onto the white gravel drive that led up to two resplendent gates.

He waved and opened them, letting the van enter and stop next to his Land Rover.

"Cheery fellow." Georgina said as she watched him close the gates again and walk over smiling.

"His name's Mr Staggs." Nora said, glancing up from the calls file.

Mr Staggs was dressed in dark green cords with heavy boots and a thick check shirt. He had floppy brown hair, a ruddy face and twinkling blue eyes.

"Hallo there." He welcomed them.

Georgina greeted him and introduced herself and Nora and he led his way to the house.

"Quails!" Nora exclaimed in delight as they passed a little enclosure full of the funny little birds next to the front door.

Georgina paused to look at them too and then they were led into the house.

"So he left me his whole library, the dear old fellow." Mr Staggs was saying, leading them through a rustic house with a sophisticated feel to it. "It was delivered here two weeks ago but as you will see I just don't have room for all the books. I've been through and pulled out all of the ones I want to keep but the rest, well, it would be nice for them to go to people who will read them and appreciate them."

He opened a black door that revealed a library with a magnificent black grand piano in the middle of the room taking up most of the floor.

"Ah yes, and he left me the piano too." Mr Staggs added.

"It's beautiful." Georgina admired.

"Sadly that has to go too. It's already been sold and is being collected tomorrow." Mr Staggs sighed. He then indicated to the books on the floor. "Those are the ones I would like to sell."

Georgina looked down and nodded.

"Lovely books." She said and knelt down before them. "It's probably best I go through these, Nora, as they are quite specialist."

Nora willingly agreed and instead began examining a case of trophies.

"I'll leave you ladies to it." Mr Staggs said with a smile and headed off.

"These are lovely books." Georgina said again. "A very serious collection. Mmm, I can see how his friend thought, yes, as I expected, some of those too. Ah wonderful, we don't see that one very often. I wonder who he was; he certainly had a good taste in books."

Nora smiled as she listened to Georgina.

"Shame he doesn't want to sell these." She pointed out after a while.

Georgina was finishing adding up the whole pile of books and glanced at the case that Nora was pointing too. It was a complete collection of Nicholas Pevsner books on all the counties of England.

"Argh that really is a shame. Bother." Georgina agreed.

Mr Staggs came back when Nora called him and accepted Georgina's offer for the books, pleased. While Nora collected the last remaining boxes, packed them up and carried them to the van box by box, Georgina stood speaking with Mr Staggs about Sandalwood House after learning that he too had been at the same event as her there that past weekend.

Nora walked back to the gatehouse once the last book was in, wishing she had another chocolate bar, and stood waiting for Georgina and Mr Staggs to finish their conversation.

As they stood talking, there was a strange knocking at the back door which was opposite the front door and across a small hall between them.

"Oh, excuse me a moment." Mr Staggs said and walked across the little hallway.

When he pulled the door open, Nora's eyes almost popped out of her head to see an enormous chicken standing on the threshold. The creature promptly stepped up inside, made some clucking noises and strutted towards what Nora had thought was a cat bowl.

"Oh how lovely, a blue Columbian Brahmas!" Georgina admired.

Both Nora and Mr Staggs looked at her.

"Yes." Mr Staggs nodded.

"Lovely chickens. My mother used to keep them." Georgina said.

"Really!" Nora watched the massive chicken with delight.

"Yes. They used to let me pick them up and cuddle them." Georgina laughed. "You're lovely aren't you!" She said to the chicken as it made a loud noise and started eating.

"I want one." Nora said enviously.

"You've got dogs. And guinea pigs, fish and lots of other creatures, Nora." Georgina said and they began away.

"Bye large chicken." Nora grinned.

"Thank you very much." Georgina called to Mr Staggs.

"Enjoy the books." He smiled and walked across to open the gates.

"I would love to live on a massive estate like this. Guess I'll just have to marry the new Duke when he moves into Castletown." Nora decided.

Georgina started the van engine.

"Delusions of grandeur." She laughed and they pulled out of the park, setting off for the other side of the town and the Remainder Warehouse.

"Hello? Hello?" Georgina Pickering called into the semi-darkness of the Remainder Warehouse foyer.

Her hailing was answered by a pitter-pattering of feet, a door to the left swung open and a young man with black rimmed glasses flew into the room.

"Oh! Hello. I'm Georgina Pickering. My colleague spoke to someone named Craig on the phone." Georgina said.

"That's me!" Craig answered. "Hello. Sorry, we've got trouble with our computers all over base today, they're really slow. Are you here to buy some books?"

"Yes please." Georgina said, looking around. "We've got about an hour before we have to be somewhere for an appointment."

"Wicked." Craig stuck his thumbs up and then motioned towards a row of low trolleys. "Grab a trolley each and get going. The entrance is through there. Would you like a drink?"

"I'd love a glass of water." Georgina nodded.

"Me too, thanks." Nora agreed.

"Fab. Will grab you a glass each. Just get going and I'll leave the water here at the front. When you've finished picking out your books I'll run them through the system and you pay and take them away." He said.

"Thank you." Georgina said, more curious than enthusiastic.

She took a long low blue trolley and began to wheel it towards two swing doors and glanced back with a sardonic look at Nora. Nora clutched the long iron handle of a green trolley and followed her and they entered the warehouse of remainder books.

It was similar to a 'Cash and Carry' shop with walls and corridors of shelving units, except that instead of giant tins of baked beans or massive tubs of tomato sauce there were books; lovely bright brand new books.

"We'll split up and just grab whatever we like." Georgina said. "It doesn't matter if we duplicate what we pull out. Take out four copies of each book so that we will have two copies for each of the shops. Whatever titles you think really." Georgina instructed.

"Okay." Nora nodded and wheeled past Georgina, pushing the trolley quickly and stepping up onto the front so that it carried her swiftly down the first long high isle of books.

There were so many to choose from that Nora didn't know where to begin. She sailed slowly along a Cole section and called out to Georgina that some of the books they ordered off of the new book site Georgina has started to use were a quarter of the price here, so she loaded up her trolley with a generous helping.

There were isles of gardening books, modern cookery books, topical books, vampire books, some excellent children's books and a whole isle of crime books, the latter of which felt oppressive and opposing in the silence as Nora wheeled slowly along it, one of her wheels squeaking loudly and eerily.

Nobody else was in the warehouse and Nora and Georgina were soon in sections on their own, until Nora wheeled her trolley to find Georgina and suggested going to get their water.

"I'll go because I need to use the toilet." Georgina offered and left her trolley, walking back through the maze of corridors.

Nora glanced around her as the sound of Georgina grew faint. She was in the occult section and a large red book with a horrible image of Baphomet stared down at her.

"It's only the image of a satanic goat, Nora." She told herself but made the sign of the cross nervously and began to wheel her trolley along, scanning the shelves.

Nora grew aware of the sound of a fan high up in the roof, clicking steadily as it let in fresh cool air. She pondered the antique books and pulled off a large glossy tome about diamonds, some books about porcelain and other volumes on various other collectable objects and then she continued on with her wheel squeaking and the fan clicking.

"Oh dear." She said to herself when she found that she was back in the crime section. This time she saw that she was surrounded by the faces of serial killers and murderers as various true crime biographies and accounts of the insane and violent lined the shelves around her.

Nora wheeled her trolley along a little bit and then stopped when she heard the soft pad of footsteps walking in the isle next to her.

"Hello?" She called.

There was no answer.

Nora took a breath and told herself not to be silly. There was no one there. It was just her imagination.

But the footfalls continued and so Nora began pushing her trolley once more, listening to the wheel squeaking, the fan clicking and the soft, eerie steps from the isle beside her. Her heart began to pound and she had almost reached the end when she couldn't take it anymore so stopped the trolley.

"GEORGINA!" She yelled into the silence and then screamed when a figure turned the corner and faced her.

"Yes?" Georgina replied, lowering her glass of water.

"It was you?! Why didn't you answer me?!" Nora gasped, clutching her chest but sighing in relief.

"Sorry I was so thirsty I was drinking the whole glass of water at once." Georgina apologised and held out Nora's glass.

"I thought you were a murderer." Nora rebuked and then focused on the glass. "Unless….are you really Georgina? That water looks like it's full of poison."

"It's cloudy with chalk, so Craig told me." Georgina laughed. "It tastes okay though."

"Hmm." Nora took it dubiously and Georgina shook her head.

"Maybe I've over-worked you today, Nora." She said. "You're going all crazy on me. Come on, I'll fetch my trolley and we'll settle up and then go to the last call near your house. We'll unpack tomorrow in Castletown; I can't be bothered to do anything tonight."

"I think it was the Mushroom Farm and the howling dog outside the psychedelic shack that sent me over the edge." Nora smirked, sniffed the water and then drank some.

"Come on." Georgina chuckled and they wheeled their way to where Georgina had left her trolley.

It looked strange, standing alone in the middle of the creepy isle.

"This place gives me the heebie-jeebies." Nora said, looking around.

"Hang on. That's not where I left my trolley." Georgina said in a tense voice.

"What?" Nora looked at her sharply and then saw that she was smirking. "Oh har-har."

Georgina laughed and grabbed the handle, turning her trolley around.

"Come along then, lead the way back." She urged and Nora willingly set off, pushing the trolley faster than was really necessary but glad to be getting out of the spooky warehouse.

It took Craig ages to run the titles and quantities of the books that they had chosen through his slow computer. Although Georgina offered to come back and collect them the following day Craig said he preferred not to have them hang around in case they were misplaced.

When everything was finally completed, Georgina paid and she and Nora loaded up the van which was now filled to capacity.

"Let us hope the next call doesn't have an entire library!" Georgina said, slamming the back doors.

They climbed into the front and then set off once more, this time for Little Cove and the last call of the day.

The house in Little Cove was a neat little cottage in a quiet cul-de-sac that overlooked the cove. It was called 'Stargazing' and Nora saw with interest lots of astronomy objects and an astronomy magazine in the porch.

Mr Rigel was a friendly looking man with wild white hair and wire rimmed spectacles who sported a blue shirt, red tank top and grey trousers.

His plump smiling wife offered them a pot of tea but Georgina declined, following Mr Rigel into a long conservatory at the back of the house. Meanwhile, Nora gazed around in fascination as she travelled through the house and then stood and stared with her mouth open at the object in Mr Rigel's back garden.

"Ah, yes, yes, yes." He said, rubbing his hands together when he saw Nora's look of admiration and interest. "The telescope. Do you like astronomy, Nora?"

"Do I?!" Nora nodded eagerly. "My sister and I and one of my brothers have a telescope each. Not very powerful but we've seen the rings of Saturn and the moons of Jupiter. Yours is incredible. Do you climb inside it?"

It was a three metre fiberglass dome-shaped observatory that was open at one side revealing a huge telescope inside.

"Yes there is a seat inside so that you can lean back and look through it. It originated as a twelve inch Newtonian telescope back in nineteen seventy two but over the years it has been substantially updated and improved. We also have an eleven inch f10 Celestron Schmidt/Cassegrain telescope. More compact but GPS assisted and computerised." He explained. "Are you a member of the Little Cove Astronomical Society, Nora?"

Nora shook her head.

"Well. We have regular Star Parties here to observe the planets. I'll give you some information about joining the LCAS." Mr Rigel invited.

"Thank you." Nora was pleased.

"Now, when you come to an LCAS Star party you will have to be prepared so I will give you a leaflet…" He rummaged about on a low coffee table that was stacked with information. "…here we are." He handed Nora a homemade leaflet entitled 'LCAS Star Parties' and she took it gratefully. "You are welcome to bring friends, family and acquaintances but no pets."

"It sounds great." Nora said and glanced at Georgina who was listening with amusement.

"You can count me out." Georgina said with a smile. "I'm not one for standing around in the cold and dark looking up at the sky."

Nora smirked and Mr Rigel chuckled.

"Ah well, it's not for everyone but there are some beautiful things up in the heavens and you're always welcome to come along and see them with us." He said. "Now. To the books." He led them to the columns of literature and gestured down. "These are what we have cleared out. There are a few astronomy books, obviously, but also cookery, gardening and lace-making, my wife, not me." He said with a wink at Nora. "I didn't think you'd be interested in magazines but I popped them there anyway."

"What are they? Oh. No, not for me I'm afraid." Georgina declined when she saw that they were back issues of astronomy magazines.

Mr Rigel considered Nora thoughtfully.

"Well, if Nora would like to have them then she is very welcome. I usually just leave them around for the LCAS meetings and parties but the members tend to have their own copies so they hang around. There is a lot of information in them if you are interested in astronomy."

"I would love them." Nora nodded and looked at Georgina.

"Go on then." She chuckled, kneeling down to start going through the books.

Mr Rigel spoke with Nora about astronomy all the while Georgina sorted and priced until she was ready.

"I'm afraid I can only help you with that pile there, Mr Rigel." She concluded.

"Ah, yes, the two volume set on telescope making." He nodded and perused the other ones that Georgina had pulled out over his wire-rimmed glasses. "Mmm, yes, very good. Yes. And how much would you offer on those Miss Pickering?"

"I would offer you thirty five pounds." Georgina smiled.

"Hmm. Yes that's very fair of you. Thank you, I accept." Mr Rigel nodded.

Georgina gathered a pile in her arms while Nora paid him in cash from the wallet in the cash file. Then she took up the remaining books and her large pile of magazines and they headed off.

"I hope to see you at a Star Party one night, Nora." Mr Rigel said as he stood at his doorstep.

"I look forward to it." Nora nodded and after the last of the books had been squeezed into the back of the van and Nora and Georgina had climbed into the front, they waved goodbye and set off the short distance to Nora's home.

"What a nice fellow." Georgina said.

"He was." Nora agreed.

"Are you going to join this astronomy club?" Georgina asked.

"It does sound good. I'd like to have a look through that powerful telescope."

"And you can meet other nerds." Georgina said with a grin.

Nora laughed.

"I've always been a nerd." She sighed but then looked down at her leaflet, deciding to devour it once she was home.

"We can go through all these books tomorrow in Castletown." Georgina decided, indicating left to turn into Nora's road and going up onto the kerb slightly.

"Okay." Nora nodded, grabbing the calls file as it slid towards the gearstick.

"I'll be there for about nine-thirty and we can start unloading before we open."

"Sounds fun." Nora nodded.

They pulled up outside Nora's house, she gathered her things and climbed out of the van.

"See you tomorrow." Nora bade.

"Bright and early." Georgina sang, waved and pulled away once Nora had shut the door.

Nora waved, smiling to see the bookshop van go up another kerb and flatten some poor unsuspecting weeds on the grass verge, before speeding away, loaded with their call-day pickings ready to be priced up and placed upon the shelves in The Secondhand Bookworm.

10 GEORGINA'S ADMIRER

The following morning, while they unloaded all of the loose books from the van and a couple of the boxes, Nora told Georgina everything she had read about 'Star Parties'. Georgina listened with amusement but was even more amused to learn that Eugene Harvey attended and that he had a girlfriend.

"I recognised his name on the leaflet as the chairman so Googled it. According to the Little Cove Astronomy Group website, he and his girlfriend, Iris, are the people to ask about Star Parties. I'm going to have to go along just to meet Iris." Nora giggled, entering the shop with the first box.

They had piled up the loose books behind the counter but left room for Georgina's first shop appointment, Frank from West Town, who usually brought a couple of boxes of books in for sale and placed them behind the counter too.

"I look forward to hearing all about it." Georgina smirked. She placed her box on top of Nora's and gazed around. "Seeing as the van is in a nice parking spot just outside the delicatessen, just get one more box from it and then lock it up, Nora. We don't want to overload the shop. Then you can start marking up and get more boxes as you go."

"So my mission today is to price as much as possible." Nora deduced, grabbing the van keys from the desk.

Georgina nodded.

"I'll be leaving at about three." She said. "I've asked Humphrey if he'll come and jet hose the yard at some point. He said he would try and get in today or tomorrow to do it."

"Okay." Nora nodded and set off, smiling to herself at the thought of seeing Humphrey an extra time before a date they had arranged for Saturday night.

Once outside, Nora was so absorbed in her thoughts and the traffic tearing down the hill that she didn't notice anyone around her until it was too late.

"Eeeeeep. Morning, Nora." A giggling little voice sounded at her left elbow as she began to cross the road.

Nora turned and was faced with White-Lightning Joe, looking bleary eyed and scruffy.

"Oh hello." She replied politely and continued to cross the road.

"Nora? Eeeeeeek. Ooops haha, silly me." She heard him saying as he almost stepped out in front of a car.

Nora glanced back and watched White-Lightning Joe wait for the car to pass. She tried to ignore him when he crossed the road quickly and waddled towards her.

"Nora? Nora. Here. You don't have a few quid do you?" He asked, catching her up.

Nora grabbed a box from the van and placed it onto the kerb, narrowly missing his toe.

"Aaaaah. Oh. Hehe." He leapt aside and then flicked his greasy fringe back, shuffling close again. "Just a couple of quid. It'd really help me out."

"You know I can't. Sorry." Nora replied politely but firmly.

White-Lightning Joe's shoulders drooped.

"You were my last hope. Penny's being an old hag and refusing to give me anything and I just cut my finger, look." He held up a chubby hand and showed Nora a dirty plaster. "Luck isn't raining down on me. Oh! By the way. I saw your brother in the paper. The one who inherited the theatre. I used to work in the theatre – yaaaaaay!"

Nora frowned at him and shut the door of the van, locking it.

"The theatre." He prompted. "You know, acting and all that. I used to work on stage. If there are any jobs going, well, you know where to come. I used to work in the theatre! Yay!" He watched her pick the box up.

"I'll let my brother know." Nora said.

"Would you?! Oh eeee, oooh thanks Nora. I need a bloody job after being made redundant. No one here will employ me. Eeeep!" He almost walked into a black iron lamp post and so stopped and then remained where he was, watching her walk away. "So I'll see you later, Nora. Byeeee." He waved madly and Nora nodded a goodbye, turning back and hurrying to the shop.

When she entered through the doorway, Georgina was serving a French teenager who was buying some postcards while a second French teenager was by the folio books reading the title of a book aloud.

"The Monkeys of War." He said in his light French accent.

Nora glanced at the book in his hand. She then bit back a smile to see that the title was actually 'The Monks of War' not 'The Monkeys of War'.

"Would you like some stamps?" Georgina asked her student customer.

He stared at her blankly.

"Stamps!" She prodded the top of the postcard and when he still looked blank she opened the till draw, leaving it beeping long and loud as she took out a pack of Worldwide Postcard Stamps and opened the little grey book for him.

"Oh. Europe?" He asked.

"They will go to Europe, yes." Georgina told him.

"They stamps for Europe?" He asked, frowning. "Ah, no. They *world.* They more cost than just Europe. I not want."

Georgina stopped the till beeping, gave Nora a look and took the boy's twenty pound note for the three postcards that he had bought.

Once she had given him his change and the two students had left, a man walked into the front from the back room, carrying a book.

"There's a book here." He said, stopping before Georgina who slowly looked up. "It's called 'Stuarts of London'. Is it about the Stuarts?"

Georgina stared at him.

"One would assume so." She replied drily.

He nodded slowly and then held it out to her.

"Okay thank you. I think I'll leave it." He said and Georgina took it, watching him in bafflement as he walked around the counter and then stopped. "The maps. How much are they?"

"It depends. Usually a couple of pounds. The one there is seven pounds." Georgina replied.

"Seven pounds?" He whistled. "Fippin' Hammers!!!" He walked off, shaking his head and Nora sat down on her little stool giggling.

"You may well laugh, Miss Jolly, but this is not a good start to the day." Georgina said once the man had left the shop. "I may not last here until three o'clock."

"But you love working in Castletown with all of its eccentricities." Nora argued teasingly.

"Hmph!" Georgina muttered and continued with her paperwork on the desk. She glanced up at the clock on the wall. "Frank from West Town is due here any minute. I'm just going to pop to the butcher's for some steaks. Let him know I'll be back in a minute if he turns up."

"Okay." Nora nodded, standing up after she realised she didn't have a pencil and grabbing one from a broken mug on the desk that served as a pencil pot.

Georgina left hastily with her purse, in need of retail therapy already, even if it was only to buy steaks, and was replaced by two customers who entered while laughing and talking loudly.

"Oh darling, darling look. What a marvellous little book on 'Walking the Disused Railways of Cole'." The woman said. She was wearing a long grey wool coat, with black heeled boots and a fur hat.

"Oh wonderful!" The man exclaimed.

Nora looked him up and down. He was donned in a yellow tweed suit with a red scarf and Nora was reminded of Rupert the Bear.

"Darling look. A Johnet and Jane book!" The woman next bellowed.

Nora watched her reach for an orange reprint of the classic children's 'Janet and John' book that was on the display shelf of the window, notice her mistake of the names but remain silent and slip it back onto the shelf. Her friend wasn't listening anyway but was thumbing through the railway book.

Nora began pricing some of the books from Mr Rigel's house, which were all pretty straightforward. She observed the loud couple walk around the front room and then disappear deeper into the shop. Once they had vanished, Nora turned back to see Frank from West Town walking towards the door with a suitcase on wheels and a box under his arm.

The door was ajar so he nudged it open and strolled in.

"'Ello." He greeted in his cockney London accent. "Right on time for once."

"Hello Frank." Nora greeted him.

"I'll drop these down 'ere." He said, heading for the area behind the counter.

"Georgina has just popped out." Nora said. "She said to tell you she'd be back in a minute."

"No problem, no problem." Frank replied, leaving the stuff that he wanted to sell in his usual place. "I can pop back in about half an hour, forty minutes? I need to go to a few places."

"Okay." Nora smiled, pricing up one of Mrs Rigel's cookery books.

Frank strolled off, whistling and she heard him meet Georgina just outside, tell her that he would be back soon and head off into the town.

When Georgina came in she was followed by a French student holding a single postcard.

"You are stamp?" The student asked.

"Erm…" Georgina looked at Nora, her lips twitching and walked around the counter.

"You are stamp?" He repeated.

"Yes. We have stamps." Georgina said, reaching the till and dropping her steaks onto the cash book. "Just one?"

"Pardon?"

"JUST ONE?" Georgina repeated loudly as though he had not heard rather than did not understand.

"Yes one." He replied.

Georgina ran the sale through the till and gave him his change.

"You are little bag?" He asked and Nora sniggered into a copy of an 'Apollo 11' Haynes manual.

"No I am not a little bag, but I can give you a little bag." Georgina said flatly, pulling one off the wall.

Once the boy had left, Georgina walked off to the kitchen to pop her steaks into the fridge, muttering and leaving Nora smiling as she continued to price up the books.

"Oh. I always do this. I find so many books that I would like to have." Nora told Georgina once Georgina had returned.

Georgina smiled.

"Well make a little pile and go through it when you're done." She said.

Nora added the copy of 'The Law of Thermodynamics: a Very Short Introduction' to the cookery book and picked up the next in the box.

"Death by Black Hole: And Other Cosmic Quandaries by Neil Degrasse Tyson." Nora read out and Georgina laughed.

"Well I think I can cross that off my list of possible future deaths." Georgina said, sitting down and looking at the computer monitor.

"Did you know that Saturn's rings will be gone in about one hundred million years?" Nora read, flicking through the book.

"No. And I don't think I'd care in one hundred million years." Georgina replied.

"Oh wow. Did you know that the coldest temperature ever achieved in a laboratory was five hundred picokelvins? That's 0.0000000005 degrees K." Nora then said.

"Nora." Georgina warned.

"It's interesting." Nora laughed. She priced the book and picked up the next one. "The Privileged Planet: How Our Place in the Cosmos Is Designed for Discovery'."

"Are you going to read me all the titles of the books you pick up?" Georgina laughed, turning from the computer to start going through Frank's books.

"Sorry." Nora grinned, priced it up and then continued quietly, trying to resist flicking through the contents of each one.

By the time Nora had priced up two boxes they had had four sales, two telephone calls and Frank had come back, agreed to accept Georgina's offer of ninety five pounds and left her looking up his books on the internet for reference and pricing them.

A young man with a beanie hat stepped into the shop.

"Hello." He said, sounding confused and peering around.

Georgina glanced up from pricing some of Frank's late Observers and Nora turned from making a neat pile out of her marked up books.

"Is this 'Bellerophon Books'?" The young man asked, vaguely.

Nora stared at him.

"Erm…no. This is The Secondhand Bookworm." Georgina replied.

He stared around confused.

"Do you trade on the internet as 'Bellerophon Books'?" He asked.

"No." Georgina said, regarding him as if he was mad. "I don't sell any of my books online."

"Oh. That's weird. Are you the only bookshop in Castletown then?" He asked.

"Yes." Georgina replied tightly.

"Okay that's weird. I was dealing with a bookshop on the net called 'Bellerophon Books' located in Castletown. They're selling me some science fiction and fantasy books but I thought I'd drop by and have a browse through their stock. Very weird."

"We have a section upstairs on science fiction and fantasy." Georgina told him.

"Oh right. Well seeing as I'm here I may as well have a browse." He decided.

"Through there and up the stairs to the top." Georgina indicated and once he had gone she considered Nora.

"I've never been asked for that before. Maybe they're new?" Nora said in return to Georgina's expression.

"Anything is possible in this town." Georgina scowled in frustration, causing Nora to laugh and slide the pile towards her that she had retrieved from behind the counter to mark up.

Georgina was glowering out of the window when her expression changed and she looked surprised.

"Oh look. Nora I don't believe it! The woman across the road is actually changing her window display! It's the first time in all of the seven years that we have been here. A miracle!" Georgina exclaimed and Nora turned on her stool to peer between the shelves in the window to see.

"You're right!" She gasped and stared.

Across the cobbled square and to the left of 'Lady Lanes', which stood opposite The Secondhand Bookworm, was a small shop on the corner that often went unnoticed and was only open on Thursday afternoons and Saturdays between eleven o'clock and three o'clock.

From time immemorial the same twelve lacy Christening shawls had hung in the dusty old window, and the same assortment of brooches, rings and necklaces had been displayed along the front.

The owner was a very old fashioned old lady with huge pure white hair always up in a 1940's Pompadour style, with a beautiful pouf of hair at her crown. She wore the same white blouse buttoned up to her throat, a strange brooch and a lined black pencil skirt. Her name was Shirley.

Nora watched as Shirley stood pondering her now empty display window with a duster in one hand and a bottle of Windolene in the other. She was soon joined by Sam from the butcher's shop who, like Shirley, was changing his window. Only, he had a giant pig's head that he was putting into his.

"It's the changing of the windows." Nora said in a playfully hushed voice.

"About time too." Georgina mused. "They must be getting ready for Christmas. I saw that the people in the delicatessen were sorting out their decorations."

"Paul came in with his usual form for the town Christmas trees on Monday. But Christmas is still about six weeks away." Nora pointed out.

"Yes, the decorations in the shops go up earlier and earlier here." Georgina agreed.

"Well, as long as we hold out until at least December." Nora said. "That's about the time the Christmas trees go up around town and it really seems as though we should have some decorations in the window once the whole of Castletown is sparkling with little trees."

She then suddenly straightened up, watching as a white Ford Focus Estate car drove slowly past the shop with a familiar driver inside looking frantically about for a space.

"I think Julius Small is here." Nora said.

"Lovely." Georgina sighed, continuing to mark-up Frank from West Town's books. "We'd better leave the rest of our books in the van for a while as Julius will be unloading all of his boxes of remainders for us to go through. I do hope he's not going to fuss over each one like he usually does."

Nora winced, remembering their previous adventures with Julius and decided that they should prepare with a cup of tea. Georgina declined the offer of a beverage but told Nora to go ahead and make herself one as she would need it. So Nora headed into the kitchen, happy to disappear for as long as she could so that she wouldn't get roped into unloading Julius's car by herself while he tried to woo Georgina.

It was ten minutes later when Nora entered the front room with her cup of tea and two shortcake biscuits from a packet that her part-time colleagues Jane and Terri had left for her the week before.

Georgina was sitting on Nora's little stool by the window, already going through one of several boxes that Julius had brought inside. His car could be seen through the window, parked on the double yellow line outside, with the boot open.

Julius himself was a short man with wild brownish auburn hair, a thick pair of glasses and at least three warts on his face. He spoke with a stuttering voice and had a very pessimistic attitude. He wore the same white shirt and grey trousers and smelt of an old cup of coffee.

"Now…now….now…these I thought you m…m….m….m… might like, Georgina." He said, scurrying in with a battered box and dropping it on Georgina's foot.

"Argh!" Georgina reacted with a laugh.

Nora snorted into her tea and watched Julius almost faint with horror.

"S…s….s…sorry, oh, I'm s…s…s…s…s...s...sssssss…."

"Yes well never mind. I think I still have my toes." Georgina said good-humouredly and laughed again.

Julius was bright red in the face and looked mortified. While he bent over his box, Georgina gave Nora an enduring look as Nora sat down on the swivel chair to watch them, sipping her tea.

"These are all about Castletown. The….the…..the old ruins and the river….lots of…of…of…of….of…."

"History?" Georgina finished for him, taking the book he held out to her.

"Yes. I have f…f….f….fourteen copies. Would you like them all?" He asked hopefully.

"How much are they?"

"Five pounds each. You can sell them f…f…for eight or ten pounds?" He suggested.

"Okay. I'll take the lot." Georgina nodded.

While he wrote it on his little clipboard sheet, Georgina took up another book.

"Nora. Can you check how many of these we still have left on the shelves please? And Skype Seatown to ask them to check their stock too."

"Okay." Nora nodded, squinting across the room so as to read the title.

It was a bird book in a white dust wrapper.

"Warblers of Europe, Asia and North Africa – a Helm Identification Guide, hardback by Kevin Baker." She said as she typed it into the Skype and asked them to check. She then ran up onto the next floor and scanned the shelves in the bird section, spotting a copy there already.

When she came back down there was a message on the Skype.

"We have one." Nora told Georgina. "Seatown says *'Hello, Nora, this is Betty, lovely book, Cara has found two copies of that title left. Thank you.'*

"No thank you to this then." Georgina told Julius and he looked annoyed, took it and popped it into the box of books that Georgina had already looked at.

"This one here I think will sell well…it's a…."

"No thank you." Georgina refused straight away, causing Julius to look annoyed again.

He didn't say anything but popped that book into the box as well. He then went off to collect another box from his car.

"I love how he gets furious when you refuse a book." Nora grinned, sipping her tea.

Georgina laughed, pulling a large tome out of a box.

"Can you run up and check and see how many of these we have left. And ask the other shop too?" She asked, holding up another bird book.

Nora recognised the cover from having checked on other occasions. It was one that sold better but which had a long title.

"Shrikes and Bush-shrikes: Including Wood-shrikes, Helmet-shrikes, Shrike Flycatchers, Philentomas, Batises and Wattle-eyes - Helm Identification Guides - by Tony Harris…" Nora read out as she typed.

"Probably only 'Shrikes' will suffice." Georgina suggested with a laugh, pulling out another book. "Oh and can you check for this one too?"

She held up 'Gertrude Jekyll and the Country House Garden: From the Archives of Country Life by Judith B Tankard' which Nora recognised as well.

"Okay. Onto it." She said, typing fast and then running up the stairs to check.

When she returned a moment later, Georgina was serving a familiar customer who was wearing a large brown hat, a big red coat and had a long, thin nose.

"Hello, Mr Rutler!" Nora greeted the Castletown resident who often popped in and browsed through the architecture section.

"Ah Nora, Nora. How are you?" He asked.

"Very well thank you."

"Mr Rutler spotted a book that you had placed in the window to tempt him." Georgina said, pausing as she slipped the large tome into a blue carrier to show her the title.

"Oh yes. 'Abandoned Mansions of Ireland' by Tarquin Blake." Nora nodded. "I was so tempted by that one myself."

"Were you now?" Mr Rutler replied.

"I love books about mansions and ruins." Nora explained.

"Well you tempted me into parting with another twenty pounds." Mr Rutler said, jokingly annoyed.

"That's why I employ her." Georgina smiled, handing him the bag.

Mr Rutler laughed heartily and set off happily with his purchase, pausing to let Julius in with another box.

"More books." Georgina said ironically and began away to look through them.

There was a whole list of 'Antique Collector's Club' books to check in various sections throughout the shop. These were lovely large hardback tomes, very well presented with lush photographs and information throughout on a variety of specific topics.

Nora set off with the list and spent almost half an hour searching through the various sections of gardening, collecting and antiques, art, motoring, architecture, photography, ceramic and glass, writing down how many there were of each in stock.

When she returned, Julius was taking some of his boxes back to his car. Georgina added any that Nora had been unable to find on the shelves, wrote him a cheque and popped it onto his clipboard.

"These will be with you early next w…w…w…week, Georgina." Julius said, perspiring across his forehead as he hurried in and out of the shop with the boxes.

"Lovely." Georgina nodded, not even looking from the Skype as she typed on the keyboard.

He stared at her as he hurried out and then stared at her when he came back in, causing Nora to regard him in a bemused manner as she sat down to price the fourteen copies of the books on Castletown.

When the last of the boxes was in his car, Julius stood before the desk mopping his brow with a brown hanky, staring at Georgina.

"There all…all…all…all done, Georgina." He said.

"Thank you, Julius." Georgina sang and when she sensed he was still standing there she looked at him.

"Ye…yes…I was wondering, Georgina…would you like to have a coff…coff… coff…coff…"

Georgina stared at him and he trailed off, looking nervous.

"Have a cough sweet? No. My throat is fine thank you." She said.

"…coff…coff…coff….coff…coff…coffee?" Julius finally managed to conclude.

Nora buried her face behind a copy of the book in her hands and Georgina looked surprised.

"Oh!"

"I don't usually date customers." Julius then added gravely. "But…would you….be interested in…din…din, …din ….din, …din…din…"

"Din-dins?" Nora put in helpfully, desperately trying not to laugh.

Georgina stared across at her querulously but Nora could see that she wanted to laugh too.

"Din…din…din…din…dinner." Julius finally finished with a gasp.

Georgina smiled politely.

"Oh, no thank you, Julius. I don't usually date tradesmen." She returned politely and that was too much for Nora, who bent over the pile of books, laughing as silently as she could.

"Oh, f…f….f….f…..f….f….f…." Julius stammered loudly.

Nora looked up and both she and Georgina stared at Julius as he stuttered loudly and desperately with his face bright red.

"F….f…f….f…f…fair enough." He finally said and mopped his head again with his handkerchief.

Georgina continued to smile politely and turned slowly back to her typing.

"I'll get the books out t…t…to you early next week, Georgina. See you again, s…s…s..s..sssssss..sssss.. ssss..ss….s…ssss…."

Nora thought it sounded as though a large snake was in the shop and when Julius gasped the word 'soon' and walked off, she could see that he still wasn't deterred from his relentless pursuing of Georgina.

"Goodbye." Georgina sang in an irritated voice, not even looking at him.

When he had gone Nora turned and regarded Georgina but Georgina said: "Don't say a word, Nora", in a slightly amused tone.

Nora giggled into her book.

Finally, ten minutes later, Georgina had had enough of Nora's giggling and, almost laughing herself, told Nora to go and have some lunch.

Grinning to herself, Nora grabbed her bag and set off into the town to grab a large sandwich and a richly deserved slice of cake.

11 THE LADYBIRDS AND THE JET HOSE

While Georgina was eating her lunch in the kitchen sometime later, Nora dealt with several rude customers. After five minutes of peace, two German men arrived and stood laughing while looking at some books Nora had displayed on the counter.

"Yar look! 'Vot to say ven you talk to yourself'." One German said and almost doubled up laughing.

The other German picked up a second book.

"'How to be happy though human'." He said and spluttered with laughter. "Vot about 'Correctly English in Hundred Days'."

The man with the brightest blue eyes asked Nora if the books were for real.

"Yes. They're all real books." Nora nodded, sending them into fits of laughter again.

"You sell stamps?" The other man asked.

"Yes."

"To Germany?"

"They go anywhere." Nora explained.

"Please don't call Germany 'anywhere'." The man warned her teasingly and she smirked, organising their stamps.

When the Germans left, an old man walked up to Nora.

"I see that 'Seven Pillars of Wisdom' is priced at seventy five pounds." He snarled, nodding his head to behind the counter where the pricier books were kept. "I was expecting it to be ten pounds. Good luck selling it!"

Nora stared at him and then watched another man, who looked like a sailor, come up to the counter, holding a book.

"I'll give you ten pounds for this but I can't justify paying twelve pounds fifty for it." He said, passing her the book and a ten pound note that he had placed on top.

Nora automatically took them and opened the cover.

"It's priced at twelve pounds fifty." She pointed.

"Yes and I can't justify paying that. I'll give you ten pounds." He persisted.

Nora closed the book.

"It says twelve pounds fifty and I am not allowed to change the price." She replied firmly.

He stared at her so that his white whiskers bristled.

"How much for cash?" He asked.

"Twelve pounds fifty." Nora replied.

His lips pursed.

"It costs money to pay cash in." Nora added, refusing to be intimidated by him.

"Oh I'll pay by card then." He said and snatched back the ten pound note, dug out his wallet and added the tenner to a large wad of what looked like fifty pound notes and twenty pound notes.

Nora was silent as his card processed and smiled politely when she asked if he wanted a bag.

"No." He said, took the book and stomped off.

When Georgina finally returned, Nora felt exhausted. She went back to her marking up and managed to price all of the ladybird books from The Mushroom Farm and take them upstairs into the children's room. She had just brought in two more boxes to price up from the van when a familiar man walked in.

"Hello again." The man said, standing before Georgina.

Georgina looked up from her large purple diary and beheld him blankly.

"Oh. Sorry. Phil Bond from Environmental Health." He introduced.

"Ahhh, yes sorry, I do recognise you now." Georgina said. "Ah so you've been next door then."

"I have just spent a delightful two hours with Mr Duleepsinhji, examining the drains and the kitchens." Phil explained.

"Oh yes, how delightful for you." Georgina replied sarcastically.

"Quite. I have given them another warning but if I was you I would take the matter to court. I am advising Southern Water to come out and conduct a full survey of the drains. It will cost about two thousand pounds but it will be worth it. They will put cameras down the drains to confirm my findings but from what I have seen myself, the kitchen workers are still pouring cooking oil and fat down the sinks and drain every day and have been doing so for years."

"Why are people like that?!" Georgina said in disgust.

"It's ridiculous isn't it. I told them again about A and B Oil Collection coming and collecting cooking oils each week like they do with the fish and chip shop over the bridge and Mr Duleepsinhji lied and says that they do. I checked with A and B Oil and they have no record of the restaurant so they don't. And I don't expect they use any other company either."

"I've never seen any come." Nora chipped in.

"Well, I'm taking it further because the damage that they are doing to the environment alone is criminal." Phil said.

"Good. Well thank you for letting us know." Georgina appreciated.

"I will keep you informed of any developments. Meanwhile, do take them to court to get all your money back. You will certainly win." Phil advised.

"I will." Georgina nodded. "My niece is a lawyer. She'll delight in taking on the case."

Phil smiled, said his goodbyes and left.

"Good!" Georgina said passionately once he had gone. "Ridiculous people, pouring oil into the drainage system. If I see Charming-Max I'll have a few words to say to him!"

"It's the poop that freaks me out." Nora admitted.

Georgina laughed and then Nora jumped when her phone, which she had forgotten was in her pocket, rang out with a text message alert.

"What was that?" Georgina laughed at the sound of the duck quack.

"Sorry. My phone. I don't usually get a signal in here but I have been lately." She said and drew it out. It was a message from Humphrey so Nora read it.

'Are you in the shop? I'll come and jet hose the yard if you are. xxx'

Nora smiled to herself and replied that she was.

'*See you in ten minute*s!' He texted back.

"Humphrey will be here in about ten minutes." Nora told Georgina.

"Oh good!" She said, pleased. "We can lay that stinky yard saga to rest."

"It will forever haunt me." Nora admitted.

Georgina smiled and they continued with their work until ten minutes later Humphrey walked in wearing Wellington boots, chewing something and carrying the jet hose.

"Humphrey!" Georgina greeted cheerfully.

"Hi." He grinned and looked around for Nora. "Hello." He smiled fondly when he saw her, swallowing his mouthful. "How are you?"

"Hello." Nora replied, putting a priced book aside. "Worn out from the usual madness."

He smirked, standing before her.

"Here." He passed her the book that he saw she was going to pick up and she smiled and took it from him.

"How's your day going?" She asked him.

"Busy. I've got an hour to spare before I have to be over in Walltown. I thought I'd get this done as I knew it would be freaking you out." Humphrey told Nora.

Georgina was listening with a smirk and cleared her throat playfully, pretending that she was offended at being ignored and so making herself known.

Humphrey glanced at his sister and grinned.

"I'll get onto it. Is the back door open?" He asked his sister.

"I don't know." Georgina replied.

"No it isn't." Nora said.

Georgina passed Humphrey the keys and he glanced back at Nora before heading off. When he had gone Georgina regarded Nora knowingly so she just smiled and continued pricing.

A moment later, Georgina's voice drew Nora from her thoughts as she was flicking through a book about the Battle of the Bulge.

"Arrrrrghhhhh. It's the Ravens." Georgina said in a strangled tone.

Nora's blood froze and she straightened up.

"You're joking!"

"I'm afraid not." Georgina said with a slight smile and Nora leaned aside to look in the direction that Georgina was indicating.

Heading across the square close together, whispering and sporting their favourite duffle coats and bobble hats were Mrs and Miss Raven. They were carrying their usual assortment of carrier bags and black sacks and Nora noticed that Miss Raven was dressed in her favourite pastel blue flannelette knee length shorts, white socks and white plimsolls.

They stopped outside of the shop and whispered together and then only Miss Raven entered. Nora and Georgina pretended to be absorbed in their work and so Miss Raven walked straight through and headed off upstairs.

"Close one." Nora whispered. "We should hide the Seatown leaflets before they steal them all."

Georgina smirked.

Nora went to pick up another book to price when there was a distant yell from the kitchen.

"NORA?" Humphrey's voice called.

Nora leaned aside to look through the isle down to the kitchen but the kitchen door was practically closed so she could only see as far as the back room.

Georgina wrote something in her diary.

"Better go and see what he wants." She told Nora while concentrating and so Nora put down her pencil and stood up as Humphrey called Nora's name again.

She headed through the stairwell area, stepped up into the back room, paused to push a history book in place, drew open the back door and then gasped.

Her breath was silenced as a hand covered her mouth and another hand drew her into the kitchen and then closed the door behind her.

Humphrey was laughing as he uncovered Nora's mouth.

"What are you doing?! I should batter you over the head with the jet hose attachment." Nora gasped.

"I needed a hand." He said, chuckling.

"What with?" Nora asked, shaking her head at his twinkling blue eyes.

"Where's the tap extension for the hose that is usually here? I've looked everywhere." He explained, popping something from his pocket into his mouth innocently.

"Did you check in here?" Nora asked him suspiciously and opened the cupboard under the sink, reached down and picked it up.

She held it out to him and he grinned, took it and shrugged.

"Must need new glasses." He said, chewing.

"You don't wear glasses." Nora laughed.

"Maybe I should start?" He suggested and Nora slapped his shoulder.

Humphrey attached the hose to the sink, the jet nozzle to the other end of the hose and then leaned past her to plug the pressure washer into the mains.

"I have to get back to work." Nora grinned and headed off, leaving him turning on the water and starting to clean the yard while whistling happily.

She stepped into the back room and let out a small yelp.

"Any regimental histories?" A regular customer named Don asked, grinning at having made her jump.

"Erm…I don't think so." Nora assured, slightly baffled at his relentless visits.

"Na, na, I'll have a look though." He said and turned around to browse the military and war sections. Nora shook her head, continuing from the room.

In the front of the shop Georgina was dealing with Miss Raven who had returned from her visit upstairs.

Nora went back to her stool by the window and sat down to continue marking the books up, glancing at Miss Raven who was frowning over a little pile of books in her hands.

Georgina was watching Miss Raven ironically.

"Could you put these by?" Miss Raven finally asked Georgina in her high voice accompanied by her sweet smile.

"No problem." Georgina nodded.

"And there is a small pile of ladybirds that I couldn't manage to bring down. It has 'King Charles the First' on top. Put them by until tomorrow. I may come in today but I have hay fever."

Georgina stared at her and then cleared her throat, standing up.

"No problem." She repeated as Miss Raven began away.

Once she had gone, Nora watched Georgina head upstairs for the ladybird books while Don came out of the back room, said goodbye and left. When Georgina came down she was carrying a tiny pile of about four more ladybird books which she pretended were really heavy and that she was having immense difficulty carrying.

Nora laughed.

"It was actually 'Elizabeth Fry' on top, not 'King Charles the First'." Georgina said, and added them to the other few, made out a reservation slip, placed them all into a clear bag and put them under the counter. "Oh by the way, a man called about bringing some books in and I…oh this might be him."

Nora glanced from Georgina to the doorway as a man stepped into the shop carrying a box of books. He walked with an arrogant swagger straight up to the counter where he casually took off his sunglasses and looked Georgina slowly up and down. Nora's eyebrows shot up.

"Hi. I believe we spoke earlier." He said loudly and confidently.

"Did we?" Georgina replied politely. "I have had lots of phone calls."

The man's dashing smile faltered but he continued in the same supercilious tone.

"Mr Ackroyd." He prompted. "I have some books for sale."

"Shall I take a look?" Georgina suggested, keeping her face and voice polite. Nora could tell she was less than thrilled with having to deal with him.

"Sure. While you have a gander where's your history section?" Mr Ackroyd asked.

"In the back room." Georgina smiled without looking at him.

"Top notch. I'll just have a gander." He said and walked off.

When Georgina opened the box and began to go through the books she pulled out a couple of photography tomes and a book on psychology but had a look of disgust as she rifled through the rest.

"What's the matter?" Nora whispered.

"You don't want to know." Georgina replied, shaking her head. "It's all German erotica. You didn't hear the phone call I had with him. And I told him not to bring any in. Creep."

Nora looked revolted.

"Gross." She said and then saw that he was coming back.

When he was finally before Georgina she closed the flaps on the box and smiled so falsely at him that her expression looked as though she was in pain.

"I can only help you with these three here I'm afraid." She told him, holding the three chosen books and edging the box towards him.

"Oh. Right." Mr Ackroyd said.

"And these would be worth fifteen pounds to me if that's any good for you?" Georgina said, showing him the photography and psychology books.

He chewed his bottom lip for a moment and then nodded.

"Okay."

When Georgina opened the till to get him the cash he said: "I suppose I should have haggled."

"It wouldn't have made any difference." Georgina told him.

Mr Ackroyd was silent and Nora could sense that he was prickling.

When Georgina handed him the cash he handed her a business card.

"Here's my card. Just to show you who I am and why I should have haggled." He said.

Georgina took it, screwing up her nose and looking at him as if he was mad, which made Nora want to laugh.

He then picked up his box and headed off without another word.

"What the…?" Georgina exclaimed in bafflement as she read his card. She turned it over as if expecting to see something significant. "He's a nobody."

Nora laughed.

"Maybe he's the king of German erotica?" Nora joked and Georgina laughed too. "Kind of insulting if he expected you to have heard of him."

"Quite!" Georgina glowered and continued marking up her piles of books.

Nora then gasped but didn't get a chance to warn Georgina, for coming through the doorway was Mrs

Raven, sporting her usual long red puffy duffle coat and breathing and huffing loudly.

Georgina turned and stiffened upon seeing Mrs Raven approaching the counter. After the initial shock, she recovered her disposition.

"Hello." Georgina greeted Mrs Raven brightly. "How are you?"

"I'm…fine…thanks." Mrs Raven whispered breathlessly, this time ignoring the pile of Seatown leaflets. "My daughter put…some books aside."

"Oh yes. They're just here." Georgina said, still sounding cheerful and she took them from under the counter, unwrapped them and handed them to Mrs Raven.

While Mrs Raven scoured through the ladybird books, Georgina looked across to Nora with an expression that told her she was just about ready to flee the town screaming. Nora bit back her smile and pencilled a price into the copy of 'The Last Abbot of Glastonbury' on her knee.

Once Mrs Raven had looked through the books she asked Georgina if she could have a discount. Georgina appeared irritated but agreed and out came a small plastic bank bag full of coins which were then counted out for ages on the desk.

"TWO…bags…please!" Mrs Raven whispered hard.

"They're just ladybirds." Georgina argued.

"I would like…two. To double them up!" Mrs Raven stated aggressively.

Annoyed, Georgina did as she was told and handed Mrs Raven the doubled up blue carrier bag that contained eight little ladybird books.

Without saying anything else, Mrs Raven turned and waddled off towards the door, puffing loudly like a steam train. She stepped up and stood outside and Nora wondered why Georgina wasn't venting her annoyance.

She leaned forward and saw the younger Raven fill the doorway.

"If you ever see the 'Henry the Eighth' ladybird could you please let us know?" Miss Raven asked in her sugary voice.

Georgina stared at her.

"Well, I see so many ladybirds…"

Nora watched Miss Raven's face contort, almost like in the Exorcist film, and she glared steadily at Georgina.

"IT would really mean a lot if you could let us know if you do!" She said and turned, paused and looked back quickly. "If you could let us know!" She added and moved away, whispering hard with her mother and heading off across the square.

Georgina made the motion of strangling with her hands and Nora laughed.

"I sometimes wonder if it is worth keeping those types of customers. They hardly spend money and make such a fuss about it." Georgina grouched.

"Oh please ban them. I'll inform them they're banned." Nora volunteered and Georgina chuckled.

"I'll think about it." She said.

Smiling, Nora finished marking up her box of books, collapsed it, took up a few other empties, grabbed the van keys and set off to replace the empty boxes with some more full ones and continue pricing.

When she had placed three more full boxes on the carpet, Georgina decided it was probably enough for Castletown and that she would price the rest at Seatown the next day.

"Hurray." Nora sighed.

"If you want to make yourself and Humphrey a cup of tea quickly before I go, I think I'll make a move." Georgina mused. "I've had it here."

"Okay. I'll go and pop the kettle on." Nora nodded.

"Oh, and can you bring my steaks out on your way back?"

"Will do." Nora said and set off, leaving Georgina reaching for the telephone that had started to ring.

The back door into the yard was open and Nora could hear Humphrey whistling over the loud hissing sound of high pressured water. She peered out and saw that he had done an amazing job on the whole yard, including the walls which were usually covered in cobwebs and dirt. He currently had the jet hose on a fan setting and was directing the dirty water towards the drain in the far corner. The air smelt fresh and mossy and all trace of excrement had vanished.

"Cup of tea?" Nora called over the water sounds.

Humphrey turned.

"Tea? I'd love one. Four sugars please." He nodded.

"Four?" Nora repeated and laughed.

"What?" He smirked and lifted the hose up so that the water sprayed in her direction.

Nora let out a scream and Humphrey's laughter filled the little yard.

Shaking her head she turned to fill up the kettle and saw that the hose was attached to the cold tap.

"Hmm." She opened the fridge and smiled to see a large bottle of Evian inside so used some of that to fill up the kettle, switch it on, and then organise the mugs.

"I'll leave your tea on the side here, Humphrey!" Nora called to him.

"Thanks." He nodded. "I'm almost done."

"It's a good machine. You've done a brilliant job." Nora said.

"I removed a wasp's nest from a distance with it in a neighbour's garden yesterday." He explained. "I've cleaned all the window frames in here, even up on the top floor."

Nora smiled, watching him glance upwards. He looked wet and worn out but was always laid back and happy about doing endless favours for people. He smiled back at her and she left him to finish off, heading out of the kitchen with her tea and Georgina's steaks.

Georgina turned to Nora who placed the tea on the counter.

"Guess what I just saw." She challenged, chuckling to herself as she gathered her boxes, handbag, steaks and books.

"What?" Nora asked.

"The Ravens climbing into a taxi and leaving Castletown. The taxi company was called 'Swift'." She said.

Nora laughed too.

"That's brilliant." She agreed.

"How's Humphrey getting on?" Georgina then asked.

"He's doing a brilliant job." Nora replied.

"Good. I'll leave you both to it. I think I'll avoid the yard while there are still remnants of the revolting episode out there. Tell him I said goodbye." She decided, screwing up her nose.

"I will."

"Have a good day tomorrow with Heather. I'm not sure what the weather will be like but I know there's no farmer's market in the square so it shouldn't be too messy."

"Oh, shame. I do love their carrots." Nora grinned.

Georgina smirked and headed off, slipping her sunglasses on and clip-clopping off in her high heels towards The Secondhand Bookworm van.

"All done." Humphrey announced fifteen minutes later, strolling into the front room with the jet hose slung over his shoulder like a lasso.

Nora was writing her last sale into the cash book as the customer left, closing the door behind her.

"Have you? Thanks for doing that." Nora appreciated.

"My pleasure." He smiled, standing at the counter.

She continued to write the title of the book she had just sold until she finished and looked up to meet his eyes.

"What are you doing tomorrow night?" He asked.

"Going on a date." Nora replied with a small smile.

"Lucky guy." Humphrey said smugly and leaned forward to kiss her.

"Humphrey!" Nora edged back. "You'll scandalise the customers."

He laughed.

"Fine. I'll just have to content myself with smooching you tomorrow night." He shrugged.

Nora chuckled, shaking her head.

"Blast, I really have to go over to Walltown." He checked his watch. "I'll pick you up at seven tomorrow?"

Nora nodded.

"Look forward to it."

"Me too." He grinned and headed off.

Nora smiled when he glanced back at her in the doorway, saluted and left, strolling up the road with his jet hose, whistling.

There weren't many customers left in the shop and the town looked empty outside. In the remaining hour and a half, Nora busied about organising the books that she and Georgina had priced, tidied up the antiquarian shelves, rearranged some first editions, gave the shelves in the walkway a quick polish, sold some postcards and an eight volume set of Edgar Allen Poe bound in green cloth for £150 to a very pleased collector from Rivertown, and then set about packing up for the day.

It was dark outside as Nora turned the key in the lock to keep any stragglers out as she banked up. She ran upstairs to the top room to make sure that it was empty. Then she made her way down, checking each room as she did so and finally turning off the lights behind the travel books on Russia.

"A good day today." She said to herself as she wrote down the final figure of takings. "Six hundred pounds, and in November too."

She cashed up the till, banked the PDQ machine, tidied everything away, switched off the lights, set the alarm and legged it around the counter to the door. Once outside, Nora turned the key in the lock, organised the 'just-in-case-of-a-flood' sandbags and was relieved to make a smooth getaway without any fuss.

Her car was parked up the hill that day by the Roman Catholic Church so Nora slipped inside before the priest locked up, to light a candle and say a prayer before she jumped in her car and sped away, leaving Castletown behind after a very busy day.

12 THE WOMAN IN GOLD AND THE MAN IN THE KIOSK

Heather Jolly sometimes worked on a Saturday with her sister in The Secondhand Bookworm and that weekend she was anticipating a day of amusing book-wormy madness. Georgina employed Heather 'ad hoc' and paid her cash in hand which suited Heather well and meant she got to spend the day with Nora too.

They parked up the hill again in a nifty space not far from 'The Duke's Pie' restaurant when an old man happened to reverse out as they were going past. Heather was still giggling about the sound Nora's tires had made when she had slammed her brakes on and come to an ear-splitting screeching stop that had almost given Albert from the Print Shop a heart attack and sent thirty crows screaming into the air.

They strolled down the steep roads, avoiding a dog poop in the middle of the pavement before crossing to the side of The Secondhand Bookworm.

"Oh look!" Heather exclaimed as Nora dug around her pocket for her key.

Nora turned to see Heather pointing at the new shop opposite which had promised to open that Saturday. It was called ‘Marbles’ and now had a huge gold figurine of a woman on the pavement outside, an enormous brown coat stand next to it and a big flowery armchair by the door. Nora stared.

“Kind of lowers the tone a bit don’t you think?” Heather grinned.

“Somewhat.” Nora smirked and turned back to unlock the door.

“Are you open?” A man asked, stopping behind Heather.

“In about five minutes.” Nora heard Heather’s muffled voice say from bending down to drag in the sandbags.

“Oh. Okay.” He said grumpily.

Nora ran and punched in the alarm code, kicking over the stool with a crash.

Smothering her laugh at the racket, Heather politely shut the door in the man’s grim face, turned the key and joined Nora behind the counter.

The phone then began to ring so Nora dived for the receiver and picked it up.

“Good morning, The Secondhand....Book...worm....” Her voice trailed off when she heard familiar heavy breathing.

“Is that Nora?” The voice at the end of the line asked.

“Yes it is.” Nora replied warily, grimacing at Heather who was looking at her curiously.

“Nora, it’s Mr Hill.”

“Hello, Mr Hill.”

“Nora, I’m in a kiosk, could you phone me back please!” He asked.

“Erm....”

“The number is 555000, did you get that? You had better write it down, it’s 555000.”

Nora grabbed a pen.

"Okay I've written it down."

"Good, that's 555000."

"Got it!" Nora assured.

"I'll replace the receiver and you can phone me back. I'll await your call. B-bye. 555000." He rang off coughing and Nora pressed the connection button.

"What was that all about?" Heather asked, starting to throw the float into the till.

"Mr Hill is in a kiosk and wishes me to phone him back."

Heather smirked as, with a sigh, Nora dialled the number.

"Why, oh why am I doing this?" She asked.

It rang for a second and was picked up.

"Hello?" Mr Hill breathed heavily.

"Hello, Mr Hill." Nora said, sitting down in the chair.

"Is that Nora?" Mr Hill breathed deeply.

"Yes!"

"Nora. In the back room, on the left, third shelf down in the middle, do you have a copy of 'King Charles II' by Antonia Fraser? It's black cloth." He asked, followed by heavy breathing.

"I can have a look for you." Nora said and stood up.

While he repeated the exact instructions once again, Nora reached the book, which emitted the faint scent of Mr Hill.

"I have it." Nora pulled it out, leaned it against the shelf and opened it.

"Oh! Oh! You have? And how much is it please?" Mr Hill asked.

Nora shook her head in exasperation when she saw the right hand side of the title page covered almost artistically in faint pencil markings. It seemed like a hundred faded pound signs were almost visible from the countless times the price had been rubbed out by Mr Hill when he had purchased the book and then written back in again by Nora or some other member of staff when he had sold it. It currently had Cara's marking inside seeing as Mr Hill had sold it to her on Thursday.

"It's seven pounds fifty Mr Hill." Nora said, knowing that he was already aware of the price.

"Seven pounds fifty is it? Hmm, can you put it by for me Nora and I'll be in to purchase it this afternoon."

"This afternoon?!" Nora repeated, walking back to the front of the shop. "Here? Are you sure you don't want it sent over to our lovely Seatown branch or..."

Mr Hill coughed and spluttered and breathed loudly.

"No I shall be making a trip to Castletown by bus this afternoon and shall arrive by four fifteen." He said.

Nora looked at the clock, anticipating six hours of Hill-freedom.

"I am currently in Seatown and will come to Castletown to purchase 'King Charles II' by Antonia Fraser for seven pounds fifty. I shall pay by cheque. B-bye." Mr Hill said hastily.

"I'll have to make sure that we are accepting cheques from you Mr Hill by asking Georgina first." She said, remembering last month's saga of the cheques written by Mr Hill all bouncing.

A long and loud onslaught of heavy breathing and spluttering ensued until Mr Hill assured Nora that Georgina had just accepted a cheque from him for six volumes of the 'Decline and Fall of the Roman Empire' by Gibbons. Nora had put those in the transfer box the day before for Georgina to take with her in the hope that Mr Hill would plague Seatown instead.

"Okay, I'll keep it aside for you Mr Hill." Nora said and dropped 'King Charles II' onto the desk.

He repeated his travel plans two more times to Nora until he hung up without saying goodbye.

Heather had filled up the till and turned on the computer.

"Oh is that Mr Hill's book?" She asked innocently.

"One of a few." Nora nodded, shoving it under the counter with the reserved books.

The phone then rang so Nora grabbed the receiver.

She didn't speak first but waited a few seconds when she heard the loud and heavy breathing.

"Hello Mr Hill."

"Is that Nora?" Mr Hill's voice rang out.

"Yes, Mr Hill."

"Nora. I shall be arriving at Castletown to purchase the 'King Charles II' book by Antonia Fraser and I would just like to check the price." He breathed.

"It's seven pounds fifty Mr Hill." Nora said.

"Seven pounds fifty you say?"

"Yes." Nora almost groaned.

"Seven pounds fifty. Hmmm. Okay I shall be catching the number 700 bus to Castletown this afternoon and shall be arriving to purchase 'King Charles II' by Antonia Fraser for seven pounds fifty. I shall be paying by cheque."

Nora was about to say that she hadn't made sure that was alright yet but decided to remain silent.

"B-bye." Mr Hill said, breathed loudly and hung up.

Heather snorted with laughter.

"Oh it's going to be one of *those* days is it?" She chuckled.

"You won't be laughing if he really does turn up." Nora smirked, heading for the door.

"I hope he does."

"You'll regret that."

"Shall I help you with those or turn on the upstairs lights?" Heather asked.

"Perhaps turn on the lights. I think Mr Grumpy-Face is keen to come in, although he looks like a bit of a werewolf so might be able to see in the dark."

Heather hurried off laughing, while Nora opened up.

"Hello." Nora greeted pleasantly.

"Oh you're open then." Mr Grumpy-Face said grumpily, walking inside.

"Yes, can I help at all?" Nora asked, heaving a postcard spinner up the step and onto the pavement.

"You have a book in your window. Is it for sale?"

"Er…yes, which one is it?"

"It doesn't have a price" The man said.

"All of our prices are inside. Shall I get it for you?"

"I'll take a look but I'm not committing to buying it." He said adamantly.

Nora stared.

"No, of course, you're welcome to browse through it and decide." She said, leaving the postcard spinner to the left of the door and heading inside to get the book.

She was aware of a scratchy-rolling sound and then a car emitted several loud beeps. Turning around, Nora saw the postcard spinner heading towards the kerb and the road.

"Agh, excuse me a moment!" She cried and ran out and grabbed it just as it teetered on the edge and would have careened into the road and probably hurtled to the floor sending several thousand postcards into the air. Quickly she wheeled it back towards the shop.

"Thank you!" She hailed to the car driver who was a red-haired man about her age and was grinning with amusement.

He beeped again chuckling and drove away. Nora made sure the brakes were on the spinner before returning to the shop rather breathless.

"Dratted things." She muttered and returned to the window where the man was waiting grumpily.

"It's the book called 'Memoirs of a fox-hunting man' by 'Siegfried Sassoon'." The man indicated.

"Oh yes, I know the one. It's a first American edition and first printing, a nice clean copy so it is priced at seventy pounds." Nora explained before she reached for it.

"Oh, leave it then, I was only interested in it because I'm a supporter of fox-hunting and thought it would help the cause." He shrugged, turning to go.

Nora blinked, watching him leave.

"Horrible old werewolf." She muttered and continued putting the rest of the spinners and black boxes outside.

Heather returned from upstairs.

"Cup of tea?" She offered hopefully.

"I think we'll need it to start us off." Nora agreed.

There was a message on Skype chat from Seatown where Georgina was working with Roger.

'Morning girls! When you get a chance pls look for a copy of Wuthering Heights, it has to be a penguin paperback, black with a tree on the front.'

Nora sat down.

'Okay will do. Can we accept cheques from Mr Hill?' She typed.

While she waited for a reply, a couple of customers entered and after saying hello headed off into the depths of the shop. She saw the pen moving on Skype.

'Yes no problem. Make sure you take his cheque card though!' Georgina Skyped.

'Ok!' She replied.

When Heather returned with the tea she volunteered to run up and look for the 'Wuthering Heights'. Nora took a swig of tea, swallowing her mouthful as a man appeared from the back of the shop and stood in front of Nora.

"Do you ever sell the dust wrappers from your books?" He asked.

"Erm..." Nora began.

"It's not a trick question." The man said. "I'm serious. Would you ever consider selling the dust wrappers separately from your books? I have one of the clock books at home that you have on your shelves but I don't have the wrapper. Would you sell me the wrapper from that one?"

"No. Sorry." Nora replied.

"Oh, well I won't beef about it but I had to ask." The man muttered and set off towards the door.

Heather came back carrying a paperback.

"Do you think this is the one? It's a penguin classic." She asked.

"Oh it looks like it." Nora said. "I'll describe it."

She Skyped a message to Seatown.

'We have a Wuthering Heights; it has a landscape hilly thing with some trees to the right.' Nora wrote.

Heather smirked, sipping her tea.

'Is it this one?' Georgina replied and added a link.

The link didn't work so Nora grinned.

'Sorry, but the link doesn't work. Shall I photograph it and send you a picture?'

'No don't worry. Put it in the transfer box for a Mrs Holt. It sounds like the one but they can be fussy about that kind of thing. Thx.'

Nora smirked, grabbed a slip of paper and organised the book just as one of their regular customers who obsessively bought books on the Pre-Raphaelites entered the shop.

"Oh. Hello." Nora greeted.

"Hello, Nora. How are you?" He was wearing his usual grey woolly fleece jacket and the top of his large nose was bright red. "Anything for me today? I know there are some on order but I was just passing."

Nora disappeared behind the counter as she looked through the reserved books.

"It doesn't look like there are at the moment." She said.

"Na, na that's okay. Georgina ordered some for me yesterday so there will be some coming in." He said. "I'll have a look around while I'm here though."

He walked off with his hands in his pockets.

Heather moved around to the front of the counter and picked up a book.

"Oh this is lovely." She said.

"That's one that we bought yesterday from the Mushroom Farm." Nora explained.

"It's not about mushrooms."

"Silly, the mushroom people don't sell them to us. One of the warehouses is used by 'The Piertown Lions'." Nora chuckled.

Heather laughed.

The door opened and Nora and Heather watched an old man enter the shop with a walking stick and puff about the front room. Heather put down the book.

"Can I help, sir?" Heather asked the old man with the stick.

"No." He replied curtly.

Nora watched the man head into the back before she looked at Heather.

"Sorry I asked." Heather mouthed.

Nora bit back a smile.

They sat down behind the counter for a while, drinking their tea as people gradually filled up the front of the shop, disappearing into its depths or buying local guides, postcards and a few books from the window. When it had quietened down a bit, Heather clipped a walkie-talkie to her belt and headed off to see if any books needed putting away around the shop before it became busy. Nora organised the books behind the counter, had a tidy, served some customers and dealt with a trade customer who bought some first editions and two sets of leather without a fuss, leaving happily and wishing her a Happy New Year in case he didn't see her over the next seven weeks.

When Heather returned, she made another round of tea and once Nora had added up their sales so far and Skyped it over to Seatown they stood by the window looking at the new shop opposite.

"Perhaps I'll check it out on my lunch break." Nora decided.

"I wonder if it's a shop that sells just marbles or bric-a-brac." Heather mused.

"Well, the Woman in Gold and the armchair and coat stand indicate the latter." Nora said.

"Hmm, seems so." Heather agreed.

"Oh look, that must be the owner." Nora watched a scruffy man with wild wavy hair, a holey red jumper and faded blue jeans step out the doorway and settle himself into the armchair with a mug of tea. Nora and Heather looked at one another.

"Definitely lowers the tone." Nora chuckled.

They then saw Albert from the Print Shop walk past, staring at the man and then the Woman in Gold statue. Phil, who doubled as a postman and waiter at 'The Duke's Pie' strolled past next and stopped to chat to the scruffy man. After a moment they disappeared inside 'Marbles'.

"Curious." Heather smirked.

The bookshop door opened and this time a lady with a walking stick stepped down onto the flagstones.

"Good morning." Nora greeted cheerfully.

At that moment, the old man who had entered earlier with his own stick came into the front room from the back.

"There you are! I've been upstairs two flights searching in every corner for you. I must have missed you." The man said loudly, rapping his stick on the floor.

The woman closed the door behind her.

"Oh I'm sorry. I've been in the charity shop. I thought I had time." She replied, looking keenly around at the shelves of books.

"Well I looked everywhere. Up two flights, every corner, nook and cranny. I thought I'd find you in here but I was wrong so I thought I'd better wait." The man said. "It must have been about an hour."

"Yes you're right; you were gone for an hour." The woman bristled.

Nora and Heather fled to behind the counter, half expecting them to engage in a walking stick fight. While Heather pretended to tidy up the blue carrier bags, Nora watched from the corner of her eye as the woman hobbled over to the books on display in the window area and picked up a large white tome with the photograph of an old looking toy on front.

"Ten pounds. Must be a collector's item." The woman decided as the man joined her.

"Well I have a collector's item but I didn't pay ten pounds." He said.

The woman put it back on the shelf.

"Listen. I'm sorry for keeping you waiting." She apologised again, leaning on her stick.

"Well I had a look upstairs for you and I was looking and waiting for a good hour."

"I am sorry. I didn't think you could manage the stairs."

"Well I can manage to take them slowly." The man returned irritably.

"Listen. I'm ready to go when you are, Rod." She cast a look around the shop longingly, obviously wanting to spend some time inside. Nora watched the old man begin to force her out as he tapped his stick repetitively on the carpet.

"Is that a book by Carpenter?" The woman then noticed in the Cole section.

"Ah yes, I remember her." The man nodded. "Ready when you are."

"Yes, alright." The old woman said, turning and leading the way out.

Nora watched them go, amused by their strained conversation. Heather grinned and the phone began to ring so Nora grabbed the receiver.

"Good afternoon, The Secondhand Bookworm, Castletown." Nora greeted.

"It's still morning, Nora. I know it feels like the afternoon already." Georgina's amused voice returned.

"Oh, hello. It's been a *long* morning." Nora chuckled and sat down. "How are things in Seatown?"

"Busy here." Georgina said.

"How's all the marking up going?" Nora asked, moving aside for Heather as a customer asked for directions to the needlecraft section.

"Oh, we're getting there. There are still five boxes to price from our calls but Roger has brought them all in from the van now and they're all in front of the art section. I just had my head in the boot of another car for half an hour and then had a run in with the ridiculous woman at the bank. Anyway." She sighed and Nora could hear her tapping on the computer. "What? Oh, what a ridiculous man." She said and Nora laughed, assuming she was reading her emails. "Percival is asking me to meet him at Sea Road Café with all the books I've been putting aside for him in the back of the van. Honestly, I feel like we're conducting a suspicious transaction going through boxes in the back of the van in the car park of Sea Road Café. I suppose I'll have to go.

He also wants me to go shopping with him to help him choose a pair of new trousers again."

Nora giggled.

"Now the reason I telephoned is that Terri has handed in her notice today." Georgina then said.

"Oh! That's a shock!"

"Yes, I know. She's worked on Saturdays since she was fourteen but she's been accepted into the local agriculture college, a late application but their term starts in January, which is why she's not in today as she had an interview, so, you mentioned that your brother or your cousin is after a Saturday job?"

"Oh yes." Nora nodded. "Well, Milton was asking but Seymour has decided to pilfer him for the theatre when it opens at Christmas, but our cousin Felix has been asking for ages and I know he'd be more than keen."

"Okay, how old is Felix?"

"He's seventeen." Nora said.

"Does he drive?"

"Yes, he's just passed and has his license. He's still at college but he's leaving in July. He is thinking about journalism so is keen to work with literature."

"Hmm, sounds worthwhile. And I am a fan of nepotism."

Nora chuckled.

"Okay, I'll make a note of Felix and you can ask him to come into the shop or telephone me in the New Year if he doesn't have a job by then."

"Great!" Nora nodded.

"Nora I have to go as a man has just arrived with a huge amount of books!" Georgina then said abruptly and rang off leaving Nora chuckling to herself.

While she returned the phone to the cradle, Nora's attention was drawn to the window and the Woman in

Gold opposite which was now wearing an enormous fruit hat. She choked on a laugh, shaking her head.

Heather returned holding an armful of books for the needlecraft woman which they ran through the till and bagged up for the happy lady who left humming.

"Yikes!" Heather then exclaimed. "It looks like it's raining."

"Whaaaaaaat!" Nora gasped and they ran out the shop to drag the postcard spinners and free map box inside. They left the black boxes full of cheap paperbacks clipped to the wall seeing as the rain wasn't heavy and then they stood observing the new shop opposite as the scruffy man leapt out his door and proceeded to wrap the Woman in Gold in a hideous yellow plastic mac. Heather and Nora looked at one another and then burst out laughing.

A customer arrived, battling to get through the doorway with his umbrella still up.

"What the blazes!" He grimaced.

Nora and Heather watched as he dragged the sides of his umbrella along the door and the display shelves, sending two walking books sailing to the floor with a crash. He then closed his umbrella and picked up the books muttering.

"Good morning, sir." Nora greeted politely, returning to the counter.

Heather straightened up some display books by the window, smirking.

"Hello." The man said and finally walked to the counter after looking around. His dark bushy brown eyebrows were dotted with raindrops.

"Would you have a section on asbestos?" The man asked.

Nora stared at him.

"A section?"

"On asbestos." The man repeated.

"No." Nora replied, baffled.

"Oh. No technical books then?" He said, beginning away from the counter and heading deeper into the shop.

Nora screwed up her nose, looking at Heather who was giggling.

"Typical Saturday." Nora sighed.

When the telephone rang again, Nora picked it up only to be greeted with slow, dodgy heavy breathing.

"Hello, Mr Hill." She said with a strained smile.

Heather snorted behind her hand.

"Hello, hello? Who's that?" Mr Hill's wheezy voice demanded.

"It's Nora, Mr Hill!" Nora exclaimed.

"Oh, Nora, it's Mr Hill."

"Hello, Mr Hill." Nora said in a strangled voice.

"Nora, I'm in a kiosk so I would like you to phone me back. Shall I give you the number?"

"Not if it's 555000." Nora said.

A massive onslaught of heavy breathing occurred followed by spluttering and what Nora thought was the sound of breaking wind. She closed her eyes, forcing herself not to laugh.

"I'll read out the number, Nora." Mr Hill suddenly decided amidst coughs.

"Well, if you just tell me what it is you would like Mr Hill I can…"

More heavy breathing and spluttering.

"The number is 555000 have you go that? I'm in a kiosk so you can phone me back. B-bye." He said and the line went dead.

"Aaaaaaaagh!" Nora half laughed, half cried.

Heather tried to control her expression of laughter as two customers came in holding handfuls of paperbacks and she hurried around the counter to serve them.

When Nora phoned the kiosk, after about eight rings a foreign-sounding voice answered.

“Yar?! This phone box.” He said.

“Erm…is there an old gentleman there?” Nora asked warily.

There was the sound of shuffling, wrestling and distant conversation before immense heavy breathing filled Nora’s ear and she held the phone away at arm’s length.

“Nora…is that Nora?” A distant voice asked.

Nora put the receiver back to her ear.

“Hello, Mr Hill, this is Nora.” She said wearily.

“Oh Nora, it’s Mr Hill.” He said and Nora almost threw the phone. “I’ve put a book aside to be collected…it’s called ‘King Charles the II’ and it’s written by Antonia Fraser…”

“Yes.” Nora shook her head.

“And it’s priced at…at…seven pounds fifty.”

“Yes!”

“Well, I’ve had a change of plans and I won’t be able to make it to Castletown today after all.”

Nora felt her world suddenly get lighter.

“Oh dear, what a shame.” She said politely.

“Yes….yes, indeed. Could you have it sent over to your branch in Seatown to arrive on Monday morning?” He asked.

“Erm…” Nora thought it possibly would get there so rather than warn him it might not and have to endure another ten phone calls of heavy breathing she assured him it would.

“So I shall catch the bus to Seatown on Monday morning and collect the copy of ‘King Charles II’ by Antonia Fraser. I look forward to doing business with you. B-bye.” He said and hung up.

For a long moment Nora held the phone, expecting it to ring again, but after a while she returned it to its cradle and shook her head.

“More tea?” Heather suggested with a grin.

"My thoughts exactly." Nora nodded and Heather headed off for the kitchen, leaving her sister smirking at her clear view of the Woman in Gold who was in the process of having her enormous fruit hat wrapped in a waterproof headscarf.

13 NORA IN WONDERLAND

While Heather was at lunch the sun came out so Nora battled endless customers trying to enter the shop as she attempted to put the postcard spinners and free map box back outside. Not long after, a large man came into The Secondhand Bookworm closely followed by a woman. Nora thought that they might be together but they didn't speak to each other as the man sauntered around to look at the art books and the woman the topography books by the door.

Nora was watching the woman when the man spoke.

"Do you have any books on Mormons? Or Mormonism?" He asked.

"We have a section on religions up…" Nora began but he interrupted.

"You don't have your books listed?"

"No, I'm afraid not."

"You should do, it would save you a lot of time."

The man turned away, walking quickly into the back room, leaving Nora staring.

The door opened and another woman walked in. She paced towards the woman in the topography section and then stopped.

"Oh I'm sorry! I thought you were my husband." She said.

Nora glanced at the topography woman who just laughed and continued browsing.

"Oh there you are!" The first woman said as the man sauntered back out into the front of the shop. "Shall we go? Are you cold?"

"No I'm baking now." He replied but paused at the counter and looked at Nora. "Where are your religious books?"

"On the top floor." Nora replied.

"NEVER!" The man said and laughed loudly. "Ah, nearer to God I suppose."

He walked off and Nora turned to the monitor.

"Haven't heard that one before." She sighed.

A man came in and bought a few postcards and when he left the shop he was replaced by a little plump man all dressed in black, with a round face, one slightly crooked eye and a fake smile. He was carrying a large case.

"Hello, how are you today?" He greeted Nora in a strong Australian accent and then he giggled.

Nora smiled suspiciously at him.

"I'm fine thank you." Immediately she sensed that he was going to try and sell her something.

"Can I just take a few moments of your time? We're here in the area doing a promotion of natural make-up products."

"It wouldn't be for me I'm afraid. I have very sensitive skin so I'm very careful what make-up I use." Nora explained.

"Oh like me." He giggled. "But you're just the person we are looking for as these are all dermatologically tested and perfect for sensitive skin."

"Oh that's nice, but I wouldn't want any anyway." Nora insisted.

"Oh well let me just show you."

"If you are selling it I really wouldn't be interested. It probably isn't worth your while." She explained frankly.

"Well, let me show you anyway." He pulled out a fat ugly black leather case with an unsightly zip around it, seemingly from thin air. Nora stared as he opened it up on the counter.

"Now this is the foundation with a natural bristle brush." He said, holding up a black stick with some hair squashed in one end. He turned the bottom slowly so that the brush opened, slightly wonky. "And the shimmery foundation is in this compartment here so it flows out naturally, look." He held out a chubby hand which shimmered like cheap gold make-up from the nineteen eighties.

"Oh. That's er...lovely." Nora smiled falsely.

"Yes it is. Now that retails at forty pounds but we are selling it today for twenty pounds. That's half price, which means everything else in this case is free."

"That sounds like a very good deal."

"It is." He agreed hopefully.

"But I wouldn't be interested in it for myself. Honestly." Nora assured him.

"For any family members perhaps?" He asked, refusing to be deterred.

Nora shook her head.

"No."

"Don't any of your family wear make-up?" He asked astonished.

Nora had a fleeting thought about saying that her brother Seymour did, then changed her mind with a smirk.

"My mother wears make-up, but she has loads due to birthdays and Christmases and certainly doesn't need anymore. My sister is like me and..."

"Prefers the natural look?" He finished for her. "Like me." He said and giggled again.

"Hmmm." Nora said, and decided she should pretend to be busy and so randomly pressed a load of keys on the keyboard.

"Well." The man said loudly, reached into the hideous leather case once more and took out a bulky square black box. "Let me show you a magic trick. Are you ready?"

Nora looked at him and watched as he extended the box to reveal two sections of rather dull shades of make-up in little squares.

"This is a neat little box of beeswax lipstick, so it doesn't stick to your teeth, yes?" He pointed to a dreary pink square that looked like it was sweating and made a motion with his finger over his lips. Nora stared. "This is erm...erm..." He giggled and clicked his fingers. "Eye stuff." He said and Nora made a strangling sound of suppressed laughter so he pointed at her. "Thank you, *eye shadow*, thanks." He giggled and pointed to a miserable shade of blue.

Nora frowned, thinking back and wondering if she had said 'eye shadow' without realising it.

"It lasts all day." He said, making a light arched movement with his finger over his left eye. He then closed it and held it out. "It retails at er…eighty five pounds."

"Wow." Nora said, thinking what an unbelievable rip off it was.

"Yes!" He enthused heedlessly. "But today it will be free." He smiled broadly.

"That's very good." Nora lied politely and tapped again on the keyboard, longing for a customer to come along.

"Would it be for you?" He asked hopefully.

Nora shook her head.

"Sorry not for me but thank you for showing it to me."

A man and a woman entered the shop and Nora straightened up, hoping they would interrupt them and the annoying salesman would leave, but they headed for the Cole section and stood in the corner talking about the titles they were looking for.

"Ah well thank you anyway. What's your name?" The make-up seller asked, putting the box into the case.

"Oh, Nora." Nora replied.

He stuck out his chubby hand.

"Thank you for listening Nora." He said and she shook his hand, which was clammy and made her cringe. "Is this your shop?" He then asked, looking around.

"No." Nora replied.

"Ah I've never worked in a bookshop or with books but I know I would just be in heaven. I would just read and read and read."

"Yes it is a lovely place to work." Nora agreed.

"I'm writing a novel at the moment." He stated, zipping up the case.

"Oh that's good." Nora replied.

"But I read so much I fear that I plagiarise. And also I'll go back to it and write something like: 'he walks down a dark alley to investigate the crime, and tries to sell some make-up', hahahaha." He said.

Nora smiled.

"It's a sci-fi novel, with fantasy. Do you read fantasy?" He asked her.

"No but my colleague loves it." Nora said, thinking of Cara.

"Ah it is great. Have you read David Eddings?"

Nora shook her head.

"He's very good, and also Feist and Hobbs." He continued.

"She loves Robert Jordan." Nora said.

The man looked blank.

"Wheel of time?" Nora prompted, surprised that he didn't seem to know the author.

"Oh, yes, Jordan is good, but the best writer is George R. R. Martin. Have you read any of his?"

"He's on my list." Nora admitted.

"They are INCREDIBLE!" The man gushed with an ecstatic look. "You should read the series! You realise the author must be INSANE to be able to write so well and such an incredible story. The books are a thousand times better that the television series."

"I'm sure I'll get around to it one day." She smiled politely.

"I can lend you my copy if you like?" He offered smarmily.

Nora tried not to look horrified.

"Oh, thank you but I'm afraid I can't borrow books from customers. It's…erm…illegal." She refused.

The man stared at her and for the first time he was silent.

"Illegal?" He finally asked.

"Yes. I could be arrested." Nora said, hoping he would leave.

Fortunately, after a long moment of muteness, the make-up man smiled broadly.

"Well I would love to stay and talk shop but I must be off. Goodbye." He said, hurrying hastily away with his revolting black case of ugly make-up.

Nora watched him go and chuckled to herself just as Heather returned from her lunch.

"He sells marbles!" Heather exclaimed.

"Really?"

"A whole room of them. Some bric-a-brac too but mainly marbles, up on the second floor."

"I'll have to go and check it out." Nora decided, standing up as Heather moved around the counter and began to take off her coat.

"It's nice out there now. I sat on a bench by the castle ruins watching the building work taking place on the new castle." She said. "It was lovely until some teenagers came and started shoving each other into the dustbin."

"I'll go and snoop around 'Marbles' and then grab a sandwich." Nora said. "By the way, you just missed a make-up salesman."

Heather laughed, unravelling her scarf.

"What a shame."

When she stepped out of the shop a few minutes later, Nora headed straight for 'Marbles'. The Woman in Gold had had her rain mac and head scarf removed and was gleaming brightly in the sunshine. The armchair was already wrapped in plastic so hadn't needed covering during the shower.

The door to 'Marbles' opened into a small lobby with a staircase directly in front. Nora climbed up, turned left at the top and entered a large room. There were glass cases and bookcases against all the walls and a glass counter in the centre where the scruffy man was sitting in a large sofa, talking on the phone. He nodded to Nora, continuing his loud conversation about spectacle repairing so Nora had a browse.

There were enormous jars of every kind of marble ever made, vintage marble games, handmade glass robins, marble runs, nuggets and glass pieces, world map and planet marbles as well as incredible collector marbles by Tim Keyzers, Anna Tillman and Fred Rossi.

Nora had never heard of them but stared in fascination at the pieces.

After a while she left, smirking at the Woman in Gold as she passed and heading off to the delicatessen to buy a sandwich, cake and coffee and eat her lunch.

When Nora returned to the shop half an hour later, Heather was speaking with White-Lightning Joe who stood in a cloud of cider-scent.

"Do you mind if I ask you a personal question?" White-Lightning Joe was saying and giggled.

"What?" Heather replied with a polite smile.

"Oh…it's a little embarrassing really…oh, erm….eeeeeep, well….are you pregnant?"

Nora almost tripped over the swivel chair and dived behind the stairs leaving Heather staring at White-Lightning Joe in affront.

"Do I look pregnant?"

"Oh, no! I….erm…hehe, I wondered if you were…because…eeeeep…."

"No, I'm not pregnant." Heather assured patiently.

"Ah, I thought not….so, erm…I was wondering…would you like to go out for a drink?"

"No thank you." Heather replied tightly.

"Oh…okay, yeah, I understand haha….oh hi Nora." White-Lightning Joe said as Nora stepped up to the counter beside Heather.

"Goodbye." Nora said with a smile causing Heather to smirk.

"Hahaha, ah I must be going anyway. I saw that you didn't have any new local history books in so nothing for me today…by the way, Nora, I think that Sam in the butcher's shop fancies you." He said, grinning stupidly.

"Does he? I'll tell him you said so." Nora replied.

"Oh, haha, no don't do that else he sock me one, eeeeep!" White-Lightning Joe implored before waving frantically in her face and heading for the door. "Bye eeeeek." He almost swung back as the door opened to emit several customers before heading off, his cider-belly leading the way, and hastily legging it up the hill.

Nora and Heather looked at each other.

"Do I look pregnant?" Heather then asked again, although her lips were twitching.

"NO! He's just a bozo." Nora assured, laughing.

They chuckled together and then Heather grabbed the walkie-talkie and clipped it to her belt, heading off upstairs to look for a list of requests from Seatown.

When she had disappeared, Nora sat down on the swivel seat before the till as another customer arrived. He was a well-dressed middle aged man with a blue suit and a red tie.

"Good afternoon. Do you sell piggy banks?" He asked.

"Books on piggy banks?" Nora returned.

"No. Piggy banks. Oh, perhaps you don't. Are these just all books?" He scanned the room.

"Just books I'm afraid." Nora said, watching him.

"Okay, there is a book I'm looking for actually. What was it? Oh what was the name? Oh I think it was called 'Red for Danger'. Do you have it?" He asked.

"Who wrote it?"

"I don't know." The man said. "Can't you look on your computer?"

"I can look on the internet but we don't have our books listed." Nora explained. "What's the subject?"

"It's a book." He said seriously and Nora stared at him. "So it must be about reading or something."

She decided to just type the title into Google but had the feeling she was wasting her time. She typed it in and scanned down the results.

"Well. There's a book called 'Red for Danger' about railways." She told him.

"No that wouldn't be it. I don't think I'm interested in railways." He replied.

"Er…well there's a result here talking about the effects of red hair in surgical practice – it's called 'Red for Danger'…" She said.

"No. Doesn't sound like it. Maybe it's not the right title. Oh, what was it called? Do you know?" He asked her.

Nora stared.

"Know what the title is?"

"Well, what it could be? Something like 'Red for Danger'." He prompted.

"If you had an idea of the topic it might help…"

"Well something readable. Something you read." He said and then paused. "Is that the right time up there?" He gestured towards the clock above the alarm pad.

Nora was still regarding him in bafflement but then glanced at the clock too.

"Yes. It's almost two." She nodded warily.

"Cripes, I'd best be off. Have a nice day." He said and turned, leaving the shop quickly.

Nora watching him go, wondering if she had fallen into a Lewis Carroll book.

While Heather was upstairs, a customer asked Nora if there were any Georgette Heyer novels in stock so Nora radioed Heather on the walkie-talkie to have a look.

"Hello! We have three titles here." Heather's voice crackled out of the device. "Over."

"Okay what are they, over?" Nora asked with a grin.

The woman listened as Heather read them out.

"Oh no, I have all of those, thanks for looking though." She said.

"I can ask our Seatown shop to check their shelves?" Nora offered.

"No I live in Seatown. Goodbye."

When the woman had gone, Nora picked up the walkie-talkie.

"No on those Heather. Thanks though."

"No problem. Over and OUT!" Heather replied and Nora laughed.

"Where are all the customers?" Heather wondered when she came back down five minutes later with a handful of books.

Nora watched as a woman immediately threw open the door.

"You spoke too soon." She smirked.

The woman stood on the mat in a turquoise shell suit, pink sweat band and pink trainers.

"TONY?!" The woman shouted loudly.

Heather flinched and Nora watched her slam the door.

"Where is he? Maddening man! Can I shout up the stairs?" She asked, stomping across the carpet. "I need to tell my husband that we're going up the road. He's in here somewhere."

"Would you like me to run up and tell him for you?" Nora offered as Heather sat down to Skype the titles she had found to Seatown.

"Could you?" She replied, pleased.

"Yes. What does he look like?"

The woman followed Nora.

"He's about sixty, with grey hair and cycling clothes." She explained, walking with Nora to the bottom of the stairs. "TONY! TONY CAN YOU HEAR ME? TONY!" She screamed up.

Nora resisted covering her ears and raced up the stairs at a sprint. On the second level, Nora ran into the front room that overlooked the square. It was empty so Nora edged back out, ran up three little steps onto the landing and walked into the next room which was devoted entirely to children's books.

She picked up an 'Eagle Annual' leaning against the shelves, slotted it into the annual section and, seeing that Tony wasn't in that room either, continued up the next staircase. The sound of creaking announced that someone was walking about in the attic room above.

Nora could hear the woman still calling from below and so ran up the last staircase and around into the attic room where she came face to face with a man holding a small pile of fantasy novels.

"Hello. Is your name Tony?" Nora asked.

The man arched an eyebrow.

"Yes. Is the old ball and chain after me?" He asked with a sigh.

Nora bit her bottom lip.

"Your wife would like you to know that she is going up the road." She explained.

He smiled with a pained expression.

"Thank you. I shall resist coming down and facing her as I am enjoying my parole time up here."

"I'll tell her you'll be here." Nora smiled and turned around, running all the way down the winding, twisting staircase to the ground floor.

"Well?" The woman asked, still standing at the bottom.

"He is immersed in the paperback room and said he will be here." Nora explained.

"It'll take a miracle to get him out. Very well, we shall continue up and collect him when we've finished." She said, more to herself and headed off.

Back in the front room, Nora was about to suggest a cup of tea to see them through to the end of the day when she paled and sunk slowly into the swivel chair, for walking casually along the street with a large dog at his side was The Terminator.

The Terminator's name was really Harry and he was a smooth-talking local who had moved into the town several months ago and walked the dog that belonged to the Florist Shop under the flat where he lived. He seemed to think that he was also the most dashing resident and that the ladies of the bookshop waited eagerly for him to drop by. He had received his nickname due to the first impression he had given to Nora when he had turned up dressed like Arnold Schwarzenegger with dark sunglasses and bulging muscles and said 'I'll be back' to her the first day they had met.

Nora watched him saunter past, glance in through the window, slow down and then turn back.

"Terminator alert." Nora nudged Heather's arm.

"What?" Heather asked, looking up from the keyboard.

The door opened and Harry stepped in with Bella the dog at his heels. Because it had been raining earlier, Bella had obviously gotten wet and smelt more strongly than usual. The pong of wet dog engulfed Nora. Thankfully, Harry left the door open.

"Hiiiiii." Harry said smoothly, lifting his sunglasses.

"Hello." Nora returned.

"How are you?" The Terminator asked, winking at Nora.

"Fine." She replied.

"Do you know if you have any Garfield books? For my nephew." He then asked.

"There may be some in humour." She replied. "Would you like me to have a look for you?"

"Ah, would you mind? That would be really nice of you, Nora." Harry replied fondly.

He smiled, flashing his straight white teeth.

Nora stood up quickly.

"Won't be a moment." She said and headed away, hoping that Heather would be safe with him.

The humour section was at the top of the stairs and around slightly on the next floor landing, standing alone in its own case with a shelf of Christmas books at the top. The side of the case had each letter of the word 'humour' cut out and coloured in and tacked at funny angles all the way down. There was a whole heap of Giles annuals as usual on the bottom shelf but the shelves in between were higgledy-piggledy with various other tomes of a humorous nature.

Nora stood and scanned through each shelf. She then checked in the children's room in case any Garfield books had been put in there, but she couldn't see any. Empty handed, Nora began back down the stairs slowly.

Harry seemed pleased when Nora returned, even when he noticed that she didn't have any books with her.

"Sorry, no luck at the moment." Nora said.

"No worries. Thanks for looking. By the way, do you like dressing like that?" He asked.

Both Nora and Heather stared at The Terminator.

"Like what?" Nora asked warily.

"In loose sweaters. You would look much better in tighter clothing."

Nora's eyes almost popped and Heather's mouth dropped open.

"Yes as a matter of fact, I do like dressing like this." Nora said tightly.

The Terminator grinned.

"Have a nice weekend. I'll be back." He said and sauntered off with Bella.

Once he had gone, Nora and Heather looked at each other.

"So I'm pregnant and you dress like a hip-hop artist." Heather said and Nora burst out laughing.

"You could get a complex working here." She decided.

Nora glanced at Harry through the window as he swaggered off up the hill and was tempted to spray the air freshener around but the opened door let in some fresh air, as well as the sound of a psychotic seagull on the cobbles. After a while, Nora went and closed it, noticing with a small start that the Woman in Gold was now sporting a black and white gangster fedora.

"I feel like Alice down the rabbit hole." She told Heather as the phone began to ring.

"And I expect this is the Mad Hatter calling again." Her sister agreed, referring to Mr Hill.

Nora grabbed the receiver, leaving Heather corresponding with Seatown on Skype Chat.

"Good afternoon, The Secondhand Bookworm, Castletown." Nora greeted the caller.

"Oh hello!" A high voice cried out on the other end. "Do you have the telephone number for your shop in Seatown please?"

"Yes of course." Nora said and started to reel it off.

"Just a minute!" The high voice interrupted Nora as she was half way through the number. "Let me just get a pencil."

Nora paused.

"If she phoned for a number why didn't she have her pencil ready??" She whispered to Heather, whose shoulders shook with silent laughter.

"Okay dear! Continue!" The high voice ordered upon its return.

Nora repeated the number and the caller thanked her and hung up.

Heather was laughing and pointing at the monitor so Nora leaned in to read the one long word written on Skype.

'HILLLLLLLLLLLL!!!'

Laughing, Nora headed off to make a well-earned cup of tea.

Inevitably, at ten minutes to closing time, a man stepped into the shop. Nora was adding up the day's takings, feeling exhausted after two hours of madness that included three trade customers buying numerous antiquarian tomes as well as two boxes of books a lady brought in for sale that she had had to rummage through, all of which either had mould, bogies or cobwebs over them. It had been quiet at times but thanks to the trade customers they had passed the one thousand pound mark so Nora was chuffed.

"Hello." Nora greeted. "Can I help?"

"Just browsing thank you." The man said, looking around.

"We're closing in ten minutes." She warned him politely.

"Oh. Okay." He said and she watched him head off towards the walkway that led deeper into the shop.

"Grrr." Nora glowered. "You've had all day to browse, why pick ten minutes before we close."

She sent the figure through to Georgina in Seatown and then began to lug the postcard spinners into the shop.

"Hi Nora." Sam called from outside the butcher's shop.

He was locking up his own shop and so she waved, picking up the free maps box which was empty of all the free maps.

"Hey, Sam." She called back, suddenly remembering White-Lightning Joe's comment about Sam fancying her so blushing red slightly.

"Nora." It was Penny, who was collecting all the windmills from her window baskets in front of her shop window. "How did you find it today?"

"A little bit quiet at some points." Nora said.

"You're telling me! I don't know if I've made enough to even cover my wages today. It was the pits!" Penny said, shaking her head.

"It has been a dreary week. I think the weather is to blame."

"Roll on summer eh!" Penny sighed, picked up a smiling ladybird on a long stick and headed back inside her shop.

"Are you still open?" A large man in a floppy black hat asked Nora.

"We're just about to close I'm afraid." She replied politely.

"Darn." He grimaced. "Is the owner here?"

"No, I'm afraid not. But I'm the manager of The Secondhand Bookworm. Was there anything specific that you were looking for?" Nora asked him, throwing the empty map box against the wall with a crash.

"No, no, no just a browse." He looked through into the shop, past her shoulder, hopefully.

"Oh, well sorry, we close at half past five." Nora said firmly.

"Shame, shame, shame. What time are you open tomorrow?" He asked, watching her struggle to manoeuvre the postcard rack down the step.

"Well the owner will be here tomorrow and as it is Sunday the opening times are eleven o'clock until four." She said in a strained voice as she rolled the spinner over the flagstones.

"Okay, okay, okay. I'll pop back tomorrow." He said, cast one last look behind her and then set off.

Nora unclipped the black boxes containing the bargain paperbacks fastened either side of the door, heaved them in, leaned them against the topography section, quickly shut the door and turned the sign to 'CLOSED' just as the clock read five thirty. She grabbed her keys, locked the door to prevent anyone else barging in and called to Heather who was cleaning the kitchen that she was turning off the lights upstairs. Nora then set off to find the last 'browser'. He was in the paperback room and so Nora shadowed him to make sure he would leave, although he lingered on each level and paused to pick up a book to browse through in the front room.

He finally left without buying anything, as Nora had predicted.

"Kitchen's all nice and clean." Heather said, returning with the keys having locked up.

"Great. Let's get going."

"Oh, there's a message from Seatown." Heather noticed.

'*Pls give you and Heather £30 bonus each for today. Well done on the takings! Have a nice evening.*' Georgina wrote.

"Ooooh that's nice!" Heather exclaimed pleased.

Nora agreed and wrote a thank you before she and Heather counted out their bonuses, counted out the float in the till, said goodbye on the Skype and closed down the computer, bagged up the money, banked the PDQ machine, tidied the front and once everything was finally finished, opened the door.

Nora set the alarm, grabbed her bag and jacket, turned off the light and ran almost screaming to the door to step out and lock up the shop.

As she closed the door, put her key in the lock and turned it, a woman stopped next to Heather.

"Are you closed?" The woman asked in an airy voice.

Nora jumped and took her key from the lock.

"Yes. I'm afraid so." Heather said and pointed to the 'CLOSED' sign.

The woman stared at the sign and then took hold of the handle and pushed the door to make sure that it was locked. Nora stared at her.

"Do you have a cookery section?" She asked Nora.

"Yes." She replied, dragging the sandbags in front of the door followed by the black board.

"I want a recipe to cook something for dinner tonight. So you're closed. Will you be opening later?" The woman asked her seriously.

"No. That's it for the day I'm afraid." Nora assured her cheerfully and grabbed Heather's arm, beginning away.

"What the devil can I cook for dinner?" The woman asked herself and pressed her face against the glass of the door, peering tragically into the shop.

Nora walked hastily away, glancing back while Heather spluttered with laughter.

"Note to self. Clean face print off window on Monday." She said.

"And make sure you open twenty-four hours a day." Heather suggested sarcastically.

They began up the hill, pulling up their hoods as it began to rain.

"Look!" Heather pointed, bemused. "The man is holding an umbrella over the Woman in Gold."

"What?!" Nora exclaimed and almost collided with the bin on the pavement, shaking her head.

Outside 'Marbles', the scruffy owner was standing holding a huge golf umbrella over his statue as he puffed on a cigarette, oblivious to the rain falling on his own head. Laughing, Nora and Heather crossed the road, heading for the corner where 'The Duke's Pie' restaurant stood with a little row of cars parked just outside.

"I'm rather pleased I'm not in again until Tuesday." Nora admitted with a chuckle.

"Ah, you don't mean that. You're looking forward to another week of bookworms." Heather grinned.

"I suppose." Nora shrugged, casting a glance back down the hill at the new Woman in Gold sheltering happily under her umbrella. “And then of course, there’s Christmas.” She said, her eyes twinkling.

“Oh yes. Christmas at the Secondhand Bookworm.” Heather agreed with a giggle. “Who can resist that?”

They laughed and set off up the hill to where Nora’s car was parked. Nora paused as she took out her keys, her gaze sliding to the distant turrets and windows in the Duke of Cole’s newly built castle, unable to help but smile, wistfully.

“Come on, dreamer.” Heather giggled, wiggling the handle of the passenger door.

Nora blinked and remembered where she was. She grinned, unlocked the door and the sisters jumped inside. They were soon driving down out of Castletown, Nora looking forward to her evening with Humphrey, and Heather working out how many sleeps there were until that magical festive season of Christmas at The Secondhand Bookworm.

Up above the shops, over the tall stone walls, across newly landscaped gardens to the towering bulwarks, ramparts, buttresses and turrets of the expanding, magnificent, rebuilt castle, James, the Duke of Cole stood at a tall, mullioned window.

His blue eyes surveyed the sprawling landscape and town beyond his enormous, recently finished and freshly stocked library, a smile upon his face, a miniature schnauzer sitting at his feet.

“Well, Marlow. Here we are at last.” He told his canine friend.

Marlow looked up, his head to the side.

The Duke smiled down and took a sip of tea from the antique cup and saucer in his hands.

“Woof?” Marlow queried, wisely.

"A bookshop, you ask?" James nodded, returning the cup to the saucer. "Of course. One can't live without a bookshop." His blue eyes twinkled.

Marlow twitched his nose.

"Woof, woof?" The miniature schnauzer next enquired.

"Hmm." The Duke crouched down to tickle behind one of Marlow's ears. "You're wondering if we'll make some new friends." His eyes lifted towards a coffee table, set before one of two large sofas in front of a large inglenook fireplace. "I'm sure we will. And who knows…" The Duke straightened up, walked over to the coffee table and picked up a sheet of paper. He pondered it thoughtfully before looking down and meeting Marlow's intelligent black eyes. "…perhaps even more than friends."

"Woof." Marlow agreed.

James grinned again, sat down in the sofa and rested his woolly-socked feet upon the table top, crossing his ankles. Marlow jumped up beside him and pawed the sheet of paper. The Duke kept his eyes upon it.

"The Secondhand Bookworm." James read for the umpteenth time. "What interesting treasures you appear to hold."

His eyes moved across the page of information, one of one hundred detailed sheets given to him by his surveyors before he had decided to come to Castletown, telling him all about the businesses, shops, holdings, estates and companies in his land. *This* sheet of paper was his favourite, the one that had made up his mind, the one he referred to the most. He smiled and rubbed his chin.

"Over twenty-seven thousand books." He read, his gaze then dropping to the word '*manager*' beneath a now familiar photograph.

He picked up his cup of tea, saucer and leather bound book from the coffee table with a smile.

"What interesting treasures, indeed."

THE END

ALSO IN THE SERIES

'The Secondhand Bookworm'
'Christmas at the Secondhand Bookworm'
'Summer at the Secondhand Bookworm'
'Halloween at The Secondhand Bookworm'
'Black Friday at The Secondhand Bookworm'
'Book Club at The Secondhand Bookworm'
'Valentine's Day at The Secondhand Bookworm'
'Lockdown at The Secondhand Bookworm'
'Strange Things at The Secondhand Bookworm'
'Winterland at The Secondhand Bookworm'

Watch for more novels in the Bookworm series

Also by the author

'House of Villains'
Available now from Amazon

ABOUT THE AUTHOR

Emily Jane Bevans lives on the south coast of England. For ten years she worked in, and helped to manage, a family chain of antiquarian bookshops in Sussex. She is the co-founder and co-director of a UK based Catholic film production apostolate ‘Mary’s Dowry Productions’. She writes, edits, produces, directs, narrates and sometimes acts for the company’s numerous historical and religious films on the lives of the Saints and English Martyrs. She also likes to write fiction based on her bookshop experience.

MARY'S DOWRY PRODUCTIONS

Mary's Dowry Productions is a Catholic Film Production Apostolate founded in 2007 to bring the lives of the Saints and English Martyrs, English Catholic heritage and history to film and DVD. Mary's Dowry Productions' unique film production style has been internationally praised for not only presenting facts, biographical information and historical details but a prayerful and spiritual film experience. Many of the films of Mary's Dowry Productions have been broadcast on EWTN, BBC and SKY.
For a full listing of films and more information visit:

www.marysdowryproductions.org

Made in the USA
Las Vegas, NV
08 September 2023

77252640R00152